The Year's BEST HORROR STORIES

Series VII

Edited by
GERALD W. PAGE

DAW BOOKS, INC.
DONALD A. WOLLHEIM, PUBLISHER

1301 Avenue of the Americas
New York, N.Y.   10019

COPYRIGHT ©, 1979, BY DAW BOOKS, INC.

All Rights Reserved.

Cover art by Michael Whelan.

DEDICATION

To Deborah Ruth Page
and Daniel Steven Page,
unrivaled siblings.

FIRST PRINTING, JULY 1979

1 2 3 4 5 6 7 8 9

DAW TRADEMARK REGISTERED
U.S. PAT. OFF. MARCA
REGISTRADA. HECHO EN U.S.A.

PRINTED IN U.S.A.

TABLE OF CONTENTS

INTRODUCTION
The Editor — 7

THE PITCH
Dennis Etchison — 11
Copyright ©, 1978, by Stuart David Schiff. From *Whispers*, Oct. 1978. By permission of the author.

THE NIGHT OF THE TIGER
Stephen King — 20
Copyright ©, 1977, by Mercury Press, Inc. From *The Magazine of Fantasy and Science Fiction*, Feb. 1978. By permission of the author and the author's agent, Kirby McCauley.

AMMA
Charles Saunders — 34
Copyright ©, 1978, by Charles de Lint. From *Beyond the Fields We Know*, Autumn 1978. By permission of the author.

CHASTEL
Manly Wade Wellman — 54
Copyright ©, 1979, by Manly Wade Wellman. First publication by arrangement with the author and the author's agent, Kirby McCauley.

SLEEPING TIGER
Tanith Lee — 78
Copyright ©, 1978, by Charles de Lint and Charles R. Saunders. From *Dragonbane*, Spring 1978. By permission of the author.

INTIMATELY, WITH RAIN
Janet Fox — 87
Copyright ©, 1978, by *Collage*. From *Collage*, Nov. 1978. By permission of the author.

THE SECRET
Jack Vance — 94
Copyright ©, 1978, by Jack Vance. By permission of the author's agent, Kirby McCauley.

HEAR ME NOW, MY SWEET ABBEY ROSE
    Charles L. Grant   103
  Copyright ©, 1978, by Mercury Press, Inc.
From *The Magazine of Fantasy and Science Fiction*, March 1978. By permission of the author.

DIVERS HANDS
    Darrell Schweitzer   118
  Copyright ©, 1979, by Darrell Schweitzer. First publication, by arrangement with the author.

HEADING HOME
    Ramsey Campbell   144
  Copyright ©, 1978, by Stuart David Schiff. From *Whispers*, Oct. 1978. By permission of the author and the author's agent, Kirby McCauley.

IN THE ARCADE
    Lisa Tuttle   149
  Copyright ©, 1978, by Ultimate Publishing Co., Inc. From *Amazing Science Fiction*, May 1978. By permission of the author.

NEMESIS PLACE
    David Drake   159
  Copyright ©, 1978, by Ultimate Publishing Co., Inc. From *Fantastic*, April 1978. By permission of the author, and the author's agent, Kirby McCauley.

COLLABORATING
    Michael Bishop   173
  Copyright ©, 1978, by Lee Harding. From *Rooms of Paradise*, edited by Lee Harding. By permission of the author and the author's agent, Virginia Kidd.

MARRIAGE
    Robert Aickman   192
  Copyright ©, 1978, by Mercury Press, Inc. By permission of the author's agent, Kirby McCauley.

Introduction

Robert Bloch, who has written some of the best horror stories ever penned, has also written some of the funniest. He once made a very cogent remark about humor: he said it was a funny thing. That can be said about horror fiction, too.

Each year I have the opportunity to read as many of the recent short horror stories as I can lay hands on, so that I can select the best of them for anthologization. It's a rewarding job, but it has certain frustrations.

This year's contents were found in fantasy magazines like *Fantasy & Science Fiction*, small press publications like *Whispers* and *Dragonbane*, an anthology, a literary paper, and even a science fiction fanzine. Our writers live in the U.S., Great Britain and Canada. But despite the range of our sources, I make no pretense that no good horror story has slipped past me. I hunted through a lot of publications, but horror fiction can be anything, and almost any magazine that carries fiction can run a terror tale. The only way to catch all of them would be to read everything published during the year, and there just isn't time for that. That's what my frustration rises from: the feeling that somewhere out there something that's very good is going unnoticed, and that just can't be avoided. Once or twice in the past, excellent stories have failed to appear here: usually because the publication rights were simply not available. But on occasion I've missed something simply because it first appeared in a source I would never think of, or never heard of. Sometimes I luck into them anyway, as with Janet Fox's "Intimately with Rain," which appeared in a San Francisco area publication I would never have seen if the author hadn't provided me with a copy. Horror fiction is the scatter-gun genre. You can find it anywhere.

It's just a shame you can't look everywhere, which, in a way, is the rationale of this anthology series. We can't look everywhere, either, but we can look in a lot of places, and a lot more of them than most.

One of the reasons for this scatter-gun publication of our type of fiction is that the hallmark of any form of imaginative writing is diversity. You never truly know where a good imaginative story will take you, whether it's science fiction, fantasy or horror. And that's true not only of the genre, but of its best writers. Diversity was the rule for Poe, H.G. Wells and John Collier, and it remains the rule for Fritz Leiber, Richard Matheson, Robert Aickman, Ramsey Campbell and the rest of today's best writers. Good horror fiction may be good fiction of any type, and no editor who wants the best he can get his hands on will reject a good story simply because it's horrifying.

For this same reason, the most satisfying of those publications that regularly feature macabre fiction are the ones like *Fantasy and Science Fiction* and *Whispers* and *Weirdbook*, and such anthologies as Ramsey Campbell's *Superhorror* and Kirby McCauley's *Frights*, where the writer is given the fullest rein to his imagination. Those who insist on restrictions, whether by demanding that the setting be opulently fantastic or drably ordinary, have never quite managed to produce a fully satisfying publication; and any such policy is a betrayal of the reader.

For *Year's Best Horror Stories*, I've tried to set up as few restrictions as I can. First, the story must be a horror story, by whatever stretch of the definition possible. Second, it has to have some sort of positive effect on the only reader whose reactions I can be completely sure of: me. And that's it. I don't pretend that it's an infallible policy, but I do think that any imposition of standards beyond my own reactions would only increase that infallibility. If it's news to you that we live in an imperfect world, then perhaps this introduction will do you the service of informing you of the fact.

But if you've picked up this book and hope to read some pretty good horror fiction, I want to share with you the hope that this might not be too imperfect a world. I think these stories are all of a kind in that they're pretty damned good, but other than that I claim no common ground for them.

They'll take you into the past, the present, the future; they deal with the ordinary and the extraordinary; and their themes run a pretty broad range. If you want other than that, I'm sorry; the book isn't for you.

But I don't think you can ask for more.

—Gerald W. Page

Atlanta, Ga.

THE PITCH

Dennis Etchison

In commenting on Dennis Etchison's "I Can Hear the Dark," in *Year's Best Horror Stories: Series VI*, I used the term "psychologically vivid." I could also have used the phrase, "finely crafted," because in addition to being a superb horror writer, Etchison is a masterful writer per se. In the case of this small chiller both descriptions apply. "The Pitch" is a story so effective that it ought to be printed with a warning on it, and indeed it is: the Etchison name, which to the knowledgeable reader is an adequate warning—and a grand reassurance. You are about to read something very special.

The third floor came down to meet him.

As far as he could see, around a swaying bunch of sphagnum moss that was wired to one of the brass fire nozzles in the soundproofed ceiling, a gauntlet of piano legs staggered back in a V to the Kitchen Appliance Department like sullen, waiting lines of wooden soldiers. C-Note shuddered, then cursed as the toe guard clipped the rubber soles of his wedgies.

He stepped off the escalator.

He turned in a half-circle, trying to spot an opening.

A saleswoman, brittle with hairspray, dovetailed her hands at her waist and said, "May I help you, sir?"

"No, ma'am," said C-Note. He saw it now. He would have to move down alongside the escalator, looking straight ahead, of course, pivot right and weave a path through the pink and orange rows of the Special Children's Easter Department. There. "I work for the store," he added, already walking.

"Oh," said the saleswoman dubiously. "An employee! And what floor might that be? The, ah, Gourmet Foods on One?"

If it had been a joke, she abandoned her intention at once. He swung around and glared, the little crinkles fanning out from his eyes, deepening into ridges like arrows set to fire on her. Her make-up froze. She took a step back.

A few women were already gathering listlessly near the demonstration platform. Just like chickens waiting to be fed. Ready. All angles and bones. *May I help you, sir?* I'll plump them up, he thought, swinging a heavy arm to the right as he pushed past a pillar. A small ornament made of pipe cleaners and dyed feathers hooked his sleeve. He swung to the left, shaking it off and heading between tables of rough sugar eggs and yellow marshmallow animals.

They looked up, hearing his footsteps. He considered saying a few words now, smoothing their feathers before the kill. But just then a sound pierced the muzak and his face fisted angrily. It was "Chopsticks."

He ducked backstage through the acetate curtain.

"They don't even notice," he wheezed, disgusted.

"Why, here he is," said the pitchman, "right on time." Seated on a gold anodized dining room chair borrowed from the Furniture Department, he was fooling with the microphone wired around his neck and waiting blankly for the next pitch. "All set to knock 'em dead, killer? What don't they notice?"

"They don't notice my hand goin' in their pocketbooks in about fifteen minutes." C-Note sprawled over the second chair, also upholstered in a grained vinyl imprinted with lime-green daisies.

"Ha ha! Well, you just rest your dogs for now," said the pitchman. He spooled out a length of black plastic tape and began dutifully winding another protective layer around the microphone's coat hanger neckpiece.

C-Note saw that all was in ready: several cartons marked Ace Products, Inc., barricaded either side of the split curtain and behind the pitchman, leaned against two large suitcases, were lumpen bags of potatoes, a pried-open crate of Califor-

THE PITCH

nia lettuce and a plastic trash can liner brimming over with bunched celery and the wilted cowlick tops of fat hybrid carrots. C-Note flexed his fingers in preparation, turned one wrist up to check his watch and pulled a white-gloved hand through his lank hair. He was not worried; it would not fall in his eyes, not now, not so long as he did not have to lean forward on a stool over another scale. Sometimes he had thought they would never end. Up and down, down and up.

"We got fifteen units out there," said the pitchman, "another forty-eight in the box here. I don't think you'll have to touch 'em, though. The locations we do our best is the discount chains. You know."

"Sure," C-Note lied, "I know."

"These *ladies*—" He overlaid the word with a doubtful emphasis. "—They're all snobs, you know?" The pitchman cut the tape and then paused, eyeing him as he pared dirt from under his fingernails with the vegetable knife.

C-Note stared at the man's hands. "You want to be careful," he said.

"Check, kid. You got to slant it just right. But you can sell anything, can't you? You talked me into it. I believe you."

That was what C-Note had told him. He had come up to the platform late yesterday, hung around for a couple of sets and, when the pitchman had scraped off the cutting board for the last time and was about to pack up the rest of the units in the big suitcases and carry them out to the station wagon, he had asked for a job. *You want to buy one? Then don't waste my time.* But C-Note had barged through the curtain with him and picked up a unit, covering one of the kitchen chairs as if it had always been his favorite resting place. As he had done just now. And the pitch. The pitch he auditioned was good, better even than the original mimeo script from Ace. If he pitched as well out there today in front of the marks, the head pitchman just might earn himself a bonus for top weekly sales. Of course, C-Note would never know that. The pitchman had agreed to pay him cash, *right out of my own pocket*, for every sale. And how would C-Note know how much commission to expect? He would not bother to go to the company, not today and not next week, because that would mean W-2s, withholding—less take-home. And the new man looked like he needed every dime he could lay his hands on. His white-gloved hands.

"Here you go," said the pitchman. "I'll hold onto your

gloves. Shake out a little talcum powder. That way you won't go droppin' quarters."

"The gloves," said C-Note, "don't come off." And the way he said it told the pitchman that he considered the point neither trivial nor negotiable.

The pitchman watched him bemusedly, as if already seeing juice stains soaking into the white cloth. He stifled a laugh and glanced aside, as though to an audience: *Did you catch that?*

"Well, it's two o'clock, pal. I'm goin' up to the cafeteria. Be back in time to catch your act. You can start, uh, on your own, can't—?"

"Take it easy," said C-Note, waiting.

"Don't worry, now. I'm not gonna stick you with no check. Ha ha. Cash!" He patted his hip pocket. "Not every demonstrator's that lucky, you know."

"I appreciate it. But I'm not worried about the money."

"Yeah." The pitchman handed him the neck microphone. "Sure." He looked the new man over again as if trying to remember something more to ask him, tell him. "Check," and he left, looking relieved to be leaving and at the same time uneasy about it, a very curious expression.

C-Note left the microphone on the chair and set to work on the units. He had to prepare them and these few minutes would be his only chance. If the pitchman had not volunteered to go to lunch, C-Note would have had to beg off the next demonstration and remain backstage while his boss pitched out front in order to get to them in time. He tightened his gloves and dug his fingertips into the big Ace carton and ripped the cardboard. They did not hurt at all anymore; he was glad of that, in a bitter sort of way.

". . . And today only," droned C-Note, "as a special advertising premium from the manufacturer, this pair of stainless steel tongs, guaranteed never to rust, just the thing for picking baby up out of the bathtub. . . ."

He lifted a potato from the cutting board and plunked it ceremoniously into the waste hole. Most of the ladies giggled.

"That's right, they're yours, along with the Everlast glass knife, the Mighty Mite rotary tool, the Lifetime orange juicer *and* the fruit and vegetable appliance complete with five-year written warranty and two interchangeable surgical steel blades, all for the price of the VariVeger alone. *If* you all

THE PITCH

promise to go home and tell your friends and neighbors about us, extend our word-of-mouth. Because you will not find this wonder product on the shelves of your stores, no ma'am, not yet. When you do, next fall sometime, the new, improved VariVeger alone will list for a price of seven dollars and ninety-five cents. That's seven ninety-five for the shredder, chopper and julienne potato maker alone. You all remember how to operate this little miracle, don't you, so that you'll be able to put it to work on your husband's, your boyfriend's, your next door neighbor's husband's dinner just as soon as you get home tonight?"

More laughter.

"Just crowd in close as you can now, 'cause this is the last time I'm going to be demonstrating this amazing..."

"Say, does that thing really work?"

"Three years of kitchen testing..." C-Note saw that it was the head pitchman, watching from the aisle, a sporting smirk on his lips. "Three years of testing by the largest consumer laboratory...."

There was something else.

Distracted, he let his voice roll off for a brief moment, heard the reverberation replaced by the dull din of milling shoppers, the ringing of cash registers and the sound of a piano playing on the other side of the Special Children's Easter Department. He hesitated, his teeth setting and grinding. Why wouldn't she let him stop? He hovered over the soggy cutting board, waiting for the sharp crack of the ruler on the music rest, just missing the knuckles.

A gnarled hand reached up, grasping for a VariVeger. C-Note snapped to.

"Just another minute, ma'am, and I'll be handing out the good-will samples. If you'll just bear with me, I'm sure you'll go away from this store feeling...."

And so on and on. He peeled a potato, set it on the grid of the VariVeger and slammed his hand down on the safety guard handle. Dozens of slim, pallid, finger-like segments appeared underneath. A susurrus of delight swept the crowd.

"No need to hold back—the patented safety grip bar makes sure you won't be serving up finger stew tonight!"

Then he took up the Mighty Mite, needled it into a radish and rotated the blade, holding to the protective finger guard. And a good thing, too: without that tiny ridge of aluminum the blade would continue turning right down through glove, finger and jointed bone. Five seconds later he pulled the radish apart in an accordion spiral.

"Here's just the thing for that mother-in-law you thought you'd never impress!"

Oohs and ahhs. Nothing worked like a non sequitur.

He diced onions, he ripple-cut potato chips, lateral, diagonal and criss-cross, he sliced blood-red tomatoes into inflationary slips—

"This is one way to stretch that food bill to cover the boss, his wife, your in-laws, your husband and all sixteen screaming kids!"

—He squeezed gouts of juice from a plastic spout like a magician with a never-empty lotta, he slivered green beans and cross-haired a turnip into a stiff blooming white flower. He shredded lettuce head after head, he riced more potatoes, he wavy-edged a starchy-smelling mound of French fries, he chopped cabbage, he separated a cucumber into a fleshy green Mobius strip, he purled twists of lemon peel, he segmented a carrot, grated another, then finished by describing the Everlast glass knife, stacking the packages into a protective wall in front of him. You know. You know what he said. And he gave the signal and the money came forth and he moved forty-three unit combinations at a price less than one-half of the fanciful manufacturer's retail, the bills folded between his fingers like Japanese paper water flowers, blooming and growing in the juices as his gloves became green, green as Christmas trees made of dollars.

He scraped the garbage into a hole, mopped his forehead, put away twenty unsold packages, stripped off his plastic apron, unplugged the mike and departed the platform.

Just as he was about to peel the drenched gloves from his hands, the head pitchman appeared at the slit in the curtain.

C-Note left his gloves on.

The pitchman flashed his hand forward, then thought better of it.

"Hell of a salesman," he announced.

"We thank you," said C-Note. "But—"

"Don't let it go to your head, 'though."

"No, sir. I got—"

"Hell of a salesman. But what the hell was that business with the knife?"

"I sold the knife. 'Long with the rest of the package. Isn't that all right, sir? But if you don't mind, I got to—"

THE PITCH 17

"But you didn't *demonstrate* the knife. What's with that? You afraid you're gonna cut yourself or—"

C-Note's sharp eyes nailed him where he stood.

"If you don't mind, I got to go now." He started for the curtain, head down. "I mean, this gut of mine's startin' to eat itself. If you don't mind. Sir. If you think I earned my lunch."

"Hell yes, you earned it, boy." The pitchman put a foot up on the kitchen chair. His toe brushed the carton, the one with the torn-open top. "Hey, wait a minute."

C-Note drew back the curtain.

"Look, you want your money or don't you?"

C-Note turned back.

"Ha ha." The pitchman unfolded some money. C-Note took it without counting, which made the pitchman stare. "Hell of a salesman," he muttered, smiling crookedly. He watched the heavyset man leave.

"Kid must have to take a hell of a leak," the pitchman said to himself. It was only after he had counted and stacked the limp piles of bills in the money box, counted the units, shaken his head and paced the floor several times, lost in some ambitious vision, that he noticed the torn-up carton. "Hell of a salesman," he said again, shaking his head with pleasure. He poked around inside, counting the reserve. Cutting his finger on something, he drew it back with a grimace and stuck it in his mouth. "Well goddam," he said slowly, patiently, pulling up the crease in his trousers and seating himself before the carton from which, he now realized, unpackaged units had been inexplicably switched, "what in the name of the . . ." *goddam holy hell do we have here?* he might have said.

C-Note hurried for the back stairs. On the landing he stopped and looked at his hands. They were trembling. Still moist, they resembled thick, mushy clumps of pseudopodia. Loosening the fingers one by one, he eased the gloves off at last.

His fingers quivered, fat and fishbelly-white. The tips were disfigured by a fine, shiny line. They had healed almost perfectly, sewn back right afterwards, in the ambulance; still, the fusion was not quite perfect, the ends angled out each slightly askew from the straight thrust of the digits. No one would notice, probably, unless they studied his hands at close range. But the sight of them bothered him.

He braced himself, his equilibrium returning. He swallowed heavily, his breath steadying, his heart levelling out to a familiar regular tattoo. There was no need to panic. They would not notice anything out of the ordinary, not until later. Tonight, perhaps. At home.

He recognized the feeling now as exhilaration. He felt it every time.

Too many steps to the ground floor. He turned back, stuffing the gloves into his coat pocket, and reentered the store.

He passed quickly through the boundaries of the Kitchen Appliance Department. Mixers. Teflon ware. Beaters, spoons, ladles, spatulas, hanging like gleaming doctors' tools. If one were to fall it would strike the wood, making him jump, or smack the backs of his hands, again and again. One of them always had, every day. Some days a spoon, other days something else, depending on what she had been cooking. Only one day, that last day, had she been scoring a ham; at least it had smelled like a ham, he remembered, even after so many years. That day it had been a knife.

The muzak was lilting, a theme from a movie? Plenty of strings to drown out the piano, if there was one. He relaxed.

The women had somnambulated aimlessly from the demonstration platform, their new packages pressed reassuringly to their sides, moving like wheeled scarecrow mannequins about the edges of the Music Department. From here it was impossible to differentiate them from the saleswoman he had met there, by the pianos. She might have been any one of them.

He passed the platform and jumped on the escalator. The rubber handrail felt cool under his hand. Hastily he pulled a new pair of white gloves from his inside pocket and drew them on.

At the first floor, on his way out to the parking lot, he decided to detour by the Candy Department.

"May I help you, sir?"

Her hands, full and self-indulgent, smoothed the generous waist of her taut white uniform.

"A pound-and-a-half of the butter toffee nuts, all right, sweets?"

The salesgirl blushed as she funneled the fragrant candy into a paper sack. He saw her name badge: *Margie*. There

THE PITCH 19

was nothing about her that was sharp or demanding. She would be easy to please—no song and dance for her. He tipped her seventy-five cents, stroking the quarters into the deep, receptive folds of her soft palm.

He tilted the bag to his mouth and received a jawful of the tasty sugared nuts.

At the glass door he glanced down to see why the bag did not fit all the way into his wide trouser pocket. Then he remembered.

He withdrew one of the parts he had removed backstage and turned it over, fingering it pleasurably as he waddled into the lot. It was a simple item, an aluminum ring snapped over a piece of injection-molded plastic. It glinted in the afternoon sunlight as he examined it. A tiny safety guard, it fit on the vegetable shredder just above the rim that supported the surgical steel blades. A small thing, really. But it was all that would prevent a thin, angular woman's fingers from plunging down along with cucumber or potato or soft, red tomato. Without it, they would be stripped into even, fresh segments, clean and swift, right to the bone. He slipped it back into his pocket, where it dropped into the reservoir of other such parts, some the little safety wheels from the vegetable garnisher, some the protective bars from the Mighty Mite rotary tool. But mostly they were pieces from the VariVeger, that delightful invention, the product of three years of kitchen testing, the razor sharp, never-fail slicer and stripper, known the world over for its swift, unhesitating one-hand operation.

He kept the bag in his hand, feeding from it as he walked on across the parking lot and down the block, losing himself at once in the milling, mindless congestion of Easter and impatient Mother's Day shoppers.

THE NIGHT OF THE TIGER

Stephen King

Stephen King's name, by now, is synonymous with the horror novel. Among his chillers are *Carrie*, *Salem's Lot*, *The Shining*, and *The Stand*. Significantly, he may be the only writer to work regularly the area of the best-selling horror novel without losing the readership of that smaller, more discriminating coterie of connoisseurs that *Year's Best Horror* is compiled for. And to reinforce that unique position, there are his short stories, which are among the best horror tales being produced today. This year he published two notable stories: "The Gunslinger," a strong and controversial story just a bit too long to include here, and "Night of the Tiger," which appears below. It's a story of such traditional elements as a horrifying relationship between man and beast, and a circus background . . . an old favorite for strange goings on. But King's originality seeps through all of it and lifts it out of the traditional into the special—and manages to intensify the horror, while doing it.

I first saw Mr. Legere when the circus swung through Steubenville, but I'd only been with the show for two weeks; he might have been making his irregular visits indefinitely. No one much wanted to talk about Mr. Legere, not even that

THE NIGHT OF THE TIGER 21

last night when it seemed that the world was coming to an end—the night that Mr. Indrasil disappeared.

But if I'm going to tell it to you from the beginning, I should start by saying that I'm Eddie Johnston, and I was born and raised in Sauk City. Went to school there, had my first girl there, and worked in Mr. Lillie's five-and-dime there for a while after I graduated from high school. That was a few years back . . . more than I like to count, sometimes. Not that Sauk City's such a bad place; hot, lazy summer nights sitting on the front porch is all right for some folks, but it just seemed to *itch* me, like sitting in the same chair too long. So I quit the five-and-dime and joined Farnum & Williams' All-American 3-Ring Circus and Side Show. I did it in a moment of giddiness when the calliope music kind of fogged my judgment, I guess.

So I became a roustabout, helping put up tents and take them down, spreading sawdust, cleaning cages, and sometimes selling cotton candy when the regular salesman had to go away and bark for Chips Baily, who had malaria and sometimes had to go someplace far away and holler. Mostly things that kids do for free passes—things I used to do when I was a kid. But times change. They don't seem to come around like they used to.

We swung through Illinois and Indiana that hot summer, and the crowds were good and everyone was happy. Everyone except Mr. Indrasil. Mr. Indrasil was never happy. He was the lion tamer, and he looked like old pictures I've seen of Rudolph Valentino. He was tall, with handsome, arrogant features and a shock of wild black hair. And strange, mad eyes—the maddest eyes I've ever seen. He was silent most of the time; two syllables from Mr. Indrasil was a sermon. All the circus people kept a mental as well as a physical distance, because his rages were legend. There was a whispered story about coffee spilled on his hands after a particularly difficult performance and a murder that was almost done to a young roustabout before Mr. Indrasil could be hauled off him. I don't know about that. I do know that I grew to fear him worse than I had cold-eyed Mr. Edmont, my high school principal, Mr. Lillie, or even my father, who was capable of cold dressing-downs that would leave the recipient quivering with shame and dismay.

When I cleaned the big cats' cages, they were always spotless. The memory of the few times I had the vituperative wrath of Mr. Indrasil called down on me still have the power to turn my knees watery in retrospect.

Mostly it was his eyes—large and dark and totally blank. The eyes, and the feeling that a man capable of controlling seven watchful cats in a small cage must be part savage himself.

And the only two things he was afraid of were Mr. Legere and the circus's one tiger, a huge beast called Green Terror.

As I said, I first saw Mr. Legere in Steubenville, and he was staring into Green Terror's cage as if the tiger knew all the secrets of life and death.

He was lean, dark, quiet. His deep, recessed eyes held an expression of pain and brooding violence in their green-flecked depths, and his hands were always crossed behind his back as he stared moodily in at the tiger.

Green Terror was a beast to be stared at. He was a huge, beautiful specimen with a flawless striped coat, emerald eyes, and heavy fangs like ivory spikes. His roars usually filled the circus grounds—fierce, angry, and utterly savage. He seemed to scream defiance and frustration at the whole world.

Chips Baily, who had been with Farnum & Williams since Lord knew when, told me that Mr. Indrasil used to use Green Terror in his act, until one night when the tiger leaped suddenly from its perch and almost ripped his head from his shoulders before he could get out of the cage. I noticed that Mr. Indrasil always wore his hair long down the back of his neck.

I can still remember the tableau that day in Steubenville. It was hot, sweatingly hot, and we had a shirt-sleeve crowd. That was why Mr. Legere and Mr. Indrasil stood out. Mr. Legere, standing silently by the tiger cage, was fully dressed in a suit and vest, his face unmarked by perspiration. And Mr. Indrasil, clad in one of his beautiful silk shirts and white whipcord breeches, was staring at them both, his face dead-white, his eyes bulging in lunatic anger, hate, and fear. He was carrying a currycomb and brush, and his hands were trembling as they clenched on them spasmodically.

Suddenly he saw me, and his anger found vent. "You!" He shouted. "Johnston!"

"Yes, sir?" I felt a crawling in the pit of my stomach. I knew I was about to have the Wrath of Indrasil vented on me, and the thought turned me weak with fear. I like to think I'm as brave as the next, and if it had been anyone else, I

THE NIGHT OF THE TIGER 23

think I would have been fully determined to stand up for myself. But it wasn't anyone else. It was Mr. Indrasil, and his eyes were mad.

"These cages, Johnston. Are they supposed to be clean?" He pointed a finger, and I followed it. I saw four errant wisps of straw and an incriminating puddle of hose water in the far corner of one.

"Y-yes, sir," I said, and what was intended to be firmness became palsied bravado.

Silence, like the electric pause before a downpour. People were beginning to look, and I was dimly aware that Mr. Legere was staring at us with his bottomless eyes.

"Yes, sir?" Mr. Indrasil thundered suddenly. "Yes, sir? Yes, sir? Don't insult my intelligence, boy! Don't you think I can see? *Smell?* Did you use the disinfectant?"

"I used disinfectant yest—"

"Don't answer me back!" He screeched, and then the sudden drop in his voice made my skin crawl. "Don't you *dare* answer me back." Everyone was staring now. I wanted to retch, to die. "Now you get the hell into that tool shed, and you get that disinfectant and swab out those cages," he whispered, measuring every word. One hand suddenly shot out, grasping my shoulder. "And don't you ever, ever speak back to me again."

I don't know where the words came from, but they were suddenly there, spilling off my lips. "I didn't speak back to you, Mr. Indrasil, and I don't like you saying I did. I—I resent it. Now let me go."

His face went suddenly red, then white, then almost saffron with rage. His eyes were blazing doorways to hell.

Right then I thought I was going to die.

He made an inarticulate gagging sound, and the grip on my shoulder became excruciating. His right hand went up . . . up . . . up, and then descended with unbelievable speed.

If that hand had connected with my face, it would have knocked me senseless at best. At worst, it would have broken my neck.

It did not connect.

Another hand materialized magically out of space, right in front of me. The two straining limbs came together with a flat smacking sound. It was Mr. Legere.

"Leave the boy alone," he said emotionlessly.

Mr. Indrasil stared at him for a long second, and I think

there was nothing so unpleasant in the whole business as watching the fear of Mr. Legere and the mad lust to hurt (or to kill!) mix in those terrible eyes.

Then he turned and stalked away.

I turned to look at Mr. Legere. "Thank you," I said.

"Don't thank me." And it wasn't a "don't thank *me*," but a "*don't* thank me." Not a gesture of modesty, but a literal command. In a sudden flash of intuition—empathy, if you will—I understood exactly what he meant by that comment. I was a pawn in what must have been a long combat between the two of them. I had been captured by Mr. Legere rather than Mr. Indrasil. He had stopped the lion tamer not because he felt for me, but because it gained him an advantage, however slight, in their private war.

"What's your name?" I asked, not at all offended by what I had inferred. He had, after all, been honest with me.

"Legere," he said briefly. He turned to go.

"Are you with a circus?" I asked, not wanting to let him go so easily. "You seemed to know—him."

A faint smile touched his thin lips, and warmth kindled in his eyes for a moment. "No. You might call me a policeman." And before I could reply, he had disappeared into the surging throng passing by.

The next day we picked up stakes and moved on.

I saw Mr. Legere again in Danville and, two weeks later, in Chicago. In the time between I tried to avoid Mr. Indrasil as much as possible and kept the cat cages spotlessly clean. On the day before we pulled out for St. Louis, I asked Chips Baily and Sally O'Hara, the red-headed wire walker, if Mr. Legere and Mr. Indrasil knew each other. I was pretty sure they did, because Mr. Legere was hardly following the circus to eat our fabulous lime ice.

Sally and Chips looked at each other over their coffee cups. "No one knows much about what's between those two," she said. "But it's been going on for a long time—maybe twenty years. Ever since Mr. Indrasil came over from Ringling Brothers, and maybe before that."

Chips nodded. "This Legere guy picks up the circus almost every year when we swing through the Midwest and stays with us until we catch the train for Florida in Little Rock. Makes old Leopard Man touchy as one of his cats."

"He told me he was a policeman," I said. "What do you

THE NIGHT OF THE TIGER 25

suppose he looks for around here? You don't suppose Mr. Indrasil—?"

Chips and Sally looked at each other strangely, and both just about broke their backs getting up. "Got to see those weights and counterweights get stored right," Sally said, and Chips muttered something not too convincing about checking on the rear axle of his U-Haul.

And that's about the way any conversation concerning Mr. Indrasil or Mr. Legere usually broke up—hurriedly, with many hard-forced excuses.

We said farewell to Illinois and comfort at the same time. A killing hot spell came on, seemingly at the very instant we crossed the border, and it stayed with us for the next month and a half, as we moved slowly across Missouri and into Kansas. Everyone grew short of temper, including the animals. And that, of course, included the cats, which were Mr. Indrasil's responsibility. He rode the roustabouts unmercifully, and myself in particular. I grinned and tried to bear it, even though I had my own case of prickly heat. You just don't argue with a crazy man, and I'd pretty well decided that was what Mr. Indrasil was.

No one was getting any sleep, and that is the curse of all circus performers. Loss of sleep slows up reflexes, and slow reflexes make for danger. In Independence, Sally O'Hara fell seventy-five feet into the nylon netting and fractured her shoulder. Andrea Solienni, our bareback rider, fell off one of her horses during rehearsal and was knocked unconscious by a flying hoof. Chips Baily suffered silently with the fever that was always with him, his face a waxen mask, with cold perspiration clustered at each temple.

And in many ways, Mr. Indrasil had the roughest row to hoe of all. The cats were nervous and short-tempered, and every time he stepped into the Demon Cat Cage, as it was billed, he took his life in his hands. He was feeding the lions inordinate amounts of raw meat right before he went on, something that lion tamers rarely do, contrary to popular belief. His face grew drawn and haggard, and his eyes were wild.

Mr. Legere was almost always there, by Green Terror's cage, watching him. And that, of course, added to Mr. Indrasil's load. The circus began eyeing the silk-shirted figure nervously as he passed, and I knew they were all thinking the same thing I was: *He's going to crack wide open, and when he does—*

When he did, God alone knew what would happen.

The hot spell went on, and temperatures were climbing well into the nineties every day. It seemed as if the rain gods were mocking us. Every town we left would receive the showers of blessing. Every town we entered was hot, parched, sizzling.

And one night, on the road between Kansas City and Green Bluff, I saw something that upset me more than anything else.

It was hot—abominably hot. It was no good even trying to sleep. I rolled about on my cot like a man in a fever-delirium, chasing the sandman but never quite catching him. Finally I got up, pulled on my pants, and went outside.

We had pulled off into a small field and drawn into a circle. Myself and two other roustabouts had unloaded the cats so they could catch whatever breeze there might be. The cages were there now, painted dull silver by the swollen Kansas moon, and a tall figure in white whipcord breeches was standing by the biggest of them. Mr. Indrasil.

He was baiting Green Terror with a long, pointed pike. The big cat was padding silently around the cage, trying to avoid the sharp tip. And the frightening thing was, when the staff did punch into the tiger's flesh, it did not roar in pain and anger as it should have. It maintained an ominous silence, more terrifying to the person who knows cats than the loudest of roars.

It had gotten to Mr. Indrasil, too. "Quiet bastard, aren't you?" He grunted. Powerful arms flexed, and the iron shaft slid forward. Green Terror flinched, and his eyes rolled horribly. But he did not make a sound. "Yowl!" Mr. Indrasil hissed. "Go ahead and yowl, you monster! *Yowl!*" And he drove his spear deep into the tiger's flank.

Then I saw something odd. It seemed that a shadow moved in the darkness under one of the far wagons, and the moonlight seemed to glint on staring eyes—green eyes.

A cool wind passed silently through the clearing, lifting dust and rumpling my hair.

Mr. Indrasil looked up, and there was a queer listening expression on his face. Suddenly he dropped the bar, turned, and strode back to his trailer.

THE NIGHT OF THE TIGER

I stared again at the far wagon, but the shadow was gone. Green Terror stood motionlessly at the bars of his cage, staring at Mr. Indrasil's trailer. And the thought came to me that it hated Mr. Indrasil not because he was cruel or vicious, for the tiger respects these qualities in its own animalistic way, but rather because he was a deviate from even the tiger's savage norm. He was a rogue. That's the only way I can put it. Mr. Indrasil was not only a human tiger, but a rogue tiger as well.

The thought jelled inside me, disquieting and a little scary. I went back inside, but still I could not sleep.

The heat went on.

Every day we fried, every night we tossed and turned, sweating and sleepless. Everyone was painted red with sunburn, and there were fist-fights over trifling affairs. Everyone was reaching the point of explosion.

Mr. Legere remained with us, a silent watcher, emotionless on the surface, but, I sensed, with deep-running currents of—what? Hate? Fear? Vengeance? I could not place it. But he was potentially dangerous, I was sure of that. Perhaps more so than Mr. Indrasil was, if anyone ever lit his particular fuse.

He was at the circus at every performance, always dressed in his nattily creased brown suit, despite the killing temperatures. He stood silently by Green Terror's cage, seeming to commune deeply with the tiger, who was always quiet when he was around.

From Kansas to Oklahoma, with no letup in the temperature. A day without a heat prostration case was a rare day indeed. Crowds were beginning to drop off; who wanted to sit under a stifling canvas tent when there was an air-conditioned movie just around the block?

We were all as jumpy as cats, to coin a particularly applicable phrase. And as we set down stakes in Wildwood Green, Oklahoma, I think we all knew a climax of some sort was close at hand. And most of us knew it would involve Mr. Indrasil. A bizarre occurrence had taken place just prior to our first Wildwood performance. Mr. Indrasil had been in the Demon Cat Cage, putting the ill-tempered lions through their paces. One of them missed its balance on its pedestal, tottered and almost regained it. Then, at that precise moment, Green Terror let out a terrible ear-splitting roar.

The lion fell, landed heavily, and suddenly launched itself with rifle-bullet accuracy at Mr. Indrasil. With a frightened curse, he heaved his chair at the cat's feet, tangling up the driving legs. He darted out just as the lion smashed against the bars.

As he shakily collected himself preparatory to re-entering the cage, Green Terror let out another roar—but this one monstrously like a huge, disdainful chuckle.

Mr. Indrasil stared at the beast, white-faced, then turned and walked away. He did not come out of his trailer all afternoon.

That afternoon wore on interminably. But as the temperature climbed, we all began looking hopefully toward the west, where huge banks of thunderclouds were forming.

"Rain, maybe," I told Chips, stopping by his barking platform in front of the sideshow.

But he didn't respond to my hopeful grin. "Don't like it," he said. "No wind. Too hot. Hail or tornadoes." His face grew grim. "It ain't no picnic, ridin' out a tornado with a pack of crazy-wild animals all over the place, Eddie. I've thanked God more'n once when we've gone through the tornado belt that we don't have no elephants.

"Yeah," he added gloomily, "you better hope them clouds stay right on the horizon."

But they didn't. They moved slowly toward us, cyclopean pillars in the sky, purple at the bases and awesome blue-black through the cumulonimbus. All air movement ceased; and the heat lay on us like a woolen winding-shroud. Every now and again, thunder would clear its throat farther west.

About four, Mr. Farnum himself, ringmaster and half-owner of the circus, appeared and told us there would be no evening performance; just batten down and find a convenient hole to crawl into in case of trouble. There had been corkscrew funnels spotted in several places between Wildwood and Oklahoma City, some within forty miles of us.

There was only a small crowd when the announcement came, apathetically wandering through the sideshow exhibits or ogling the animals. But Mr. Legere had not been present all day; the only person at Green Terror's cage was a sweaty high-school boy with a clutch of books. When Mr. Farnum announced the U.S. Weather Bureau tornado warning that had been issued, he hurried quickly away.

I and the other two roustabouts spent the rest of the after-

THE NIGHT OF THE TIGER

noon working our tails off, securing tents, loading animals back into their wagons, and making generally sure that everything was nailed down.

Finally only the cat cages were left, and there was a special arrangement for those. Each cage had a special mesh "breezeway" accordioned up against it, which, when extended completely, connected with the Demon Cat Cage. When the smaller cages had to be moved, the felines could be herded into the big cage while they were loaded up. The big cage itself rolled on gigantic casters and could be muscled around to a position where each cat could be let back into its original cage. It sounds complicated, and it was, but it was just the only way.

We did the lions first, then Ebony Velvet, the docile black panther that had set the circus back almost one season's receipts. It was a tricky business coaxing them up and then back through the breezeways, but all of us preferred it to calling Mr. Indrasil to help.

By the time we were ready for Green Terror, twilight had come—a queer, yellow twilight that hung humidly around us. The sky above had taken on a flat, shiny aspect that I had never seen and which I didn't like in the least.

"Better hurry," Mr. Farnum said, as we laboriously trundled the Demon Cat Cage back to where we could hook it to the back of Green Terror's show cage. "Barometer's falling off fast." He shook his head worriedly. "Looks bad, boys. Bad." He hurried on, still shaking his head.

We got Green Terror's breezeway hooked up and opened the back of his cage. "In you go," I said encouragingly.

Green Terror looked at me menacingly and didn't move.

Thunder rumbled again, louder, closer, sharper. The sky had gone jaundice, the ugliest color I have ever seen. Wind-devils began to pick jerkily at our clothes and whirl away the flattened candy wrappers and cotton-candy cones that littered the area.

"Come on, come on," I urged and poked him easily with the blunt-tipped rods we were given to herd them with.

Green Terror roared ear-splittingly, and one paw lashed out with blinding speed. The hardwood pole was jerked from my hands and splintered as if it had been a greenwood twig. The tiger was on his feet now, and there was murder in his eyes.

"Look," I said shakily. "One of you will have to go get Mr. Indrasil, that's all. We can't wait around."

As if to punctuate my words, thunder cracked louder, the clapping of mammoth hands.

Kelly Nixon and Mike McGregor flipped for it; I was excluded because of my previous run-in with Mr. Indrasil. Kelly drew the task, threw us a wordless glance that said he would prefer facing the storm, and then started off.

He was gone almost ten minutes. The wind was picking up velocity now, and twilight was darkening into a weird six o'clock night. I was scared, and am not afraid to admit it. That rushing, featureless sky, the deserted circus grounds, the sharp, tugging wind-vortices—all that makes a memory that will stay with me always, undimmed.

And Green Terror would not budge into his breezeway.

Kelly Nixon came rushing back, his eyes wide. "I pounded on his door for 'most five minutes!" He gasped. "Couldn't raise him!"

We looked at each other, at a loss. Green Terror was a big investment for the circus. He couldn't just be left in the open. I turned bewilderedly, looking for Chips, Mr. Farnum, or anybody who could tell me what to do. But everyone was gone. The tiger was our responsibility. I considered trying to load the cage bodily into the trailer, but *I* wasn't going to get my fingers in that cage.

"Well, we've just got to go and get him," I said. "The three of us. Come on." And we ran toward Mr. Indrasil's trailer through the gloom of the coming night.

We pounded on his door until he must have thought all the demons of hell were after him. Thankfully, it finally jerked open. Mr. Indrasil swayed and stared down at us, his mad eyes rimmed and oversheened with drink. He smelled like a distillery.

"Damn you, leave me alone," he snarled.

"Mr. Indrasil—" I had to shout over the rising whine of the wind. It was like no storm I had ever heard of or read about, out there. It was like the end of the world.

"You," he gritted softly. He reached down and gathered my shirt up in a knot. "I'm going to teach you a lesson you'll never forget." He glared at Kelly and Mike, cowering back in the moving storm shadows. "Get out!"

They ran. I didn't blame them; I've told you—Mr. Indrasil

was crazy. And not just ordinary crazy—he was like a crazy animal, like one of his own cats gone bad.

"All right," he muttered, staring down at me, his eyes like hurricane lamps. "No juju to protect you now. No grisgris." His lips twitched in a wild, horrible smile. "He isn't here now, is he? We're two of a kind, him and me. Maybe the only two left. My nemesis—and I'm his." He was rambling, and I didn't try to stop him. At least his mind was off me.

"Turned that cat against me, back in '58. Always had the power more'n me. Fool could make a million—the two of us could make a million if he wasn't so damned high and mighty... what's that?"

It was Green Terror, and he had begun to roar ear-splittingly.

"Haven't you got that damned tiger in?" He screamed, almost falsetto. He shook me like a rag doll.

"He won't go!" I found myself yelling back. "You've got to—"

But he flung me away. I stumbled over the fold-up steps in front of his trailer and crashed into a bone-shaking heap at the bottom. With something between a sob and curse, Mr. Indrasil strode past me, face mottled with anger and fear.

I got up, drawn after him as if hypnotized. Some intuitive part of me realized I was about to see the last act played out.

Once clear of the shelter of Mr. Indrasil's trailer, the power of the wind was appalling. It screamed like a runaway freight train. I was an ant, a speck, an unprotected molecule before that thundering, cosmic force.

And Mr. Legere was standing by Green Terror's cage.

It was like a tableau from Dante. The near-empty cage-clearing inside the circle of trailers; the two men, facing each other silently, their clothes and hair rippled by the shrieking gale; the boiling sky above; the twisting wheatfields in the background, like damned souls bending to the whip of Lucifer.

"It's time, Jason," Mr. Legere said, his words flayed across the clearing by the wind.

Mr. Indrasil's wildly whipping hair lifted around the livid scar across the back of his neck. His fists clenched, but he said nothing. I could almost feel him gathering his will, his life force, his id. It gathered around him like an unholy nimbus.

And, then, I saw with sudden horror that Mr. Legere was

unhooking Green Terror's breezeway—and the back of the cage was open!

I cried out, but the wind ripped my words away.

The great tiger leaped out and almost flowed past Mr. Legere. Mr. Indrasil swayed, but did not run. He bent his head and stared down at the tiger.

And Green Terror stopped.

He swung his huge head back to Mr. Legere, almost turned, and then slowly turned back to Mr. Indrasil again. There was a terrifyingly palpable sensation of directed force in the air, a mesh of conflicting wills centered around the tiger. And the wills were evenly matched.

I think, in the end, it was Green Terror's own will—his hate of Mr. Indrasil—that tipped the scales.

The cat began to advance, his eyes hellish, flaring beacons. And something strange began to happen to Mr. Indrasil. He seemed to be folding in on himself, shriveling, accordioning. The silk shirt lost shape, the dark, whipping hair became a hideous toadstool around his collar.

Mr. Legere called something across to him, and, simultaneously, Green Terror leaped.

I never saw the outcome. The next moment I was slammed flat on my back, and the breath seemed to be sucked from my body. I caught one crazily tilted glimpse of a huge, towering cyclone funnel, and then the darkness descended.

When I awoke, I was in my cot just aft of the grainery bins in the all-purpose storage trailer we carried. My body felt as if it had been beaten with padded Indian clubs.

Chips Baily appeared, his face lined and pale. He saw my eyes were open and grinned relievedly. "Didn't know as you were ever gonna wake up. How you feel?"

"Dislocated," I said. "What happened? How'd I get here?"

"We found you piled up against Mr. Indrasil's trailer. The tornado almost carried you away for a souvenir, m'boy."

At the mention of Mr. Indrasil, all the ghastly memories came flooding back. "Where is Mr. Indrasil? And Mr. Legere?"

His eyes went murky, and he started to make some kind of an evasive answer.

"Straight talk," I said, struggling up on one elbow. "I have to know, Chips. I *have* to."

Something in my face must have decided him. "Okay. But

THE NIGHT OF THE TIGER

this isn't exactly what we told the cops—in fact we hardly told the cops any of it. No sense havin' people think we're crazy. Anyhow, Indrasil's gone. I didn't even know that Legere guy was around."

"And Green Terror?"

Chips' eyes were unreadable again. "He and the other tiger fought to death."

"*Other* tiger? There's no other—"

"Yeah, but they found two of 'em, lying in each other's blood. Hell of a mess. Ripped each other's throats out."

"What—where—"

"Who knows? We just told the cops we had two tigers. Simpler that way." And before I could say another word, he was gone.

And that's the end of my story—except for two little items. The words Mr. Legere shouted just before the tornado hit: *"When a man and an animal live in the same shell, Indrasil, the instincts determine the mold!"*

The other thing is what keeps me awake nights. Chips told me later, offering it only for what it might be worth. What he told me was that the strange tiger had a long scar on the back of its neck.

AMMA

Charles Saunders

Charles Saunders is one of the most important figures in the small press fantasy magazine movement. He is one of a half dozen or so really capable writers whose early work has appeared almost exclusively in the little fantasy magazines. More recently, he's begun to establish himself as an important editor with his heroic fantasy magazine, *Dragonbane*. As if that weren't enough, he's the creator of Imaro, one of the few really interesting series characters to show up in fantasy fiction in recent years. All of his appearances in mass market publications to date have, in fact, featured Imaro: two stories reprinted by Lin Carter in his *Year's Best Fantasy* series, and an original selected by Hank Reinhardt and myself for our anthology, *Heroic Fantasy*. But some of the most interesting of Saunders's stories in the small press magazines have not featured Imaro at all. They've been unrelated African tales that have the feel of folklore, and which have appeared in such publications as the highly praised *Weirdbook*. Therefore, it's a pleasure to offer one such story here, from the first issue of the small press fantasy magazine, *Beyond the Fields We Know*.

A soft strain of music drifts delicately among the familiar midday noises of Gao, capital city of the empire of Songhai. Softly it weaves its way through the shrill bargaining of market women; the intrusive importunings of tradesmen; the strident admonitions of *adhana*-priests to prayer and sacrifice at the shrines of the gods; and the clink and jingle of mail-

AMMA

clad soldiers strutting through the streets. The music is easily recognizable: notes plucked by skillful fingers from the seven strings of a Soudanic *ko*.

There are other *ko*-songs that mingle with the general hum of the city, for the ko is popular, and Gao large. Yet some there are in the teeming populace who pause when the notes of this one reach their ears. By the singular quality of its melody, they know that this is no outdated local strummer of weary songs, nor love-struck youth seeking to impress the object of his callow affections. They know, these connoisseurs of the *ko*, that a new *griot* has come to Gao.

Before the final notes of the song have faded, a small crowd is gathered at the *saffiyeh*, a small square off the main marketplace where, traditionally, the newly arrived *griot* comes to display his talents. The stranger sits with his back against a whitewashed wall; his fingers dancing lightly across the strings of his instrument. More like hands hardened by the gripping of sword or plow, these, than hands accustomed mainly to the touch of laquered wood and slender wire.

Beneath the road-worn garments of a wanderer, the *griot's* frame bulks large, yet strangely gaunt, as though once-massive thews have been reduced to the minimum amount required for physical activity. His sepia-toned face is solemn and middle-aged, webbed with lines scored by adversity. Large eyes, dark and luminous, seem fixed upon a point somewhere above the heads of his audience. Two *tira*, leather charm pouches, hang from beaded cords around his neck. Beside him rests a great empty turtle shell, upturned to receive the bronze coins and quills of gold-dust he hopes to earn from his listeners.

The crowd stands quietly. There are turbaned men swathed in voluminous *johos* over cotton trousers, and turbaned women garbed in colorful *asokabas* that descend from waist to ankle, leaving the rest of the body bare. Children clad after the fashion of the adults squeeze between their elders' bodies, the better to hear the *ko* of the new *griot*. The dry-season sun burns like a torch in the cloudless sky, bathing ebony skin in a glossy sheen of perspiration.

The *griot's* song ends. His listeners stamp their feet on the dusty pave: a sign of approval. Even though no coins or quills have yet found their way into his tortoise shell, the *griot* smiles. He knows that a man of his calling is first a story teller, no better than second a musician. His *ko* has served its purpose. Now it is time to earn his day's livelihood.

"I am going to tell a story," the *griot* says.

"*Ya-ngani!*" the crowd responds, meaning "Right!"

"It may be a lie."

"*Ya-ngani.*"

"But not everything in it is false."

"*Ya-ngani.*"

The *griot* begins his tale.

Mattock resting on one broad shoulder, Babakar *iri* Sounkalo stood shaking his head in the midst of his charred beanfield. For the thousandth time he cursed the Sussu, whose raiders had swept down from the north to despoil isolate border towns like Gadou, the one closest to Babakar's ruined farm. The Sussu had, as always, been driven back to their barren mountains by the soldiers of Songhai; Babakar himself had taken up lance and shield to join the forces of Kassa *iri* Ba, the invincible general from Gao, and the blood of more than a few Sussu had washed his blade.

But now, as he surveyed the burnt acres of the field that had been in his family since the first stone was laid in Gadou, the taste of triumph had faded for Babakar. His *wassa*-beans had been reduced to a mere blackish stubble, and though he knew that the next crop would grow even faster in the ash-enriched soil, alone he could never replant his beans before the wet season ended.

Alone . . . again the bitter memory seared across his mind: the memory of his wife and two daughters butchered by the swords of the Sussu who had nearly destroyed Gadou with their treacherous attack. Sussu lives had paid for the loss of his family; Kassa *iri* Ba himself had praised Babakar's ferocity in battle.

Now, though, Babakar faced only a grim choice as his reward. He could re-till his field in the slim hope that the wet season would last long enough for a new crop to rise, saving him from starvation. Or he could join the many others already in flight southward to the provinces untouched by the border war. The idea of abandoning the land still nurtured by the spirits of his ancestors remained unthinkable to Babakar.

"You'll accomplish nothing standing here in self-debate," Babakar chided himself. With a gusting sigh, he raised his mattock from his shoulder and swung it down into the soil.

AMMA

It was then that he saw her, swinging gracefully down the road that separated his field from that of a neighbor slain by the Sussu. The mattock nearly fell from his hands. For it was from the west that she came, and Babakar knew that only the semi-arid wasteland called the Tassili lay west of Gadou. The woman couldn't have come from *there* . . . she must have run off in that direction to escape the marauders, and was only now making her way back to more habitable terrain.

As the woman came closer, Babakar saw that she was, though disheveled, beautiful to behold. Though she was not tall, a willowy slenderness lent her an illusion of greater height. The tattered condition of her *asokaba* contrasted with the neatly folded turban that clung closely to her head. Between the two garments, a pleasant expanse of bare black skin was filmed with a thin layer of road dust, reminiscent of the coating of ashes young girls smeared on their bodies before their puberty dances. A look at the way her conical breasts jounced with each step convinced Babakar that the stranger had passed beyond that age, though from the tautness of her skin she could not be much older than twenty rains. Her face, withdrawn and pensive, would not have been out of place at the Court of the Hundred Wives of the *Keita*, the Emperor of Songhai, who took only the most beautiful women of the Soudan to his golden love-chamber. Of possessions besides her garments, the young woman had none save a few neck and arm ornaments.

Babakar was just asking himself if he should call out to the stranger when she caught his glance, smiled, and came toward him. That smile stirred something in Babakar that had remained sullen and dormant since the day—over a month past now—when he had returned from his field to discover the Sussu-violated corpses of his wife, Amma, and daughters in the smoldering ruins of their home.

"Does this road lead to Gadou?" the stranger asked. Her very voice reminded Babakar of the beloved tones of another, long stilled by the slash of a Sussu sword.

"What's left of it, yes," he replied. Then, on an impulse: "Where do you come from? Only lizards and gazelles dwell in the Tassili."

The woman dropped her gaze. "I was taken by some deserters from the main body of raiders. They weren't even Sussu, but renegade Nobas who had joined the Sussu for the plunder. There were five of them. They swept me onto one of their horses and took me away to the west, and they found a patch of bush, and then they . . . they. . . ." She choked, unable to continue.

This time Babakar's mattock did drop to the ground as he crossed quickly to the woman's side and laid a hand on her shoulder.

"War makes victims," he said. "Loss is the lot of us all. My wife, Amma, and my two daughters were slain by the Sussu. You, at least, still live."

The stranger's head came up sharply. Her eyes met Babakar's. "Amma? I am also called Amma. . . ."

Babakar's hand tightened on smooth skin. The pressure was gentle, though, and she did not flinch as she well might have at the touch of a strong man's grip.

"They used me until I begged to die," Amma continued tightly. "And they might have taken me back to their own country if they hadn't been pursued by Sussu who were angry at the Nobas' desertion. There was a fight . . . I escaped while they killed each other for the gold the Noba had stolen along with me. I walked through the waste, taking food where I could find it. When I left the Tassili, there was death all around. I took these garments from the body of a woman who no longer needed them. I thought I might find something in Gadou. But there is death there, too, you say."

Again she looked down. Babakar took his hand from Amma's shoulder and clenched it as if he were gripping the hilt of a sword.

"Yes, there is death," he said bitterly. "With this hand I killed as many Sussu as I could see. But in the end, I have only this burnt-out field; my family is still dead, and there is no one to help me to replant my crop before the rains pass."

They remained silent for a time, each adrift in sad reverie. Then Amma said, "There is nothing for me in Gadou, and I weary of walking. I will stay here and help you with your crop."

Astonished, Babakar could only respond, "I have but one mattock."

Amma laughed, her smile rendering her face even more attractive than before. "I'll use this," she retorted, bending down to curl her slim fingers around a fire-blackened stake which had been part of a fence that once guarded Babakar's field. Without further words, Amma began to thrust the jagged point of the stake into the soil. Fresh earth emerged as she twisted the stake in a digging motion.

Only for a moment did Babakar watch her. Then he picked up his mattock and proceeded to work at Amma's side. A cloud appeared, in the sudden fashion of the wet season, and a hot, misty rain soon washed down on two dark, naked backs bent to the soil.

Day followed inexorable day, and newly turned earth progressively supplanted the charred remnants of Babakar's field. The rains fell with perceptibly diminishing intensity. Working against the advent of the day they knew the rain would cease, Babakar and Amma toiled from the rising to the setting of the sun. With grim determination they struggled to prepare the soil for planting while there was still time for another crop to grow.

Work they shared; work in plenty, along with the thatch-roofed house Babakar had erected on the side of the one the Sussu had destroyed. They shared meager meals of millet and beans bought only after tiresome haggling with the near destitute merchants of Gadou. The people left in the town paid little heed to Babakar's new companion; she was but one more of many refugees from the desolate countryside. At night they shared the sleep of the exhausted, their bodies touching only by chance on Babakar's single sleeping mat. For, by unspoken agreement, they shared not each other; not in the way of a man and a woman.

On occasion Babakar's gaze would linger on the smooth play of muscles beneath Amma's skin as she toiled beneath the sun. Such gazes did not last long, for the memory of his first Amma remained a shadow of sorrow in his mind. And he remembered how the Noba had ravished her. . . . Was he, a countryman who had given her shelter, to offer her similar abuse?

If Amma noticed such moments of quickly suppressed passion, she showed no sign. Indeed, she seemed more determined than Babakar to succeed with their late-sown crop. She demanded nothing of him beyond food and shelter he gave her.

Once, at sunset, they were visited by Kuya Adowa, the local *tynbibi* or diviner. Despite her advanced years, Kuya stood proudly erect, and her eyes smoldered beneath her turban like the embers of a fire. The words she spoke were addressed to Babakar, but that dark, portentous gaze never left the eyes of Amma.

"The *dyongu*, the spirit-cock that embodies the luck of Gadou, died yesterday," the old woman announced ominously.

Babakar stiffened. The death of the sacred black rooster always presaged a period of ill fortune. When the predecessor of this last *dyongu* had died, the invasion of the Sussu had followed. What new calamities the death of Kuya's bird foreshadowed, Babakar did not care to contemplate. His concern was why Kuya Adowa had chosen to come to him to speak of the matter. . . .

"War brings disruption not only to the lands of men, but to the world of the spirits as well," the *tynbibi* said. "The *kambu*, the spirits of power, manifest themselves in our world, and the *tyerkou* shed their skins at night to wander the land and drink the blood of the unwary. Beware, Babakar *iri* Sounkalo. Beware."

Only after the second "Beware" did Kuya shift her gaze from Amma's eyes to Babakar's.

"What do you mean by that, Kuya Adowa?" Babakar demanded. "Are Amma and I in danger of some kind?"

The old woman wrinkled her nose in disdain. "I leave that interpretation to you. I must go and seek the black hatchling that is to become the new *dyongu*."

With that she turned her bare, bony back on them and stalked back down the dusty road to Gadou.

Troubled, Babakar turned to Amma . . . and was taken aback by the hatred in her eyes as she glared at the dwindling figure of the departing *tynbibi*. . . .

There came the morning when the first seedlings of *wassa* poked boldly through the soil. Overnight the seeds had sprouted several inches, in the typical manner of the first growth-spurt of this type of bean plant.

A smile of satisfaction crept quietly across the face of Babakar. It was the first such smile his features had worn since the coming of the Sussu. . . .

Then he looked at Amma . . . and his smile disappeared, replaced by an expression of utter bewilderment.

In an attitude approaching reverence, Amma knelt near a cluster of seedlings. One finger stroked the fragile green stems with the delicate touch of a priestess conveying a sacrifice to the goddess of fertility. Her head inclined so far forward that her face hovered only a hairsbreadth from the tops of the plants.

Tentatively, Babakar touched the shoulder of the kneeling woman. The effect of the brush of his fingers against her skin was at once instantaneous and disconcerting. Amma sprang into the air like a frightened animal. Yet for all the suddenness of her leap, she landed lightly on her feet, facing Babakar in a tense, quivering half-crouch. It was as though she were prepared to flee at the slightest pretext. Her eyes, fixed glassily at something beyond Babakar's head, bulged wide in fright. A tremor shook her slight frame; then the glaze faded from her eyes and she suddenly pitched forward.

Quickly Babakar reached out and broke Amma's fall, saving her from a bruising impact. For a moment she lay limp in his arms. Babakar became conscious of her sleek body pressing closely to his, and this time his thoughts did not stray to the Amma he had lost, or the outrage committed by the Noba deserters....

"Amma..." he murmured into the tight folds of her turban. He had felt her stir against him. "Amma, what is wrong?"

Her head tilted upward. Never before had Babakar been so aware of the true beauty of the strange woman's face. It was as though he were gazing into a sculpture carved from polished black pearl, streaked with tracks of diamond where the sunlight caught her tears.

"I am sorry," she said softly. "It's just that I was remembering the last harvest my family had ... before the Sussu came."

"The Sussu are gone!" Babakar said fiercely, his hands tightening on Amma's arms. Silently he repeated what he had said. The Sussu *were* gone ... as was his first Amma. Sorrow was there; it always would be. But the woman he held in his arms was no memory. She was warm. She was real. He loved her.

Babakar's face bent toward Amma's. Their faces came slowly together, and when their mouths met, Amma's arms encircled Babakar's shoulders and clung to him with gentle strength. Warm as the sun that nurtured the land was this, the first embrace of their love.

"My Amma," Babakar whispered when their lips parted.

"Your second Amma...."

"No," Babakar said firmly. "I have only one Amma. And I want her to be my wife."

"You do not ask this only out of gratitude for my help with the crop?"

"How can you say that?" Babakar demanded. "It is as a woman I want you, not labor to be bargained for. What is mine is yours, even my life."

Exerting a soft but insistent pressure, Amma's arms drew Babakar's head downward, and their mouths met again. Long moments passed before they parted. It was Amma who spoke first. "When the next wet season begins, we will go to the *adhana* to be mated at the shrine of the Mother of Earth?"

Without hesitation Babakar assented, and he pressed Amma close to him. He never realized that Amma's gaze was cast downward, fixed with strange avidity on the *wassa* sprouts pushing their way through the soil. . . .

Night had fallen swiftly, as always during the waning weeks of the wet season. The glances that had passed between Amma and Babakar were no longer fleeting or hastily averted. As they walked from the field to Babakar's dwelling, Amma's hand clasped his for the first time. The soft half-light of the stars cast a shaft of muted illumination through the house's only window, and outlined the contours of Amma's half-nude form as she reclined on the sleeping-mat. Her arms opened to Babakar as he moved toward her.

All the restraint he had imposed upon his emotions melted swiftly in the heat of Amma's embrace. His hands peeled the *asokaba* from her waist, then traveled upward to untie the turban from her head, so that he could experience the sensation of her kinky hair brushing against his palms.

But as Babakar's fingers pulled at the knot of the turban, Amma uttered a low cry that had naught to do with passion or pleasure. Her hands shot up to Babakar's, and with surprising force held them away from her head. The points of her fingernails dug talon-like into his flesh as she hissed, "No! You must not touch my turban."

A bewildered "Why?" was Babakar's only response.

Amma did not reply immediately. She lay silent, her body taut and rigid next to Babakar's, her hands pinioning his wrists like clamps of steel. Then, with a shudder, she released her hold and wriggled from beneath him. Sitting up, she hooked her arms around drawn-up knees, then spoke in a flat tone.

"I did not tell you everything that happened when the deserters took me. I fought them. They became angry, and one of them decided to teach me not to defy them. He took a brand from their cook-fire, and pushed it at my face. I turned away . . . and the flame burned the top of my head! There are scars . . . it is horrible. You must not see it! You must not!"

Babakar reached out and pulled Amma down to his broad chest. She yielded easily, and nestled passively against him.

"Yet another outrage that the Sussu must answer for," he said bitterly. "Would that I'd killed as many of them for you as I did for . . . my other family." Then, more gently, "My feelings for you are not so shallow that I would turn from the sight of what the Noba did to you. But if you prefer that I not see it, I will never again put my hand near your turban."

Amma leaned forward and covered Babakar's lips with hers. His arms tightened around her; she returned his embrace with an ardor beyond any he had experienced before. Their love was consummated in a fierce flow of passion that left Babakar spent and drowsy. So deep was the slumber he soon fell into that he was not disturbed when Amma extricated herself from his embrace, hastily donned her *asokaba*, and quietly slipped out of their dwelling, being especially careful not to rustle the rectangle of cloth that hung across the doorway. Nor did he waken when, only an hour before the rising of the sun, she returned.

Amma seemed strangely subdued as she and Babakar walked to the *wassa*-field in the morning. Her fingers hung lifelessly in his grasp, and her eyes were downcast. Babakar wondered if he had unknowingly done wrong the night before. Surely Amma had enjoyed their lovemaking as much as he . . . or had she? Possibly she now recalled the depredations of the Noba who had ravished her, while in the ecstasy of the night she had forgotten. Babakar wanted to assure Amma that with him she was secure. But if she had indeed begun to forget the horrors of the past, it would be foolish for Babakar to bring them once again to the forefront of her mind. Suddenly he recalled the strange warning of Kuya Adowa. . . .

The sight that met his eyes when they reached the field

swept aside all the conflicting thoughts that roiled through Babakar's mind.

The field was ruined. All the burgeoning *wassa* sprouts were gone, bitten off to jagged, pitiful stumps that barely protruded above the line of the soil. Amid the destruction lay the mocking signatures of its perpetrators: scores of small, cloven hoofprints scattered among the rows of ravaged plants.

"Goats?" thought Babakar. No, that could not be. There were no goat-herds this far south of the Gwaridi-Milima Mountains.

When he knelt to look more closely at the damage, he realized that the prints had come in a long, disorderly line from the west, then departed in the direction of neighboring fields after they had eaten their fill of his *wassa*. There were other, fresher tracks that told him that later the animals had returned the way they had come; that way led to the Tassili. There were no wild goats in the Tassili, Babakar knew. There was not enough forage in the wasteland to support their voracious appetites. But there were . . . gazelles.

The mystery deepened. Babakar's brow furrowed in confusion. Never before had the graceful, elusive antelopes of the desert ventured this far from their wasteland environs. Never, at least, in the generations of time the *griots* could recall, and these seemed to stretch back forever. Yet what tradition said could never happen, had. The evidence lay grazed to the ground at his feet.

Shaking his head in despair, Babakar stood up and turned to Amma. She stared downward with a wooden, unseeing expression. *Gods,* thought Babakar, *she's even more affected by this than I am. . . .*

Gingerly, recalling her frightened reaction of the previous morning, he placed his arm around her shoulders. "Amma," he began haltingly, "I don't understand why this happened, but somehow we must overcome it. The land is useless to us now; there is no time to plant another crop. We can go to Gao, or some other city, and hire our services to some Merchant Lord. It's only a step above slavery, but it's better than starving. . . ."

"So, Babakar, they got you too," a voice behind them interrupted.

Babakar whirled to face two of his fellow farmers, Mwiya *iri* Fenuka and Atuye *iri* Sisi, whose fields lay closer to Gadou than his.

AMMA
45

"The gazelles destroyed your crops, too?" Babakar demanded. "Did they get everybody?"

"Mine, not his," Atuye said sourly. Like Babakar, Atuye was an ex-soldier, hard-muscled and battle-scarred. Mwiya, a stocky man of middle age, seemed even more agitated than Atuye even though it was Mwiya's crop that had been spared.

"It's like that throughout this whole area," Mwiya said. "The creatures struck haphazardly. You know Atuye, here, and I are neighbors, our fields side by side. Yet mine still stands as it did yesterday, and Atuye's looks like yours."

"Thought you might have seen something, since yours is the last field in the direction the gazelles came from," Atuye said.

Babakar shook his head. "I slept through it all, curse the luck."

"What about you?" Atuye growled, turning to Amma.

Amma started, her shoulders tensing beneath Babakar's arm.

"Nothing," she replied quickly. "I know nothing."

"Are you sure?" pressed Atuye.

"What in Motoni's wrong with you, man?" Babakar exploded, taking a step forward. "Amma couldn't have seen anything. She was with me all night."

Atuye stood his ground, though he couldn't fail to notice the clenching of Babakar's fist, nor his willingness to use it.

"All I know is that when we went to old Kuya Adowa this morning to ask if she could help us, she told us to seek the answers to our questions from Babakar *iri* Sounkalo's new woman."

Something close to fear gripped Babakar in a cold grasp as he again recalled the *tynbibi's* visit, and her warning ... angrily he shook the feeling off.

"You'd take the word of a half-mad old woman over mine?" he challenged.

The two farmers stood in silence. They knew, of course, what had happened to Babakar's family during the war, and Atuye had witnessed the man's ferocity in battle. It was unlikely to the point of absurdity that the Babakar he and Mwiya knew could be involved in the mysterious destruction of the fields. But the woman ... was her obvious nervousness due to fear ... or guilt?

The tension between Babakar and Atuye was threatening

to erupt at any moment into physical conflict. Wisely Mwiya averted it.

"Calm down, Babakar. Of course we believe you. But you and Atuye aren't the only ones to have suffered because of these marauding gazelles. We've got unanswered questions here, and somehow we must find the answers to them."

"You can depend on that," Atuya added.

"We fought side by side against the Sussu, Atuye. But anyone who seeks to harm Amma is as much my enemy as they were," Babakar said quietly.

Atuye's heated reply was quickly cut off by Mwiya. "All right, Babakar. I understand. We must talk of this again later, though. Tonight the Council of Elders meets in Gadou. Will you come?"

"To Motoni with the Elders!" Babakar snarled. "Will they save us from the gazelles as they saved us from the Sussu?"

"I am sorry you take that attitude," said Mwiya. "You may well regret it before this matter's done."

When Babakar did not reply, the visitors returned to the road that led to Gadou. Babakar turned to Amma, who had said nothing since her reply to Atuye.

"We will leave tonight," he told her. "There is nothing here for us now."

"No!" Amma said with vehemence. "If we go tonight, the old woman's suspicions will be proven correct, at least to people like Atuye. We must wait a day, maybe two before departing. By then they'll have other things to think about."

"What other things?"

"The gazelles."

"What do you really know of the gazelles?" Babakar demanded, digging his fingers into her arm.

Amma glared full into the big man's eyes and said, "Nothing."

Contritely, Babakar released her arm. Before he could say anything more, Amma spun on her heel and strode stiff-backed to their dwelling. Babakar followed only after one last, despairing glance at his twice-ruined *wassa*field.

Amma remained uncommunicative while they gathered their few belongings together, mostly Babakar's. As they ate a supper of millet cakes and thin stew, Babakar spoke encouragingly of the possibilities that awaited them in the cities of the south. He could put his war skills to use as guardsman to a Merchant Lord, or even the Emperor, he reasoned. And the

Merchant Lords were always seeking women to peddle their goods for them beneath the huge multicolored awnings of the market squares. Since the time of the First Ancestors, the market had been the province of women, and an attractive one like Amma would find little difficulty finding a place in a square. Perhaps the loss of their crop was not so disastrous as it seemed, he reassured.

Amma was indifferent to his enthusiasm. After the sun sank in a crimson blaze beyond the horizon, and they prepared to retire for the night, she rebuffed Babakar's advances, keeping her *asokaba* wrapped firmly in place as she curled close to the edge of the sleeping-mat. When Babakar reached to touch her shoulder, the skin felt cold before she flinched away. It was as though the fire and tenderness of the night before had never happened. . . .

Anger stirred in Babakar as his ardor ebbed. Then the flash of resentment faded as quickly as it had come. The experience Amma had endured since the coming of the Sussu might have driven another person over the brink of madness. The destruction of the bean-crop by the gazelles must seem to her but one more in an endless series of calamities. Though she might prefer to battle the demons of her past alone this night, Babakar vowed that when morning came, Amma would know that she need never face them alone again. Thus resolved, he drifted into a deep slumber that remained undisturbed when Amma slid quietly from the sleeping-mat and melted into the shadows outside the doorway. . . .

Hard hands shook Babakar out of sleep. His eyes flew open; bleary darkness and shadowy shapes swam before him as he was hauled roughly to his feet. Alertness came in a rush as the intruders hustled him out the doorway of his dwelling.

"What is this?" he shouted hoarsely . . . then the indignant words that were to follow died in his throat at the sight that greeted him in the moonlight.

Starkly silhouetted in the pale glare stood Kuya Adowa. Her hand was clenched firmly on the *tira*-pouch dangling between her breasts, and her face bore an expression of wrath and hatred. Behind her several of the neighboring farmers stood in a tight circle, surrounding . . . Amma. They were armed with staves and long daggers, and two of them carried torches. Quick glances to his left and right confirmed that it was Mwiya and Atuye who firmly pinioned his arms.

Enraged, Babakar surged strongly against his captors' grasp. "Damn you; you dare to invade a man's house and drag his woman from her bed? Are you Songhai or Sussu?"

The insult stung Atuye into delivering a sharp blow to the side of Babakar's head. As Babakar staggered, Atuye growled, "You know damn well she wasn't in your house, son of Sounkalo. We caught her on the way from the field of Falil *iri* Nyadi."

Babakar froze, his instinct to struggle overridden by shock. He had assumed that Amma had been torn from his side moments before he had been awakened.

"Amma . . . is it true?" he asked. She did not reply. Her head was bowed; he could not see her eyes.

Abruptly Kyua Adowa spoke. "Let him go. It isn't his fault."

"*What* isn't my fault?" cried Babakar.

"You should have come to the Council of Elders, Babakar," Kuya said. There was a note of pity in her voice. "We decided that the farmers whose fields had escaped destruction would guard their crops tonight to drive away the gazelles should they return. Falil, here, was one of those who kept watch. Tell Babakar what you told us, Falil."

Falil, whose age could not have been more than eighteen rains, stepped shyly from the knot of people around Amma. His eyes seemed to reflect moonlight in his dark face as he spoke.

"I watched our field from a tree that grows near it, so that I'd be better able to see the gazelles coming. For a long time, nothing happened. I was about to fall asleep when I heard something coming into the field. I thought it might be the gazelles. But when I looked, I saw *her*." He jerked his head toward Amma, not daring to look at her. His fear of her was obvious.

"She didn't see me, though," he continued. "I was about to climb down and ask her what she was doing in my field, when she pulled her turban off her head. I saw the moon flash off something in her hair. Then she took off her *asokaba*, and rolled on the ground. . . ."

With a bellow of outrage, Babakar leaped at the youth. Atuye and Mwiya had not released their hold on him, though, and they dragged him back.

"She didn't see me!" Falil cried, his eyes wide with fright.

"She rolled and rolled, and she *changed*. When she got back to her feet, she wasn't a woman anymore. *She was a gazelle!*"

"This is madness!" roared Babakar. "Have you people lost your senses, to listen to stories a child wouldn't believe?"

"I know what I saw!" the younger man flared. "She was a gazelle. She raised her head and gave a cry like nothing I've ever heard before. Then she stood still . . . for how long I do not know. Then I heard a rumble of hooves, and a rustle in the wind, and suddenly a whole herd of gazelles was in the field. There were scores of them, eating our millet. I should have climbed down and yelled at them to scare them off. But I was afraid. If you had seen how she *changed*. . . . At last they were done, and they ran off to the west. All of them but *her*. She rolled on the ground again after the others were gone, and when she stood up, she was a woman again. She put on her turban and *asokaba*, and walked away from the field. I climbed down from the tree and ran to the field of my neighbor. We caught her as she came down the road to this house, then took her to Kuya Adowa. The rest, you already know."

Babakar shook his head in disbelief. He looked pleadingly at Amma, but she would not return his gaze.

"*Kambu*," Kuya Adowa whispered. "An animal imbued with the power of a spirit-being beyond the realm of man. They control the actions of the animal they invade, and they can assume the shape of humankind, and speak the language of men. They read our thoughts, and tell us what they know we would most like to hear. Yet even though they may look human, they are not. Babakar! Your woman is a *kambu*. A *kambu* cannot love. She means only evil for you, Babakar. If not, then why didn't her creatures spare your field?"

"No," Babakar groaned. *"No!* I cannot believe it. . . ."

"Yes!" sceamed Kuya Adowa. A spidery black hand reached up and tore the turban from Amma's head. Babakar gasped. It was not a bare, fire-seared scalp that lay revealed in the stark moonlight, as Amma had led him to expect. Her head was covered by a cap of kinky black hair, as that of any woman of Songhai would be. Sprouting from the front of her skull, however, were two small, spiralled horns . . . the horns of a female desert gazelle.

A wave of despair swept over Babakar. He recalled Amma's words of only a night before . . . "You must not touch my turban. . . ."

"Amma," he said with a sob, wondering if even the name was a lie. She had not mentioned it before he had told her of his first Amma. . . .

For the first time that night, Amma's eyes met his. Her face, even beneath the spiralled horns, still absorbed him in its loveliness.

"One of the Sussu you killed was the son of a *sabane;* a powerful sorcerer, master of the Black Talk," she told him. "He used his skills to discover the slayer of his son. Then he used the Black Talk to bind me to his will; to force me to use my people to carry out his vengeance. I resisted, but his power was too strong. The effort it took to bind me killed the *sabane*, but the power of his Black Talk remains, and I am compelled to carry out his command: to call my people like locusts to destroy your crops. The *sabane* was mad with grief. He wanted all of your town to suffer for your deed. . . ."

"Lies! Lies!" screeched Kuya Adowa. "Can't you see this is a creature of evil, a thing that deserves death? Her very appearance is a lie!"

Amma turned her gaze to Kuya, and the old woman gasped and shrank back a step. Amma's eyes returned to the stricken farmer's.

"A *kambu* can love, Babakar," she said softly. Then, in a sudden move, she bolted through the men surrounding her. One managed to grasp her *asokaba*, but Amma tore free and raced on, a naked shadow in the moonlight.

"Stop her!" screamed the *tynbibi*. One of the farmers hurled his staff. Whirling end-over-end, it struck Amma on the back of her head. She fell heavily; before she could gain her feet again, they were upon her, striking hard with their staves. They hit her with the frenzy of man killing a poisonous snake.

Crazed with sorrow and rage, Babakar broke free from Atuye and Mwiya and rushed toward Amma's attackers. An unearthly shriek rose just as he reached them. With a ferocity he had not felt since the last days of the war, he seized two of the men and hurled them violently to the ground.

Then he stopped, looked down, and swayed like a man drunk on palm-wine. For the broken, bleeding body sprawled before him was not that of a woman. It was a dead gazelle that lay there, its eyes staring emptily upward; as emptily as Babakar's stared down. He dropped to his knees and reached out to touch the head of the fallen creature.

"That sound," Falil *iri* Nyadi said nervously. "It was just like the one she made when she summoned the gazelles."

"Listen!" said Atuye. "Can you hear it? A rumbling sound, coming from the west...."

Though they did not answer him, the others had heard it. The sound grew louder. It was like the music of some insistent drum, growing in intensity yet retaining an underlying delicacy of tone.

"Look!" cried Falil, pointing to the dark western horizon. The others followed his gaze, and beheld a shadowy mass detaching itself from the black gloom. Individual shapes became discernible; graceful forms advancing rapidly in breathtaking bounds. Spiralled horns flashed and glittered in the moonlight.

"Gazelles," whispered Kuya Adowa. Her hands clutched convulsively at her *tira*; strange words of sorcerous import spilled from her lips.

"What's wrong with you, old woman?" snarled Atuye. "What harm can a herd of timid gazelles do?"

"They don't look so timid to me," said Mwiya. "I thought you said there were scores of them, Falil. Looks more like hundreds now."

"*She* called them," Falil muttered.

"I cannot stop them," cried Kuya Adowa. "Run!"

"From gazelles?" Atuye scoffed.

A four-legged body arrowed toward him, head down, horns pointed outward. The sharp tips of the horns took Atuye full in the chest. With a strangled cry he went down, eyes wide in incredulity even as blood spurted from his mouth.

Terrified, the others turned and ran, dropping staves and torches alike in the panic that clawed at their souls. They were too slow. Living projectiles of hoof and horn hurtled like lightning among them. The speed that served the gazelles so well in flight from the great beasts of prey had now become a weapon, deadly and inescapable. Screams rose amid the quiet thunder of hooves as the antelope plunged their horns through the bodies of their human prey....

Babakar had not moved when the others fled. He seemed unaware of anything save the still form lying in front of him ... until a flying body caught him on the shoulder and bowled him over onto his back. He raised his arms defensively. The gesture was not fast enough; a pair of forehooves struck him in the stomach. His breath whooshed out and he doubled over in pain. It was then that he saw the leaping messengers of death, and heard the cries of their victims. There was a curious absence of fear as he awaited his own death. But the finishing blow never came. . . .

Clutching his injured abdomen, Babakar looked up into the eyes of a large male gazelle. In those dark orbs he saw . . . recognition? Compassion? Pity? He thought he could detect these things in the glimmer of the gazelle's eyes, but he knew only that the antelope did not attack him further.

Grunting with the pain the effort cost him, Babakar raised himself on an elbow and looked upon a scene of sad carnage. Kuya Adowa, Falil, Mwiya, and all the others lay dead as the thing that had been his Amma. The great herd of gazelles stood still now, blood dripping from their horns and caking in their hooves. Silver trails glimmered down their narrow muzzles; they were weeping.

And Babakar wept with them, for what man could endure the tears of those beautiful killers, tears that mixed with the blood trickling down the graceful spiral of their horns?

The leader of the herd came toward Babakar. The beast bent its head; its tongue flickered from its mouth and licked the blood from the wounds its hooves had made in Babakar's stomach. Then the gazelle turned and bounded off to the west. As if on signal, the other antelope followed, and within an eyeblink they were gone, only the fading drum of their hooves attesting that they had been there at all. That . . . and the ten unmoving bodies of Amma's murderers.

Disregarding the pain that shot from stomach to spine, Babakar *iri* Sounkalo gathered the broken form of Amma into his arms. He rose. Cradling her close to him, he crooned her name as the tears coursed down his ebony cheeks.

A kambu can love, she had said before she died. Were these her own true words, Babakar wondered. Or had she merely repeated the desperate thought that had leaped into his mind at the end? He would never know the truth. And, knowing that, Babakar wept bitterly.

By the time the *griot's* tale is ended, a fair-sized crowd congregates at the *saffiyeh*. For a moment the people are silent. Then the jeering begins.

"You'll never make a living in Gao telling tales like that, *griot!*"

"Whoever heard of gazelles attacking people?"

"And a gazelle turning into a woman! Hah!"

"I come from a village near Gadou, and I never heard of such a thing there."

Already some of the listeners have turned to leave when the *griot* stands up. He is a tall man, taller than he had appeared in his squatting posture. Old fires kindle in his eyes. With a savage motion he pulls his upper garment over his head. Naked to the waist, his body is spare and gaunt, though stretched over a large frame. It is not his bare torso, though, that elicits sharp exclamations of surprise from the crowd. It is the two scars that stand out against the dark skin of his stomach . . . scars in the shape of two sharp, narrow hooves; the hooves of a gazelle. . . .

The coins and quills of the listeners fill the tortoise shell of the *griot*. But the *griot* pays no heed to their generosity. He plucks at the strings of his *ko*. "Amma," he murmurs softly. "Amma. . . ."

CHASTEL

Manly Wade Wellman

Judge Pursuivant first adventured in the pages of the fabulous *Weird Tales* magazine some four decades ago. In contrast, this Lee Cobbett fellow is an upstart: he first appeared in the early seventies in *Witchcraft & Sorcery*. Both characters were created by Manly Wade Wellman under his pen-name Gans T. Field, and both proved to be more than a match for just about any supernatural manifestation that their creator could imagine—and Wellman has a notably sinister imagination. Now, in a novelet written especially for *Year's Best Horror Stories*, Judge Pursuivant and Lee Cobbett join forces and become involved in chilling doings centering on a play about Dracula. About the story, Wellman writes: "The Connecticut setting for a vampire outbreak harks back to long-ago Connecticut papers, which told of such a thing apparently happening. It's in the books cited here. Incidentally, both the poems I quote are actual ones. I've puzzled over the one from Grant's odd book, have never seen it anywhere else, and have never found anyone who had heard of it. Like Pursuivant here, I give myself to wonder if it isn't a fake antique, like Clerk Saunders's better known vampire poem to be found in Montague Summers."

"Then you won't let Count Dracula rest in his tomb?" inquired Lee Cobbett, his square face creasing with a grin.

Five of them sat in the parlor of Judge Keith Hilary Pursuivant's hotel suite on Central Park West. The Judge lounged in an armchair, a wineglass in his big old hand. On this, his eighty-seventh birthday, his blue eyes were clear, penetrating. His once tawny hair and mustache had gone blizzard-white, but both grew thick, and his square face showed rosy. In his tailored blue leisure suit, he still looked powerfully deep-chested and broad-shouldered.

Blocky Lee Cobbett wore jacket and slacks almost as brown as his face. Next to him sat Laurel Parcher, small and young and cinnamon-haired. The others were natty Phil Drumm the summer theater producer, and Isobel Arrington from a wire press service. She was blonde, expensively dressed, she smoked a dark cigarette with a white tip. Her pen scribbled swiftly.

"Dracula's as much alive as Sherlock Holmes," argued Drumm. "All the revivals of the play, all the films—"

"Your musical should wake the dead, anyway," said Cobbett, drinking. "What's your main number, Phil? *Garlic Time? Gory, Gory Hallelujah?*"

"Let's have Christian charity here, Lee," Pursuivant came to Drumm's rescue. "Anyway, Miss Arrington came to interview me. Pour her some wine and let me try to answer her questions."

"I'm interested in Mr. Cobbett's remarks," said Isobel Arrington, her voice deliberately throaty. "He's an authority on the supernatural."

"Well, perhaps," admitted Cobbett, "and Miss Parcher has had some experiences. But Judge Pursuivant is the true authority, the author of *Vampiricon.*"

"I've read it, in paperback," said Isobel Arrington. "Phil, it mentions a vampire belief up in Connecticut, where you're having your show. What's that town again?"

"Deslow," he told her. "We're making a wonderful old stone barn into a theater. I've invited Lee and Miss Parcher to visit."

She looked at Drumm. "Is Deslow a resort town?"

"Not yet, but maybe the show will bring tourists. In Deslow, up to now, peace and quiet is the chief business. If you drop your shoe, everybody in town will think somebody's blowing the safe."

"Deslow's not far from Jewett City," observed Pursuivant. "There were vampires there about a century and a quarter ago. A family named Ray was afflicted. And to the east, in Rhode Island, there was a lively vampire folklore in recent years."

"Let's leave Rhode Island to H. P. Lovecraft's imitators," suggested Cobbett. "What do you call your show, Phil?"

"The Land Beyond the Forest," said Drumm. "We're casting it now. Using locals in bit parts. But we have Gonda Chastel to play Dracula's countess."

"I never knew that Dracula had a countess," said Laurel Parcher.

"There was a stage star named Chastel, long ago when I was young," said Pursuivant. "Just the one name—Chastel."

"Gonda's her daughter, and a year or so ago Gonda came to live in Deslow," Drumm told them. "Her mother's buried there. Gonda has invested in our production."

"Is that why she has a part in it?" asked Isobel Arrington.

"She has a part in it because she's beautiful and gifted," replied Drumm, rather stuffily. "Old people say she's the very picture of her mother. Speaking of pictures, here are some to prove it."

He offered two glossy prints to Isobel Arrington, who murmured "Very sweet," and passed them to Laurel Parcher. Cobbett leaned to see.

One picture seemed copied from an older one. It showed a woman who stood with unconscious stateliness, in a gracefully draped robe with a tiara binding her rich flow of dark hair. The other picture was of a woman in fashionable evening dress, her hair ordered in modern fashion, with a face strikingly like that of the woman in the other photograph.

"Oh, she's lovely," said Laurel. "Isn't she, Lee?"

"Isn't she?" echoed Drumm.

"Magnificent," said Cobbett, handing the pictures to Pursuivant, who studied them gravely.

"Chastel was in Richmond, just after the first World War," he said slowly. "A dazzling Lady Macbeth. I was in love with her. Everyone was."

"Did you tell her you loved her?" asked Laurel.

"Yes. We had supper together, twice. Then she went ahead with her tour, and I sailed to England and studied at Oxford. I never saw her again, but she's more or less why I never married."

Silence a moment. Then: *"The Land Beyond the Forest,"* Laurel repeated. "Isn't there a book called that?"

"There is indeed, my child," said the Judge. "By Emily de Laszowska Gerard. About Transylvania, where Dracula came from."

"That's why we use the title, that's what Transylvania means," put in Drumm. "It's all right, the book's out of copyright. But I'm surprised to find someone who's heard of it."

"I'll protect your guilty secret, Phil," promised Isobel Arrington. "What's over there in your window, Judge?"

Pursuivant turned to look. "Whatever it is," he said, "it's not Peter Pan."

Cobbett sprang up and ran toward the half-draped window. A silhouette with head and shoulders hung in the June night. He had a glimpse of a face, rich-mouthed, with bright eyes. Then it was gone. Laurel had hurried up behind him. He hoisted the window sash and leaned out.

Nothing. The street was fourteen stories down. The lights of moving cars crawled distantly. The wall below was course after course of dull brick, with recesses of other windows to right and left, below, above. Cobbett studied the wall, his hands braced on the sill.

"Be careful, Lee," Laurel's voice besought him.

He came back to face the others. "Nobody out there," he said evenly. "Nobody could have been. It's just a wall—nothing to hang to. Even that sill would be tricky to stand on."

"But I saw something, and so did Judge Pursuivant," said Isobel Arrington, the cigarette trembling in her fingers.

"So did I," said Cobbett. "Didn't you, Laurel?"

"Only a face."

Isobel Arrington was calm again. "If it's a trick, Phil, you played a good one. But don't expect me to put it in my story."

Drumm shook his head nervously. "I didn't play any trick, I swear."

"Don't try this on old friends," she jabbed at him. "First those pictures, then whatever was up against the glass. I'll use the pictures, but I won't write that a weird vision presided over this birthday party."

"How about a drink all around?" suggested Pursuivant.

He poured for them. Isobel Arrington wrote down answers to more questions, then said she must go. Drumm rose to escort her. "You'll be at Deslow tomorrow, Lee?" he asked.

"And Laurel, too. You said we could find quarters there."

"The Mapletree's a good auto court," said Drumm. "I've already reserved cabins for the two of you."

"On the spur of the moment," said Pursuivant suddenly, "I think I'll come along, if there's space for me."

"I'll check it out for you, Judge," said Drumm.

He departed with Isobel Arrington. Cobbett spoke to Pursuivant. "Isn't that rather offhand?" he asked. "Deciding to come with us?"

"I was thinking about Chastel." Pursuivant smiled gently. "About making a pilgrimage to her grave."

"We'll drive up about nine tomorrow morning."

"I'll be ready, Lee."

Cobbett and Laurel, too, went out. They walked down a flight of stairs to the floor below, where both their rooms were located. "Do you think Phil Drumm rigged up that illusion for us?" asked Cobbett.

"If he did, he used the face of that actress. Chastel."

He glanced keenly at her. "You saw that."

"I thought I did, and so did you."

They kissed goodnight at the door to her room.

Pursuivant was ready next morning when Cobbett knocked. He had only one suitcase and a thick, brown-blotched malacca cane, banded with silver below its curved handle.

"I'm taking only a few necessaries, I'll buy socks and such things in Deslow if we stay more than a couple of days," he said. "No, don't carry it for me, I'm quite capable."

When they reached the hotel garage, Laurel was putting her luggage in the trunk of Cobbett's black sedan. Judge Pursuivant declined the front seat beside Cobbett, held the door for Laurel to get in, and sat in the rear. They rolled out into bright June sunlight.

Cobbett drove them east on Interstate 95, mile after mile along the Connecticut shore, past service stations, markets, sandwich shops. Now and then they glimpsed Long Island Sound to the right. At toll gates, Cobbett threw quarters into hoppers and drove on.

"New Rochelle to Port Chester," Laurel half chanted. "Norwalk, Bridgeport, Stratford—"

"Where, in 1851, devils plagued a minister's home," put in Pursuivant.

"The names make a poem," said Laurel.

"You can get that effect by reading any timetable," said Cobbett. "We miss a couple of good names—Mystic and Giants Neck, though they aren't far off from our route. And

CHASTEL

Griswold—that means Gray Woods—where the Judge's book says Horace Ray was born."

"There's no Griswold on the Connecticut map any more," said the Judge.

"Vanished?" said Laurel. "Maybe it appears at just a certain time of the day, along about sundown."

She laughed, but the Judge was grave.

"Here we'll pass by New Haven," he said. "I was at Yale here, seventy years ago."

They rolled across the Connecticut River between Old Saybrook and Old Lyme. Outside New London, Cobbett turned them north on State Highway 82 and, near Jewett City, took a two-lane road that brought them into Deslow, not long after noon.

There were pleasant clapboard cottages among elm trees and flower beds. Main Street had bright shops with, farther along, the belfry of a sturdy old church. Cobbett drove them to a sign saying MAPLETREE COURT. A row of cabins faced along a cement-floored colonnade, their fronts painted white with blue doors and window frames. In the office, Phil Drumm stood at the desk, talking to the plump proprietress.

"Welcome home," he greeted them. "Judge, I was asking Mrs. Simpson here to reserve you a cabin."

"At the far end of the row, sir," the lady said. "I'd have put you next to your two friends, but so many theater folks have already moved in."

"Long ago I learned to be happy with any shelter," the Judge assured her.

They saw Laurel to her cabin and put her suitcases inside, then walked to the farthest cabin where Pursuivant would stay. Finally Drumm followed Cobbett to the space next to Laurel's. Inside, Cobbett produced a fifth of bourbon from his briefcase. Drumm trotted away to fetch ice. Pursuivant came to join them.

"It's good of you to look after us," Cobbett said to Drumm above his glass.

"Oh, I'll get my own back," Drumm assured him. "The Judge and you, distinguished folklore experts—I'll have you in all the papers."

"Whatever you like," said Cobbett. "Let's have lunch, as soon as Laurel is freshened up."

The four ate crab cakes and flounder at a little restaurant while Drumm talked about *The Land Beyond the Forest*. He had signed the minor film star Caspar Merrick to play Dracula. "He has a fine baritone singing voice," said Drumm. "He'll be at afternoon rehearsal."

"And Gonda Chastel?" inquired Pursuivant, buttering a roll.

"She'll be there tonight." Drumm sounded happy about that. "This afternoon's mostly for bits and chorus numbers. I'm directing as well as producing." They finished their lunch, and Drumm rose. "If you're not tired, come see our theater."

It was only a short walk through town to the converted barn. Cobbett judged it had been built in Colonial times, with a recent roof of composition tile, but with walls of stubborn, brown-gray New England stone. Across a narrow side street stood the old white church, with a hedge-bordered cemetery.

"Quaint, that old burying ground," commented Drumm. "Nobody's spaded under there now, there's a modern cemetery on the far side, but Chastel's tomb is there. Quite a picturesque one."

"I'd like to see it," said Pursuivant, leaning on his silver-banded cane.

The barn's interior was set with rows of folding chairs, enough for several hundred spectators. On a stage at the far end, workmen moved here and there under lights. Drumm led his guests up steps at the side.

High in the loft, catwalks zigzagged and a dark curtain hung like a broad guillotine blade. Drumm pointed out canvas flats, painted to resemble grim castle walls. Pursuivant nodded and questioned.

"I'm no authority on what you might find in Transylvania," he said, "but this looks convincing."

A man walked from the wings toward them. "Hello, Caspar," Drumm greeted him. "I want you to meet Judge Pursuivant and Lee Cobbett. And Miss Laurel Parcher, of course." He gestured the introductions. "This is Mr. Caspar Merrick, our Count Dracula."

Merrick was elegantly tall, handsome, with carefully groomed black hair. Sweepingly he bowed above Laurel's hand and smiled at them all. "Judge Pursuivant's writings I know, of course," he said richly. "I read what I can about vampires, inasmuch as I'm to be one."

"Places for the Delusion number!" called a stage manager.

Cobbett, Pursuivant and Laura went down the steps and sat on chairs. Eight men and eight girls hurried into view, dressed in knockabout summer clothes. Someone struck chords on a piano, Drumm gestured importantly, and the chorus sang. Merritt, coming downstage, took solo on a verse. All joined in the refrain. Then Drumm made them sing it over again.

After that, two comedians made much of confusing the words vampire and empire. Cobbett found it tedious. He excused himself to his companions and strolled out and across to the old, tree-crowded churchyard.

The gravestones bore interesting epitaphs: not only the familiar *Pause O Stranger Passing By/ As You Are Now So Once Was I*, and *A Bud on Earth to Bloom in Heaven*, but several of more originality. One bewailed a man who, since he had been lost at sea, could hardly have been there at all. Another bore, beneath a bat-winged face, the declaration *Death Pays All Debts* and the date *1907*, which Cobbett associated with a financial panic.

Toward the center of the graveyard, under a drooping willow, stood a shedlike structure of heavy granite blocks. Cobbett picked his way to the door of heavy grillwork, which was fastened with a rusty padlock the size of a sardine can. On the lintel were strongly carved letters, CHASTEL.

Here, then, was the tomb of the stage beauty Pursuivant remembered so romantically. Cobbett peered through the bars.

It was murkily dusty in there. The floor was coarsely flagged, and among sooty shadows at the rear stood a sort of stone chest that must contain the body. Cobbett turned and went back to the theater. Inside, piano music rang wildly and the people of the chorus desperately rehearsed what must be meant for a folk dance.

"Oh, it's exciting," said Laurel as Cobbett sat down beside her. "Where have you been?"

"Visiting the tomb of Chastel."

"Chastel?" echoed Pursuivant. "I must see that tomb."

Songs and dance ensembles went on. In the midst of them, a brisk reporter from Hartford appeared, to interview Pursuivant and Cobbett. At last Drumm resoundingly dismissed the players on stage and joined his guests.

"Principals rehearse at eight o'clock," he announced. "Gonda Chastel will be here, she'll want to meet you. Could I count on you then?"

"Count on me, at least," said Pursuivant. "Just now, I feel like resting before dinner, and so, I think, does Laurel here."

"Yes, I'd like to lie down for a little," said Laurel.

"Why don't we all meet for dinner at the place where we had lunch?" said Cobbett. "You come too, Phil."

"Thanks, I have a date with some backers from New London."

It was half-past five when they went out.

Cobbett went to his quarters, stretched out on the bed, and gave himself to thought.

He hadn't come to Deslow because of this musical interpretation of the Dracula legend. Laurel had come because he was coming, and Pursuivant on a sudden impulse that might have been more than a wish to visit the grave of Chastel. But Cobbett was here because this, he knew, had been vampire country, maybe still was vampire country.

He remembered the story in Pursuivant's book about vampires at Jewett City, as reported in the Norwich *Courier* for 1854. Horace Ray, from the now vanished town of Griswold, had died of a "wasting disease." Thereafter his oldest son, then his second son, had also gone to their graves. When a third son sickened, friends and relatives dug up Horace Ray and the two dead brothers and burned the bodies in a roaring fire. The surviving son got well. And something like that had happened in Exeter, near Providence in Rhode Island. Very well, why organize and present the Dracula musical here in Deslow, so near those places?

Cobbett had met Phil Drumm in the South the year before, knew him for a brilliant if erratic producer, who relished tales of devils and the dead who walk by night. Drumm might have known enough stage magic to have rigged that seeming appearance at Pursuivant's window in New York. That is, if indeed it was only a seeming appearance, not a real face. Might it have been real, a manifestation of the unreal? Cobbett had seen enough of what people dismissed as unreal, impossible, to wonder.

A soft knock came at the door. It was Laurel. She wore green slacks, a green jacket, and she smiled, as always, at sight of Cobbett's face. They sought Pursuivant's cabin. A note on the door said, *Meet me at the cafe.*

When they entered there, Pursuivant hailed them from the

kitchen door. "Dinner's ready," he hailed them. "I've been supervising in person, and I paid well for the privilege."

A waiter brought a laden tray. He arranged platters of red-drenched spaghetti and bowls of salad on a table. Pursuivant himself sprinkled Parmesan cheese. "No salt or pepper," he warned. "I seasoned it myself, and you can take my word it's exactly right."

Cobbett poured red wine into glasses. Laurel took a forkful of spaghetti. "Delicious," she cried. "What's in it, Judge?"

"Not only ground beef and tomatoes and onions and garlic," replied Pursuivant. "I added marjoram and green pepper and chile and thyme and bay leaf and oregano and parsley and a couple of other important ingredients. And I also minced in some Italian sausage."

Cobbett, too, ate with enthusiastic appetite. "I won't order any dessert," he declared. "I want to keep the taste of this in my mouth."

"There's more in the kitchen for dessert if you want it," the Judge assured him. "But here, I have a couple of keepsakes for you."

He handed each of them a small, silvery object. Cobbett examined his. It was smoothly wrapped in foil. He wondered if it was a nutmeat.

"You have pockets, I perceive," the Judge said. "Put those into them. And don't open them, or my wish for you won't come true."

When they had finished eating, a full moon had begun to rise in the darkening sky. They headed for the theater.

A number of visitors sat in the chairs and the stage lights looked bright. Drumm stood beside the piano, talking to two plump men in summer business suits. As Pursuivant and the others came down the aisle, Drumm eagerly beckoned them and introduced them to his companions, the financial backers with whom he had taken dinner.

"We're very much interested," said one. "This vampire legend intrigues anyone, if you forget that a vampire's motivation is simply nourishment."

"No, something more than that," offered Pursuivant. "A social motivation."

"Social motivation," repeated the other backer.

"A vampire wants company of its own kind. A victim infected becomes a vampire, too, and an associate. Otherwise the original vampire would be a disconsolate loner."

"There's a lot in what you say," said Drumm, impressed.

After that there was financial talk, something in which Cobbett could not intelligently join. Then someone else approached, and both the backers stared.

It was a tall, supremely graceful woman with red-lighted black hair in a bun at her nape, a woman of impressive figure and assurance. She wore a sweeping blue dress, fitted to her slim waist, with a frill-edged neckline. Her arms were bare and white and sweetly turned, with jewelled bracelets on them. Drumm almost ran to bring her close to the group.

"Gonda Chastel," he said, half-prayerfully. "Gonda, you'll want to meet these people."

The two backers stuttered admiringly at her. Pursuivant bowed and Laurel smiled. Gonda Chastel gave Cobbett her slim, cool hand. "You know so much about this thing we're trying to do here," she said, in a voice like cream.

Drumm watched them. His face looked plaintive.

"Judge Pursuivant has taught me a lot, Miss Chastel," said Cobbett. "He'll tell you that once he knew your mother."

"I remember her, not very clearly," said Gonda Chastel. "She died when I was just a little thing, thirty years ago. And I followed her here, now I make my home here."

"You look very like her," said Pursuivant.

"I'm proud to be like my mother in any way," she smiled at them. She could be overwhelming, Cobbett told himself.

"And Miss Parcher," went on Gonda Chastel, turning toward Laurel. "What a little presence she is. She should be in our show—I don't know what part, but she should." She smiled dazzlingly. "Now then, Phil wants me on stage."

"Knock-at-the-door number, Gonda," said Drumm.

Gracefully she mounted the steps. The piano sounded, and she sang. It was the best song, felt Cobbett, that he had heard so far in the rehearsals. "Are they seeking for a shelter from the night?" Gonda Chastel sang richly. Caspar Merritt entered, to join in a recitative. Then the chorus streamed on, singing somewhat shrilly.

Pursuivant and Laurel had sat down. Cobbett strode back up the aisle and out under a moon that rained silver-blue light.

He found his way to the churchyard. The trees that had offered pleasant afternoon shade now made a dubious darkness. He walked underneath branches that seemed to lower like hovering wings as he approached the tomb structure at the center.

The barred door that had been massively locked now stood open. He peered into the gloom within. After a moment he stepped across the threshold upon the flagged floor.

He had to grope, with one hand upon the rough wall. At last he almost stumbled upon the great stone chest at the rear.

It, too, was flung open, its lid heaved back against the wall.

There was, of course, complete darkness within it. He flicked on his cigar lighter. The flame showed him the inside of the stone coffer, solidly made and about ten feet long. Its sides of gray marble were snugly fitted. Inside lay a coffin of rich dark wood with silver fittings and here, yet again, was an open lid.

Bending close to the smudged silk lining, Cobbett seemed to catch an odor of stuffy sharpness, like dried herbs. He snapped off his light and frowned in the dark. Then he groped back to the door, emerged into the open, and headed for the theater again.

"Mr. Cobbett," said the beautiful voice of Gonda Chastel.

She stood at the graveyard's edge, beside a sagging willow. She was almost as tall as he. Her eyes glowed in the moonlight.

"You came to find the truth about my mother," she half-accused.

"I was bound to try," he replied. "Ever since I saw a certain face at a certain window of a certain New York hotel."

She stepped back from him. "You know that she's a—"

"A vampire," Cobbett finished for her. "Yes."

"I beg you to be helpful—merciful." But there was no supplication in her voice. "I already realized, long ago. That's why I live in little Deslow. I want to find a way to give her rest. Night after night, I wonder how."

"I understand that," said Cobbett.

Gonda Chastel breathed deeply. "You know all about these things. I think there's something about you that could daunt a vampire."

"If so, I don't know what it is," said Cobbett truthfully.

"Make me a solemn promise. That you won't return to her tomb, that you won't tell others what you and I know about her. I—I want to think how we two together can do something for her."

"If you wish, I'll say nothing," he promised.

Her hand clutched his.

"The cast took a five-minute break, it must be time to go to work again," she said, suddenly bright. "Let's go back and help the thing along."

They went.

Inside, the performers were gathering on stage. Drumm stared unhappily as Gonda Chastel and Cobbett came down the aisle. Cobbett sat with Laurel and Pursuivant and listened to the rehearsal.

Adaptation from Bram Stoker's novel was free, to say the least. Dracula's eerie plottings were much hampered by his having a countess, a walking dead beauty who strove to become a spirit of good. There were some songs, in interesting minor keys. There was a dance, in which men and women leaped like kangaroos. Finally Drumm called a halt, and the performers trooped wearily to the wings.

Gonda Chastel lingered, talking to Laurel. "I wonder, my dear, if you haven't had acting experience," she said.

"Only in school entertainments down south, when I was little."

"Phil," said Gonda Chastel, "Miss Parcher is a good type, has good presence. There ought to be something for her in the show."

"You're very kind, but I'm afraid that's impossible," said Laurel, smiling.

"You may change your mind, Miss Parcher. Will you and your friends come to my house for a nightcap?"

"Thank you," said Pursuivant. "We have some notes to make, and we must make them together."

"Until tomorrow evening, then. Mr. Cobbett, we'll remember our agreement."

She went away toward the back of the stage. Pursuivant and Laurel walked out. Drumm hurried up the aisle and caught Cobbett's elbow.

"I saw you," he said harshly. "Saw you both as you came in."

"And we saw you, Phil. What's this about?"

"She likes you." It was half an accusation. "Fawns on you, almost."

Cobbett grinned and twitched his arm free. "What's the matter, Phil, are you in love with her?"

"Yes, God damn it, I am. I'm in love with her. She knows

it but she won't let me come to her house. And you—the first time she meets you, she invites you."

"Easy does it, Phil," said Cobbett. "If it'll do you any good, I'm in love with someone else, and that takes just about all my spare time."

He hurried out to overtake his companions.

Pursuivant swung his cane almost jauntily as they returned through the moonlight to the auto court.

"What notes are you talking about, Judge?" asked Cobbett.

"I'll tell you at my quarters. What do you think of the show?"

"Perhaps I'll like it better after they've rehearsed more," said Laurel. "I don't follow it at present."

"Here and there, it strikes me as limp," added Cobbett.

They sat down in the Judge's cabin. He poured them drinks. "Now," he said, "there are certain things to recognize here. Things I more or less expected to find."

"A mystery, Judge?" asked Laurel.

"Not so much that, if I expected to find them. How far are we from Jewett City?"

"Twelve or fifteen miles as the crow flies," estimated Cobbett. "And Jewett City is where that vampire family, the Rays, lived and died."

"Died twice, you might say," nodded Pursuivant, stroking his white mustache. "Back about a century and a quarter ago. And here's what might be a matter of Ray family history. I've been thinking about Chastel, whom once I greatly admired. About her full name."

"But she had only one name, didn't she?" asked Laurel.

"On the stage she used one name, yes. So did Bernhardt, so did Duse, so later did Garbo. But all of them had full names. Now, before we went to dinner, I made two telephone calls to theatrical historians I know. To learn Chastel's full name."

"And she had a full name," prompted Cobbett.

"Indeed she did. Her full name was Chastel Ray."

Cobbett and Laurel looked at him in deep silence.

"Not apt to be just coincidence," elaborated Pursuivant. "Now then, I gave you some keepsakes today."

"Here's mine," said Cobbett, pulling the foil-wrapped bit from his shirt pocket.

"And I have mine here," said Laurel, her hand at her throat. "In a little locket I have on this chain."

"Keep it there," Pursuivant urged her. "Wear it around

your neck at all times. Lee, have yours always on your person. Those are garlic cloves, and you know what they're good for. You can also guess why I cut up a lot of garlic in our spaghetti for dinner."

"You think there's a vampire here," offered Laurel.

"A specific vampire." The Judge took a deep breath into his broad chest. "Chastel. Chastel Ray."

"I believe it, too," declared Cobbett tonelessly, and Laurel nodded. Cobbett looked at the watch on his wrist.

"It's past one in the morning," he said. "Perhaps we'd all be better off if we had some sleep."

They said their good nights and Laurel and Cobbett walked to where their two doors stood side by side. Laurel put her key into the lock, but did not turn it at once. She peered across the moonlit street.

"Who's that over there?" she whispered. "Maybe I ought to say, what's that?"

Cobbett looked. "Nothing, you're just nervous. Good night, dear."

She went in and shut the door. Cobbett quickly crossed the street.

"Mr. Cobbett," said the voice of Gonda Chastel.

"I wondered what you wanted, so late at night," he said, walking close to her.

She had undone her dark hair and let it flow to her shoulders. She was, Cobbett thought, as beautiful a woman as he had ever seen.

"I wanted to be sure about you," she said. "That you'd respect your promise to me, not to go into the churchyard."

"I keep my promises, Miss Chastel."

He felt a deep, hushed silence all around them. Not even the leaves rustled in the trees.

"I had hoped you wouldn't venture even this far," she went on. "You and your friends are new in town, you might tempt her specially." Her eyes burned at him. "You know I don't mean that as a compliment."

She turned to walk away. He fell into step beside her. "But you're not afraid of her," he said.

"Of my own mother?"

"She was a Ray," said Cobbett. "Each Ray sapped the blood of his kinsmen. Judge Pursuivant told me all about it."

Again the gaze of her dark, brilliant eyes. "Nothing like

that has ever happened between my mother and me." She stopped, and so did he. Her slim, strong hand took him by the wrist.

"You're wise and brave," she said. "I think you may have come here for a good purpose, not just about the show."

"I try to have good purposes."

The light of the moon soaked through the overhead branches as they walked on. "Will you come to my house?" she invited.

"I'll walk to the churchyard," replied Cobbett. "I said I wouldn't go into it, but I can stand at the edge."

"Don't go in."

"I've promised that I wouldn't, Miss Chastel."

She walked back the way they had come. He followed the street on under silent elms until he reached the border of the churchyard. Moonlight flecked and spattered the tombstones. Deep shadows lay like pools. He had a sense of being watched from within.

As he gazed, he saw movement among the graves. He could not define it, but it was there. He glimpsed, or fancied he glimpsed, a head, indistinct in outline as though swathed in dark fabric. Then another. Another. They huddled in a group, as though to gaze at him.

"I wish you'd go back to your quarters," said Gonda Chastel beside him. She had drifted after him, silent as a shadow herself.

"Miss Chastel," he said, "tell me something if you can. Whatever happened to the town or village of Griswold?"

"Griswold?" she echoed. "What's Griswold? That means gray woods."

"Your ancestor, or your relative, Horace Ray, came from Griswold to die in Jewett City. And I've told you that I knew your mother was born a Ray."

Her shining eyes seemed to flood upon him. "I didn't know that," she said.

He gazed into the churchyard, at those hints of furtive movement.

"The hands of the dead reach out for the living," murmured Gonda Chastel.

"Reach out for me?" he asked.

"Perhaps for both of us. Just now, we may be the only living souls awake in Deslow." She gazed at him again. "But you're able to defend yourself, somehow."

"What makes you think that?" he inquired, aware of the clove of garlic in his shirt pocket.

"Because they—in the churchyard there—they watch, but they hold away from you. You don't invite them."

"Nor do you, apparently," said Cobbett.

"I hope you're not trying to make fun of me," she said, her voice barely audible.

"On my soul, I'm not."

"On your soul," she repeated. "Good night, Mr. Cobbett."

Again she moved away, tall and proud and graceful. He watched her out of sight. Then he headed back toward the motor court.

Nothing moved in the empty street. Only one or two lights shone here and there in closed shops. He thought he heard a soft rustle behind him, but did not look back.

As he reached his own door, he heard Laurel scream behind hers.

Judge Pursuivant sat in his cubicle, his jacket off, studying a worn little brown book. Skinner, said letters on the spine, and *Myths and Legends of Our Own Land*. He had read the passage so often that he could almost repeat it from memory:

"To lay this monster he must be taken up and burned; at least his heart must be; and he must be disinterred in the daytime when he is asleep and unaware."

There were other ways, reflected Pursuivant.

It must be very late by now, rather it must be early. But he had no intention of going to sleep. Not when stirs of motion sounded outside, along the concrete walkway in front of his cabin. Did motion stand still, just beyond the front of the door there? Pursuivant's great, veined hand touched the front of his shirt, beneath which a bag of garlic hung like an amulet. Garlic—was that enough? He himself was fond of garlic, judiciously employed in sauces and salads. But then, he could see himself in the mirror of the bureau yonder, could see his broad old face with its white sweep of mustache like a wreath of snow on a sill. It was a clear image of a face, not a calm face just then, but a determined one. Pursuivant smiled at it, with a glimpse of even teeth that were still his own.

He flicked up his shirt cuff and looked at his watch. Half past one, about. In June, even with daylight savings time, dawn would come early. Dawn sent vampires back to the tombs that were their melancholy refuges, "asleep and unaware," as Skinner had specified.

Putting the book aside, he poured himself a small drink of bourbon, dropped in cubes of ice and a trickle of water, and sipped. He had drunk several times during that day, when on most days he partook of only a single highball, by advice of his doctor; but just now he was grateful for the pungent, walnutty taste of the liquor. It was one of Earth's natural things, a good companion when not abused. From the table he took a folder of scribbled notes. He looked at jottings from the works of Montague Summers.

These offered the proposition that a plague of vampires usually stemmed from a single source of infection, a king or queen vampire whose feasts of blood drove victims to their graves, to rise in their turn. If the original vampires were found and destroyed, the others relaxed to rest as normally dead bodies. Bram Stoker had followed the same gospel when he wrote *Dracula*, and doubtless Bram Stoker had known. Pursuivant looked at another page, this time a poem copied from James Grant's curious *Mysteries of All Nations*. It was a ballad in archaic language, that dealt with baleful happenings in "The Towne of Peste"—Budapest?

> It was the Corses that our Churchyardes filled
> That did at midnight lumberr up our Stayres;
> They suck'd our Bloud, the gorie Banquet swilled,
> And harried everie Soule with hydeous Feares . . .

Several verses down:

> They barr'd with Boltes of Iron the Churchyard-pale
> To keep them out; but all this wold not doe;
> For when a Dead-Man has learn'd to draw a naile,
> He can also burst an iron Bolte in two.

Many times Pursuivant had tried to trace the author of that verse. He wondered if it was not something quaintly confected not long before 1880, when Grant published his work. At any rate, the Judge felt that he knew what it meant, the experience that it remembered.

He put aside the notes, too, and picked up his spotted walking stick. Clamping the balance of it firmly in his left hand, he twisted the handle with his right and pulled. Out of the hollow shank slid a pale, bright blade, keen and lean and edged on both front and back.

Pursuivant permitted himself a smile above it. This was one of his most cherished possessions, this silver weapon said to have been forged a thousand years ago by Saint Dunstan. Bending, he spelled out the runic writing upon it:

Sic pereant omnes inimici tui, Domine

That was the end of the fiercely triumphant song of Deborah in the Book of Judges: So perish all thine enemies, O Lord. Whether the work of Saint Dunstan or not, the metal was silver, the writing was a warrior's prayer. Silver and writing had proved their strength against evil in the past.

Then, outside, a loud, tremulous cry of mortal terror.

Pursuivant sprang out of his chair on the instant. Blade in hand, he fairly ripped his door open and ran out. He saw Cobbett in front of Laurel's door, wrenching at the knob, and hurried there like a man half his age.

"Open up, Laurel," he heard Cobbett call. "It's Lee out here!"

The door gave inward as Pursuivant reached it, and he and Cobbett pressed into the lighted room.

Laurel half-crouched in the middle of the floor. Her trembling hand pointed to a rear window. "She tried to come in," Laurel stammered.

"There's nothing at that window," said Cobbett, but even as he spoke, there was. A face, pale as tallow, crowded against the glass. They saw wide, staring eyes, a mouth that opened and squirmed. Teeth twinkled sharply.

Cobbett started forward, but Pursuivant caught him by the shoulder. "Let me," he said, advancing toward the window, the point of his blade lifted.

The face at the window writhed convulsively as the silver weapon came against the pane with a clink. The mouth opened as though to shout, but no sound came. The face fell back and vanished from their sight.

"I've seen that face before," said Cobbett hoarsely.

"Yes," said Pursuivant. "At my hotel window. And since."

He dropped the point of the blade to the floor. Outside came a whirring rush of sound, like feet, many of them.

"We ought to wake up the people at the office," said Cobbett.

"I doubt if anyone in this little town could be wakened,"

Pursuivant told him evenly. "I have it in mind that every living soul, except the three of us, is sound asleep. Entranced."

"But out there—" Laurel gestured at the door, where something seemed to be pressing.

"I said, every living soul," Pursuivant looked from her to Cobbett. "Living," he repeated.

He paced across the floor, and with his point scratched a perpendicular line upon it. Across this he carefully drove a horizontal line, making a cross. The pushing abruptly ceased.

"There it is, at the window again," breathed Laurel.

Pursuivant took long steps back to where the face hovered, with black hair streaming about it. He scraped the glass with his silver blade, up and down, then across, making lines upon it. The face drew away. He moved to mark similar crosses on the other windows.

"You see," he said, quietly triumphant, "the force of old, old charms."

He sat down in a chair, heavily. His face was weary, but he looked at Laurel and smiled.

"It might help if we managed to pity those poor things out there," he said.

"Pity?" she almost cried out.

"Yes," he said, and quoted:

". . . Think how sad it must be
To thirst always for a scorned elixir,
The salt of quotidian blood."

"I know that," volunteered Cobbett. "It's from a poem by Richard Wilbur, a damned unhappy poet."

"Quotidian," repeated Laurel to herself.

"That means something that keeps coming back, that returns daily," Cobbett said.

"It's a term used to refer to a recurrent fever," added Pursuivant.

Laurel and Cobbett sat down together on the bed.

"I would say that for the time being we're safe here," declared Pursuivant. "Not at ease, but at least safe. At dawn, danger will go to sleep and we can open the door."

"But why are we safe, and nobody else?" Laurel cried out. "Why are we awake, with everyone else in this town asleep and helpless?"

"Apparently because we all of us wear garlic," replied Pursuivant patiently, "and because we ate garlic, plenty of it, at dinner time. And because there are crosses—crude, but unmistakable—wherever something might try to come in. I won't ask you to be calm, but I'll ask you to be resolute."

"I'm resolute," said Cobbett between clenched teeth. "I'm ready to go out there and face them."

"If you did that, even with the garlic," said Pursuivant, "you'd last about as long as a pint of whiskey in a five-handed poker game. No, Lee, relax as much as you can, and let's talk."

They talked, while outside strange presences could be felt rather than heard. Their talk was of anything and everything but where they were and why. Cobbett remembered strange things he had encountered, in towns, among mountains, along desolate roads, and what he had been able to do about them. Pursuivant told of a vampire he had known and defeated in upstate New York, of a werewolf in his own Southern countryside. Laurel, at Cobbett's urging, sang songs, old songs, from her own rustic home place. Her voice was sweet. When she sang "Round is the Ring," faces came and hung like smudges outside the cross-scored windows. She saw, and sang again, an old Appalachian carol called "Mary She Heared a Knock in the Night." The faces drifted away again. And the hours, too, drifted away, one by one.

"There's a horde of vampires on the night street here, then." Cobbett at last brought up the subject of their problem.

"And they lull the people of Deslow to sleep, to be helpless victims," agreed Pursuivant. "About this show, *The Land Beyond the Forest*, mightn't it be welcomed as a chance to spread the infection? Even a townful of sleepers couldn't feed a growing community of blood drinkers."

"If we could deal with the source, the original infection—" began Cobbett.

"The mistress of them, the queen," said Pursuivant. "Yes. The one whose walking by night rouses them all. If she could be destroyed, they'd all die properly."

He glanced at the front window. The moonlight had a touch of slaty gray.

"Almost morning," he pronounced. "Time for a visit to her tomb."

"I gave my promise I wouldn't go there," said Cobbett.

"But I didn't promise," said Pursuivant, rising. "You stay here with Laurel."

His silver blade in hand, he stepped out into darkness from which the moon had all but dropped away. Overhead, stars were fading out. Dawn was at hand.

He sensed a flutter of movement on the far side of the street, an almost inaudible gibbering of sound. Steadily he walked across. He saw nothing along the sidewalk there, heard nothing. Resolutely he tramped to the churchyard, his weapon poised. More grayness had come to dilute the dark.

He pushed his way through the hedge of shrubs, stepped in upon the grass, and paused at the side of a grave. Above it hung an eddy of soft mist, no larger than the swirl of water draining from a sink. As Pursuivant watched, it seemed to soak into the earth and disappear. That, he said to himself, is what a soul looks like when it seeks to regain its coffin.

On he walked, step by weary, purposeful step, toward the central crypt. A ray of the early sun, stealing between heavily leafed boughs, made his way more visible. In this dawn, he would find what he would find. He knew that.

The crypt's door of open bars was held shut by its heavy padlock. He examined that lock closely. After a moment, he slid the point of his blade into the rusted keyhole and judiciously pressed this way, then that, and back again the first way. The spring creakily relaxed and he dragged the door open. Holding his breath, he entered.

The lid of the great stone vault was closed down. He took hold of the edge and heaved. The lid was heavy, but rose with a complaining grate of the hinges. Inside he saw a dark, closed coffin. He lifted the lid of that, too.

She lay there, calm-faced, the eyes half shut as though dozing.

"Chastel," said Pursuivant to her. "Not Gonda. Chastel."

The eyelids fluttered. That was all, but he knew that she heard what he said.

"Now you can rest," he said. "Rest in peace, really in peace."

He set the point of his silver blade at the swell of her left breast. Leaning both his broad hands upon the curved handle, he drove downward with all his strength.

She made a faint squeak of sound.

Blood sprang up as he cleared his weapon. More light

shone in. He could see a dark moisture fading from the blade, like evaporating dew.

In the coffin, Chastel's proud shape shrivelled, darkened. Quickly he slammed the coffin shut, then lowered the lid of the vault into place and went quickly out. He pushed the door shut again and fastened the stubborn old lock. As he walked back through the churchyard among the graves, a bird twittered over his head. More distantly, he heard the hum of a car's motor. The town was waking up.

In the growing radiance, he walked back across the street. By now, his steps were the steps of an old man, old and very tired.

Inside Laurel's cabin, Laurel and Cobbett were stirring instant coffee into hot water in plastic cups. They questioned the Judge with their tired eyes.

"She's finished," he said shortly.

"What will you tell Gonda?" asked Cobbett.

"Chastel was Gonda."

"But—"

"She was Gonda," said Pursuivant again, sitting down. "Chastel died. The infection wakened her out of her tomb, and she told people she was Gonda, and naturally they believed her." He sagged wearily. "Now that she's finished and at rest, those others—the ones she had bled, who also rose at night—will rest, too."

Laurel took a sip of coffee. Above the cup, her face was pale.

"Why do you say Chastel was Gonda?" she asked the Judge. "How can you know that?"

"I wondered from the very beginning. I was utterly sure just now."

"Sure?" said Laurel. "How can you be sure?"

Pursuivant smiled at her, the very faintest of smiles.

"My dear, don't you think a man always recognizes a woman he has loved?"

He seemed to recover his characteristic defiant vigor. He rose and went to the door and put his hand on the knob. "Now, if you'll just excuse me for awhile."

"Don't you think we'd better hurry and leave?" Cobbett asked him. "Before people miss her and ask questions?"

"Not at all," said Pursuivant, his voice strong again. "If we're gone, they'll ask questions about us, too, possibly embarrassing questions. No, we'll stay. We'll eat a good breakfast, or at least pretend to eat it. And we'll be as surprised as the rest of them about the disappearance of their leading lady."

"I'll do my best," vowed Laurel.

"I know you will, my child," said Pursuivant, and went out the door.

SLEEPING TIGER

Tanith Lee

One of the highlights of *Year's Best Horror Stories: Series VI* was a story called "Winter White," one of the strongest and most emotional pieces of good fantasy in several years. (And you saw it in these pages, first.) It was by Tanith Lee, whose career as fantasy and science fiction writer has risen like gasoline prices since publication of her *Birthgrave* a mere three years ago. "Sleeping Tiger" appeared in the Canadian small press fantasy magazine, *Dragonbane*, edited by Charles Saunders (author of "Amma," elsewhere in this book). This is, therefore, its first mass-market appearance, though we don't believe it will be the last.

Sky Tiger, the warrior, had been riding toward the city of North Mountain, his bow and quiver slung from his shoulder, his curved sword at his side. Handsome he was, the warrior Sky Tiger. A blue sheen on his unbound oil-black hair, a gold sheen on his saffron skin, the sheen of strength on the burnished iron of his breastplate. Despite that, or because of it, three miles back, where the dusty road emerged from the forest, Sky Tiger had met another warrior, similarly clad for fighting, and a fight there had been. Attack was frequent on any road, particularly in the lawless kingdom of North Mountain. And to ride in armor was generally to invite battle, just as to ride without it was to invite robbery and murder. Sky Tiger dealt as he found. He slew this challenger with commendable ease. Then, since he did not like to leave even the commonest villain in a ditch, Sky Tiger dug a shallow pit for him by way of temporary protection, and came searching for priests and a more honorable burial.

Finding a temple so swiftly seemed opportune.

It stood on the shore of a satin-smooth lake, amid a foam of blossoming peach trees. The low sun glinted on gold-scalloped roofs, scarlet pillars of painted wood and closed lacquer doors. And all about was an exceptional peace and quiet, not even the icy clink of wind chimes, or the whir of a cricket in the grass.

Having already met one source of trouble at the forest's edge, Sky Tiger suited his approach to the silence, rode cautiously among the trees, along the hillside, to the temple steps, and drew rein there.

At that moment, a beam of the declining sun shot clear and red between the peach boughs, and smote on the lacquer doors. As if in response to this solar knock, the doors slid gently open.

From a temple's entrance, one would expect priests to issue, serenely emaciated from their fasts and their spirituality, hairless and wise. But instead of priests, there issued forth two young women who might have stepped straight from the courts of an emperor, or from the ranks of an emperor's daughters.

Slender they were, and as alike as two moons. Their beautiful faces might have been fashioned from the palest and most translucent tawny ivory, their mouths of crimson cherries; their eyes were like the tilted wings of two black pigeons in flight. Nor were they rich in nature alone. Their garments, one robe pictured by lotus buds, one by orchids, were both embroidered with gold, and in their black hair sparkled tall diamond pins.

Sky Tiger regarded the young women a moment, his countenance as enigmatic as theirs but he thought his own thoughts. Then they bowed to him, and he to them, and the Lotus Moon spoke.

"Brave prince, we greet you in humility, and humbly ask why you have come to this place?"

Sky Tiger's horse had grown restive. He dealt with it, and said: "I am on the road to the city. I have come to offer to the gods of travelers."

Lotus Moon bowed again, more deeply.

"Brave prince, pardon my discourtesy. I am ashamed to rebuke you with your own lie."

"Why do you say I lie?"

"Your arrows and your sword say you lie, and the stain of another's blood on your sleeve."

Sky Tiger also bowed a second time.

"Your wit matches your loveliness. I admit I have slain a man. I would ask the priest for the rites."

The Orchid Moon spoke:

"The priests are gone. We alone are left to tend the temple."

Women did not tend temples, least of all in rough and lawless lands. Mystery deepened in the air as the sunset deepened among the peach trees.

"It is our joy to offer to those that visit us, the hospitality of this holy temple," said Orchid Moon.

Sky Tiger had heard of weirdly orgiastic houses here in the north. He sat his horse, considering the women, who lowered their gaze in simulated modesty. Back at the forest's edge, lay the unknown dead enemy, whom he had no actual obligation to attend to.

Curiosity and weariness getting the upper hand, Sky Tiger dismounted. He saw the women watching him under their lids, weighing his skills and looks, as if each eye were a delicate balance of polished jet.

The sun had descended; blue darkness clung to the lake, the trees, the temple. Somewhere Sky Tiger's horse had been tethered, fed and watered. Lotus Moon and Orchid Moon now waited upon the comfort of Sky Tiger himself, as if he were an esteemed guest in their master's house—save that this house had no master. After he had submitted to the hot and cool baths and the robe laid out for him, the women conducted him, through a hall of gleaming gods, to a courtyard open to the stars and hung with gilded parchment lamps. Here among the scented shrubs, while the golden fish glanced and glittered in the marble basin, dishes of food were offered to Sky Tiger and fragile cups of fragrant yellow wine. While one woman knelt to serve him, the other played softly and most suitably upon a moon-guitar, plucking dainty and aesthetic notes from its four silken strings.

Everything was performed with the utmost taste and harmony, and Sky Tiger was letting curiosity slip into abeyance. Soothed, well fed, a little mellowed by the wine, his thoughts were turning to other pleasures with an irresistible but quite unhurried motion. Certainly, it was strange, the isolated temple magnificently provided with meat and matter. (How sweet the perfume of flowers and feminine flesh, how subtle the aroma of the wine.) A man lived hard and adventurously, as Heaven intended. But there was also rest. Even the tiger must sleep. And was the tiger less of a tiger when he slept? Naturally, hunters might steal upon him, but there were no hunters here. (And would the women come both together to the bed of lacquered wood and white silk curtaining they had artlessly shown him?)

Sky Tiger half closed his eyes, and the notes of the moon-guitar hummed in his brain.

"Does he drowse?" asked Lotus Moon, very distinctly.

"Yes, the hog drowses, ripe with food and drugged by the powder we prepared for his wine," said Orchid Moon, as distinctly.

Sky Tiger, eyes half-shut, rather than feeling unease, found himself amused by this statement. Had they drugged him? It must be true. Now they mentioned it, he could perceive it in himself, a buoyant happy floating of the senses.

"How long must we wait?" asked Lotus Moon. She did not sound impatient or anxious. Her voice was ritualistic and quite flat.

"The hour of the moon's rising above the lake."

This too was an automatic response.

Sky Tiger wished to ask his concubines what venture they planned for the hour of moonrise, but he was quite unable to enter their dialogue, his tongue cleaved to the roof of his mouth. *It is as the woman says, I am a worthless hog*, he chid himself mildly. *A warrior accustomed to battle, but a bending reed before her vixen's wiles.*

"I wonder," said Lotus Moon, "if he will suffer, as men presumably do, when death claims him."

"It is no matter to us. He is a wicked and despised person. And we have only to follow the instructions of our august lord."

Sky Tiger stirred, lazily. He was going to die. This should worry him, should it not? Honorless and purposeless death at the hands of two harlots? (Ah, but the scent of—) No. He must rouse himself. He had no belly for death just now.

Futilely, he struggled. The struggle made no impression on his relaxed body.

"But," said Lotus Moon, "the water will fill his eyes, his mouth and nostrils."

"So it did with our pious and peerless lord. And we, who had been set to guard him, failed to save him."

"But was it not, perhaps, a foolishness to seat himself upon the brink of the lake—" Lotus Moon's voice had abruptly gained personality. An odd excited breathless sort of personality.

"Younger sister, be still," yapped Orchid Moon. "Do not presume."

An argument ensued.

Sky Tiger, lying prone upon the cushions, the wine bowl fallen from his hands, could do nothing but listen helplessly.

It appeared one priest had remained in the temple when the others had abandoned it. A holy and miraculous man he had been, who had ordered the courts alone by means of wizardry, for he could govern divers magic arts. Otherwise, he would pray and meditate upon the divine Path of Knowledge, and sometimes his soul would leave his body to explore the psychic regions. He had sat himself at the lake's edge beneath the shade of a mulberry tree, when just such a thing occurred. His soul had flown, leaving his body senselessly propped on the tree trunk. Presently, an evil man chanced that way. Always he had feared the priest's marvelous powers, being himself a robber and brawler of the district, who had once lost his prey due to the priest's intervention. Never before had he dared visit the temple, but having done so and discovering the priest helpless, he could not resist such a fortunate opening. Even the two women guardians of the priest, on their own admission, had dropped asleep in the warm grass. They awoke to witness their master's body, having been thrown in the lake, sinking like a stone, while the robber was heard laughing and congratulating himself in the distance. Thus, the body of the priest perished. When the soul returned, finding itself homeless, it must descend to Hell.

Thereafter, three years had passed. Tonight, at the moon's rising—

A paroxysm of panic seized Sky Tiger's inarticulate and unresponsive frame. He knew now what fate awaited him—and it was worse, worse by a thousand, thousand degrees, than mere death.

Hell, the Land of the Dead, where wrongdoing was mercilessly punished and good explicitly rewarded, was not in itself an area of loathing. Virtuous men might cross a silver bridge and observe the gods walk by on a bridge of gold. Besides, rebirth into the world would inevitably come at length. Unless the man or woman who entered Hell had died before their allotted time. That being the case, they were doomed to an eternity of futile howling, without hope of rebirth—save in one instance. After three years, a soul was permitted to return to the scene of its mortal fatality. Once there, if it could cause another to die in like manner to itself, thereby exchanging that luckless soul for its own, it could regain life.

The priest, drowned in the lake, was returning after three years, at the rising of the moon. He had ordered his women to take a traveler to the lake and drown him. The priest's soul would then be exchanged for the traveler's in the most wretched quarter of Hell. Sky Tiger's was to be the luckless soul.

Rebelling at last, and utterly, all his excellent young body could manage were a series of writhing spasms.

The women giggled in nasty yappy sharp little bursts. Next, to his dismay, he learned they were able to haul him from his seat and across the flowery court.

They were taking him to the water.

He had dreamed of a sensuous couch. Instead, it would be the lightless floor of the lake, and after that, an eternal yard in Hell.

Presently, his feeble resistance exhausted, he trailed from the women's spiteful grasp (they had even fastened their teeth in his shoulders). In this way, Sky Tiger the warrior left the temple, and was borne joltingly over the roots of the night-veiled peach trees.

No longer satin, the lake, but cold black jade, and set in it a round peony of white jade, slowly rising, as it rose in the heaven.

The women were dragging Sky Tiger forward inch by inch. Strands of his long hair already swam before him on the water, omens of what was to come. The inexorable progress continued, until there was a sudden, spontaneous check. The women left Sky Tiger lying, and lifting their heads, let out terrible thin wails of delight. Somehow, Sky Tiger managed to turn his head at an unlikely angle. He was then able to look aslant into the air, and see, between shore and moon, a ghastly pallid shimmering.

The ghost had all the appearance of a figure painted on a scroll and the color and the fine-drawn lines of ink and brush half washed away by rain or some other fluid. A priest for sure he was, lean and narrow as when living, shaved and solemn, with wide and ancient eyes.

At first these eyes were fixed dispassionately upon his female minions, then they lowered themselves to glare upon Sky Tiger. With a frantic shriek, the women floundered their victim forward again. In a total surrender of despair, Sky Tiger's head submerged. Choking, he swallowed and inspired the frigid liquid of the lake. Another second, and he would have lost consciousness, except that a vague din broke out above the surface, and in that vital second he was wrenched up again to the air. From the center of his coughing and crowing for breath, Sky Tiger was aware of an insane diatribe taking place.

"Stupid bitches!" shouted the whistling ghost-voice of the drowned priest's rage. "Can you do nothing right? Yes, grovel you may, you brainless ones. What would my further punishment be in Hell, if I were to have on my conscience the death of this valiant young hero? Say, exalted prince, are you recovered?"

Sky Tiger became aware that the effects of the drug seemed to have been driven out by the water. Trembling in every limb, he bowed three times to the ghost.

"Most venerable priest, I am a miserable item, not worthy of your notice."

"It is I who am miserable," said the priest. "My shame is insupportable, and brought about by these, my idiot servants. I assure you that you were not the man I had elected to drown in my stead. Know that through my powers some of which I have retained even in Hell, I was able to divine that my own murderer, that accursed bandit of the road who cast me in the lake, would ride by the temple tonight. And recalling his partiality to young women, I had arranged matters, instructing these two on what they must do at his arrival. But, the fools, the grasshoppers, they snared you in error, a warrior deserving of long life."

His mind rapidly clearing, Sky Tiger contemplated the events of the day in retrospect.

"Dread venerable," he finally said, "would you, from your great kindness, describe to me this bandit who murdered you, and whose soul you wished to bargain with in Hell?"

The ghost agreed, and promptly described the warrior Sky Tiger had fought with and slain at the edge of the wood some hours earlier. Sky Tiger revealed this fact.

"Unhappily, revered one, I have thereby cheated you of your hope of exchange," Sky Tiger apologized, "though there is this consolation, that, since you had predicted the robber would have come here, had it not been for the intervention of my sword, he too has died before his allotted span was accomplished, and must therefore eternally languish in Hell, saving some trick of his own."

The ghost smiled.

"That surely is a consolation, but there is more. By my power I shall be able to heal his wound and enter his body, for it has been dead but a few short hours. Thus shall I regain my interrupted life, and in the flesh of a healthful man of middle years. Might my mediocre self prevail upon your generosity to bring the corpse to the lake?"

Sky Tiger and the ghostly priest bowed several times.

The two young women lamented in the grass.

Soon after, Sky Tiger was riding back up the road toward the forest.

When he returned, leading his horse, with the dead bandit across it, the dawn was opening chrysanthemum petals in the east. Sky Tiger feared he was too late but nevertheless went to the lakeshore, and laid the corpse down there.

Despite the rekindling of the light and his own wondrous escape, Sky Tiger had begun to abhor the spot, and a grim horror caused his muscles to shiver. Glancing about, he saw no sign either of the ghost or his two handmaidens. With a relinquishing shudder, Sky Tiger spurred his horse in retreat through the peach trees.

On the road above, he did look back, but only once. He was not reassured to see, through the blossoming boughs, an armoured figure walking from the lake toward the temple. Nor to hear it calling, in a commanding voice, to two beings named Lotus and Orchid.

But less reassuring even than that, was the encounter a minute later with two little ivory and black lap-dogs, which came bounding from the shrub at the roadside, passed yapping under Sky Tiger's horse's hooves, and on, racing toward the temple. Plainly, in answer to the voice of a beloved master, vehemently calling their names.

INTIMATELY, WITH RAIN

Janet Fox

Janet Fox is a high school English teacher in Osage City, Kansas. Her first story appears to have been "Materialist," published in the lamented *Magazine of Horror*, back in 1970. She's had stories in *Weirdbook, Fantastic, Eerie Country* and other publications, and was represented in *Year's Best Horror Stories, Series VI* with "Screaming to Get Out," a story that featured the sort of title that prompts other writers to say, "Why didn't I think of that?" But more importantly, "Screaming to Get Out," had the sort of plot that prompts the same reaction as the title. It was a safe bet we wouldn't see so perfectly nasty a story again for some time. But it was a sucker bet, because here's another story with an idea that's just as chilling, and chillingly told—and by the same writer. Inasmuch as its previous appearance was in a literary magazine published on the West Coast, it should be unknown even to the majority of the really rapid collectors of horror yarns.

The land had a barren, torn-up look, the dark soil churned up by the workmen and their machines, native brush cleared away to the last ragged stand of timber along the creek. Annmarie clutched her black plastic patent purse against herself, shivering a little in the raw March wind, for all the portliness of her figure. Her matching shoes squished ridges of mud as she stood staring off toward the creek; she knew those bends, the sluggish trickle of mud-brown water dimly mirroring overhanging foliage. She knew where to seine for minnows and the deeper spots where skinny-dipping had been possible. Her heavy bosom heaved a little as she remembered.

She felt a hand on her elbow. "We can go inside. Nothing's finished in there yet, of course." She looked at William Dudley with almost a sense of shock—a round face, chins doubling down to his white shirtfront, a laurel wreath of thin gray hair garlanding a bald head, a permanent red flush beneath the skin. She was surprised, not that he seemed so old but that she could remember him no other way.

"It's cold out here," she said, hearing the whininess of her own voice, but unable to alter its tone. "I must get back soon. I have a Women Workers Club meeting at four."

They entered the unfinished house that would be their new home. There was the woody smell of new lumber and a rawness to it, though she could not have said it had an empty feel. It was as though the place was inhabited by something—shy but ineffably present. "A good omen," she thought, even though she knew it was imaginary. Something almost childlike about it, creeping about unseen with a suppressed giggle. It had been 20 years since Angela, her youngest, had been a child. Now they were all grown and gone. And she couldn't really say she was sorry about that; there were always so many good uses to which time could be put.

She wandered away from William, who was inspecting the basement, and went from room to room, trying to imagine how these bare chambers would look when all was complete. She supposed her nerves weren't all they should be, for the feeling of someone else in the house just wouldn't leave, even though she knew it was imagination. She could almost have sworn that she was being watched by wide, wondering eyes, that there had been a blur of motion at the window. So strong was the impression that she rushed to the window, a glassless frame, gripped the sill and looked out. The sun was bright, making everything appear terrifically real. Nothing was there except a small brown lizard, its back as rough as tree bark, sunning on a pile of bricks. Disturbed, it lifted its head to survey her out of one bead-black eye and then slithered down into the pile between bricks. Leaf shadows fluttered under one vulnerable tree left standing by the work crew.

She looked down and saw that a splinter of wood had

pierced her wrist when she'd grabbed the sill. She pursed her plum-colored lips and with a shudder of distaste, drew out the sliver; a thin line of blood was drawn down her arm, almost reaching the cuff of her best gray dress. Somehow the day seemed spoiled for her. "Let's go, William. My club meeting. . . ."

"Calm down, Annie," he said. He'd begun calling her that after the last child had left, she realized. Odd how it startled her now. "We've got plenty of time. This is a nice place. A nice place to settle in. You'll have to agree now that I had a good idea there. And for you it's coming home."

"Things change. In over thirty years people die . . . people leave. I can't really say it's home."

"But look how well you fit in, even though we've only been living here for six months."

She smiled. One learned things, what to join, whom to cultivate. Money helped too, and William had plenty of that.

The decor was a little stodgy, even to her taste—fat chairs and divans with chintzy prints, pictures of children and grandchildren propped everywhere, but William liked it and it was comfortable. Annmarie sat by the window in her housecoat, warming her hands on a coffee cup. The mornings were still a little cool. The house was becoming familiar now, though sometimes she awoke in the night and thought she was in older homes, and so the contours of these rooms would be a shock until she remembered. The feeling that she was never alone in the house had deepened with residence, though she'd never said anything like that to William. He lived in a pretty matter-of-fact world. He'd simply deny that anything like that existed, and maybe he was right.

She looked away from the sun-filled window back into the darkened room. Her vision filled with dancing spangles; she thought she saw something by the fireplace, a slight figure poised for flight, the suggestion of glossy dark hair. When her vison cleared, of course nothing was there, except a dust-winged moth that fluttered a moment and then darted up the chimney. Still there was that impression of a childlike figure—a kind of sprite. She finished the bitter dregs of the coffee with a grimace. She hardly had time to sit here dreaming. There was the church bazaar to manage.

She smiled as she put on the layers of undergarments that strapped her bulk into a firmer but no slenderer package and applied the makeup that really did nothing to hide the lines of her face. She had been a little afraid to come back to her home town, though she never would have admitted it to William. She was afraid that someone would remember Annie Byrd, the daughter of old Crikbank Ed—Anytime Annie. She had heard the name, though it was always in whispers and giggles. And there were those who should have remembered, stolid old citizens whom she passed in the streets or greeted in church with a circumspect nod. It must have been the time that had passed and the way that she had changed in the meantime. Perhaps it was as if that other person, that other life hadn't existed at all.

Full summer made the scraggly trees along the creekbank swell with layers of foliage. Annmarie had begun, now that it was warm, to walk here. The shack where she and her father had lived, now long torn down, was some miles from here. She had no desire to return to that place, but it was pleasant to walk among the trees, and she never walked here alone.

She had accepted it because there was literally no one she would talk to about it. She could see it, in the undulant green gold shadows under the trees, a figure straight, slender, but barely female with breasts that were no more than bud-swellings. The skin was butterscotch brown—all over. The hair, with the color and texture of moss, hung raggedly in peaks about the small face, and the eyes were large and luminous, the color between sunlight and leaf shadow. A woodspirit—sprite—dryad.

For all its lucent beauty, the thing still made her uneasy as it paced her through the trees. She knew that if she tried to approach it, speak to it, it would be gone and a squirrel, or garter snake would disappear into the tangle of underbrush, so much had it grown to be one with the natural life of this wood. She felt she could almost run with it through the aisles of forest, bare feet intimate with soil and moss, diving into the tepid brown water on a sultry dog-day evening with the water a long coolness against the skin—a sheath of silk. Then toward morning, dressed in the rough garment of the tree, just peering out a little to see the sunlight falling in slanted shafts to the forest floor.

She shook off the feeling and turned toward the path back to the house. Whenever she found her thoughts running free like this, she pulled them up, as if she were approaching memories she did not dare relive. And she had to get sandwiches ready for her bridge club, which would meet that afternoon.

The country club was decorated with streamers of red, white and blue, but they were drooping and wilted as the dance drew to a close. Smoke wreathed a few somnambulant dancers. While William was enmeshed in some interminable talk of politics, she stepped outside a moment to get out of the smoky atmosphere. A bulky shape approached her, and for a moment she thought it was William; then she saw that it was not.

"Mrs. Dudley?"

She nodded, frostily, as this kind of meeting didn't seem exactly proper to her.

"Annmarie—Annie Byrd?"

She searched the sagging gray face, with its dewlaps and eye pouches, but she couldn't remember the name.

"David—Davy Brubaker." He stood a little unsteadily, leaning forward to exhale a breath of stale alcohol on her. "Don't you remember me?"

She felt she should deny acquaintance, yet somehow she couldn't.

"We had us some good times back there in those woods," he said hoarsely. His poor, time-broken face tried for an obscene wink, but couldn't quite bring it off. "Us guys never knew where you went after—"

She pushed him away from her and fled back to the dance, feeling in one way naked, in another almost relieved. Was there an undercurrent of talk she'd been unaware of all this time, she wondered. William greeted her loudly, having had a little too much to drink. She managed to get him to the car, to drive him home. A slight, free figure seemed to fly before them in the beam of headlights. She put William to bed, but she was unable to sleep. As she roamed the house, she felt an awful constriction and a desire to be free of it. It was as if she were slipping from the confines of her tree, her body light and firm, her hair vegetable cool when it blew against her cheeks. She ran lightly to the deep pools and waited there. Through an endless twilight they came to her, one by one, shaggy boyish satyrs, the moon bringing coppery highlights from the curling hair of chest and flanks, young forest gods, their faces and bodies as self-consciously perfect as those of Greek statues. Her buttocks had squirmed their shape into the moist earth of the bank, not once—many times. They were all young, all beautiful; no wonder she had difficulty distinguishing one from another. She supposed one of them had been David Brubaker, ludicrous as that seemed. Sated, she returned to draw the substance of the tree close about her and in the morning she awoke on the divan, struggling to draw the rough blanket tighter against morning's coolness.

The following day was not as difficult for her as she had thought it would be; there were all those things to do. She visited the beauty parlor, had lunch with several of the girls. After lunch there was her volunteer work at the hospital in a nearby city. She had gone through the day like a sleepwalker; there were ways to let routine take over and the time passed very quickly, but as she undressed in her bedroom, removing the tight layers, the bindings, she was remembering things. She had heard herself mouthing platitudes at a woman who was in the process of dying, a little at a time, and who had looked vaguely amused. She had read greeting-card type verse to a man in a body cast.

William was sitting open-mouthed and snoring in front of the TV set. She turned off the set but didn't wake him. It seemed that there was a tension in the air; the wind blew in the scent of rain. She remembered that smell. A few fireflies blinked above the grass as she hurried toward the shelter of the trees. It did not seem odd to her to be running out barefoot, dressed only in a thin robe. The wind whipped stingingly cold drops against her skin, but she ran on. She knew she would recognize the glade with its soft floor of forest debris and its single great twisted oak. A dryad could never lose its own tree. She thought as she ran that she had almost forgotten what it was like to feel this free—not since the days when she'd gone skinny-dipping with the town boys, one and then another, in the deep pools. She knew now that it had been done in true innocence, not in guilt as they had made her believe, and if she ran swiftly she might yet recapture that innocence.

Breathless, she reached the glade at last and fell panting to the soft forest floor. Lying there brought back that other time.

She'd escaped another of her father's fits of rage, the names he'd called her burning in her ears. She'd blundered clumsily along the bank until she'd come to this place, where she'd collapsed, the pains beginning in earnest, as the midwife had warned they would. All the other tales the old woman had told her were in her head, too; and she'd been sure she was going to die as the pain washed over her, coming and going in waves and rhythms that had nothing to do with what she wanted. Some old knowledge that she hadn't known she possessed had taken over then, must have, for she'd survived.

The rain was quite steady now, comforting, a kind of release. She rose, the thin robe gaping, pieces of brush and straw clinging to her white, doughy flesh. She approached the tree with a rapt expression. There was a hollow there and the dryad lay cocooned in rough bark in organic-smelling darkness. She reached in; her fingers scraped brittle wood pulp, felt a dry, twisted mass. "How strange to realize now," she thought, "that you are all I have ever had of beauty and innocence. I'll make them wear the name—bastards—and give them back their guilt." She cradled the dark object in the crook of her arm; it was shriveled and brown like some old, earth-buried tree root. "Won't William and the others be surprised," she said, "when they see how beautiful you've become."

THE SECRET

Jack Vance

If there is any writer alive whose name is synonymous with imagination, that writer is Jack Vance. If you've read such works as his *The Dying Earth*, *Big Planet*, *The Last Castle*, *The Dragon Masters*, the Demon Princes novels or the Alastor books, then you know why. Vance boasts an unfailing eye for the glitteringly strange, a knack for writing compelling narratives, and an unsurpassed talent for the music of invented words. The following story appeared in a British publication without Vance's knowledge, but its first authorized publication was in a science fiction fan magazine edited by Robert Offutt Jr., called *The Many Worlds of Jack Vance/The Horns of Elfland*. When you consider that Offutt's fine magazine doesn't begin to reach the number of readers it deserves to, that makes this story a very well-kept secret, indeed, and we are pleased to be able to share it with you.

Sunbeams slanted through chinks in the wall of the hut; from the lagoon came shouts and splashing of the village children. Rona ta Inga at last opened his eyes. He had slept far past his usual hour of arising, far into the morning. He stretched his legs, cupped hands behind his head, stared absently up at the ceiling of thatch. In actuality he had awakened at the ususal hour, to drift off again into a dreamlike doze—a habit to which lately he had become prone. Only lately. Inga frowned and sat up with a jerk. What did this mean? Was it a sign? Perhaps he should inquire from Takti-

THE SECRET

Tai. . . .But it was all so ridiculous. He had slept late for the most ordinary of reasons: he enjoyed lazing and drowsing and dreaming.

On the mat beside him were crumpled flowers, where Mai-Mio had lain. Inga gathered the blossoms and laid them on the shelf which held his scant possessions. An enchanting creature, this Mai-Mio. She laughed no more and no less than other girls; her eyes were as other eyes, her mouth like all mouths; but her quaint and charming mannerisms made her absolutely unique: the single Mai-Mio in all the universe. Inga had loved many maidens. All in some way were singular, but Mai-Mio was a creature delightfully, exquisitely apart from the others. There was considerable difference in their ages. Mai-Mio only recently had become a woman—even now from a distance she might be mistaken for a boy—while Inga was older by at least five or six seasons. He was not quite sure. It mattered little, In any event. It mattered very little, he told himself again, quite emphatically. This was his village, his island; he had no desire to leave. Ever!

The children came up the beach from the lagoon. Two or three darted under his hut, swinging on one of the poles, chanting nonsense words. The hut trembled; the outcry jarred upon Inga's nerves. He shouted in irritation. The children became instantly silent, in awe and astonishment, and trotted away looking over their shoulders.

Inga frowned; for the second time this morning he felt dissatisfied with himself. He would gain an unenviable reputation if he kept on in such a fashion. What had come over him? He was the same Inga that he was yesterday. . . . Except for the fact that a day had elapsed and he was a day older.

He went out on the porch before his hut, stretched in the sunlight. To right and left were forty or fifty other such huts as his own, with intervening trees; ahead lay the lagoon blue and sparkling in the sunlight. Inga jumped to the ground, walked to the lagoon, swam, dived far down among the glittering pebbles and ocean growths which covered the lagoon floor. Emerging he felt relaxed and at peace—once more himself: Rona ta Inga, as he had always been, and would always be.

Squatting on his porch he breakfasted on fruit and cold baked fish from last night's feast and considered the day ahead. There was no urgency, no duty to fulfil, no need to satisfy. He could join the party of young bucks now on their way into the forest hoping to snare fowl. He could fashion a brooch of carved shell and goana-nut for Mai-Mio. He could lounge and gossip; he could fish. Or he could visit his best friend Takti-Tai—who was building a boat. Inga rose to his feet. He would fish. He walked along the beach to his canoe, checked equipment, pushed off, paddled across the lagoon to the opening in the reef. The winds blew to the west as always. Leaving the lagoon Inga turned a swift glance downwind—an almost furtive glance—then bent his neck into the wind and paddled east.

Within the hour he had caught six fine fish, and drifted back along the reef to the lagoon entrance. Everyone was swimming when he returned. Maidens, young men, children. Mai-Mio paddled to the canoe, hooked her arms over the gunwales, grinned up at him, water glistening on her cheeks. "Rona ta Inga! Did you catch fish? Or am I bad luck?"

"See for yourself."

She looked. "Five—no, six! All fat silver-fins! I am good luck! May I sleep often in your hut?"

"So long as I catch fish the following day."

She dropped back into the water, splashed him, sank out of sight. Through the undulating surface Inga could see her slender brown form skimming off across the bottom. He beached the canoe, wrapped the fish in bi sipi-leaves and stored them in a cool cistern, then ran down to the lagoon to join the swimming.

Later he and Mai-Mio sat in the shade; she plaiting a decorative cord of colored bark which later she would weave into a basket, he leaning back, looking across the water. Artlessly Mai-Mio chattered—of the new song Ama ta Lalau had composed, of the odd fish she had seen while swimming underwater, of the change which had come over Takti-Tai since he had started building his boat.

Inga made an absent-minded sound, but said nothing.

"We have formed a band," Mai-Mio confided. "There are six of us: Ipa, Tuiti, Hali-Sai-Iano, Zoma, Oiu-Ngo and myself. We have pledged never to leave the island. Never, never, never. There is too much joy here. Never will we sail west—never. Whatever the secret we do not wish to know."

Inga smiled, a rather wistful smile. "There is much wisdom in the pledge you have made."

THE SECRET

She stroked his arm. "Why do you not join us in our pledge? True, we are six girls but a pledge is a pledge."

"True."

"Do you want to sail west?"

"No."

Mai-Mio excitedly rose to her knees. "I will call together the band, and all of us, all together: we will recite the pledge again, never will we leave our island! And to think you are the oldest of all at the village!"

"Takti-Tai is older," said Inga.

"But Takti-Tai is building his boat! He hardly counts any more!"

"Vai-Ona is as old as I. Almost as old."

"Do you know something? Whenever Vai Ona goes out to fish, he always looks to the west. He wonders."

"Everyone wonders."

"Not I!" Mai-Mio jumped to her feet. "Not I—not any of the band. Never, never, never—never will we leave the island! We have pledged ourselves!" She reached down, patted Inga's cheek, ran off to where a group of her friends were sharing a basket of fruit.

Inga sat quietly for five minutes. Then he made an impatient gesture, rose and walked along the shore to the platform where Takti-Tai worked on his boat. This was a catamaran with a broad deck, a shelter of woven withe thatched with sipi-leave, a stout mast. In silence Inga helped Takti-Tai shape the mast, scraping a tall well-seasoned pasiao-tui sapling with sharp shells. Inga presently paused, laid aside the shell. He said, "Long ago there were four of us. You, me, Akara and Zan. Remember?"

Takti-Tai continued to scrape. "Of course I remember."

"One night we sat on the beach around a fire—the four of us. Remember?"

Takti-Tai nodded.

"We pledged never to leave the island. We swore never to weaken, we spilled blood to seal the pact. Never would we sail west."

"I remember."

"Now you sail," said Inga. "I will be the last of the group."

Takti-Tai paused in his scraping, looked at Inga, as if he would speak, then bent once more over the mast. Inga presently returned up the beach to his hut, where squatting on the porch he carved at the brooch for Mai-Mio.

A youth presently came to sit beside him. Inga, who had no particular wish for companionship, continued with his carving. But the youth, absorbed in his own problems, failed to notice. "Advise me, Rona ta Inga. You are the oldest of the village and very sage." Inga raised his eyebrows, then scowled, but said nothing.

"I love Hali Sai Iano, I long for her desperately, but she laughs at me and runs off to throw her arms about the neck of Hopu. What should I do?"

"The situation is quite simple," said Inga. "She prefers Hopu. You merely select another girl. What of Talau Io? She is pretty and affectionate, and seems to like you."

The youth vented a sigh. "Very well. I will do as you suggest. After all one girl is much like another." He departed, unaware of the sardonic look Inga directed at his back. He asked himself, why do they come to me for advice? I am only two or three, or at most four or five, seasons their senior. It is as if they think me the fount and source of all sagacity!

During the evening a baby was born. The mother was Omei Ni Io, who for almost a season had slept in Inga's hut. Since it was a boy-child she named it Inga ta Omei. There was a naming ceremony at which Inga presided. The singing and dancing lasted until late, and if it were not for the fact that the child was his own, with his name, Inga would have crept off early to his hut. He had attended many naming ceremonies.

A week later Takti-Tai sailed west, and there was a ceremony of a different sort. Everyone came to the beach to touch the hull of the boat and bless it with water. Tears ran freely down all cheeks, including Takti-tai's. For the last time he looked around the lagoon, into the faces of those he would be leaving. Then he turned, signalled; the young men pushed the boat away from the beach, then jumping into the water, towed it across the lagoon, guided it out into the ocean. Takti-Tai cut brails, tightened halyards; the big square sail billowed in the wind. The boat surged west. Takti-Tai stood on the platform, gave a final flourish of the hand, and those on the beach waved farewell. The boat moved out into the afternoon, and when the sun sank, it could be seen no more.

During the evening meal the talk was quiet; everyone stared into the fire. Mai-Mio finally jumped to her feet. "Not I," she chanted. "Not I—ever, ever, ever!"

THE SECRET

"Nor I," shouted Ama ta Lalau, who of all the youths was the most proficient musician. He reached for the guitar which he had carved from a black soa-gum trunk, struck chords, began to sing.

Inga watched quietly. He was now the oldest on the island, and it seemed as if the others were treating him with a new respect. Ridiculous! What nonsense! So little older was he that it made no difference whatever! But he noticed that Mai-Mio was laughingly attentive to Ama ta Lalau, who responded to the flirtation with great gallantry. Inga watched with a heavy feeling around the heart, and presently went off to his hut. That night, for the first time in weeks Mai-Mio did not sleep beside him. No matter, Inga told himself: one girl is much like another.

The following day he wandered up the beach to the platform where Takti-Tai had built his boat. The area was clean and tidy, the tools were hung carefully in a nearby shed. In the forest beyond grew fine makara trees, from which the staunchest hulls were fashioned.

Inga turned away. He took his canoe out to catch fish, and leaving the lagoon looked to the west. There was nothing to see but empty horizon, precisely like the horizon to east, to north, and to south—except that the western horizon concealed the secret. And the rest of the day he felt uneasy. During the evening meal he looked from face to face. None of the faces of his dear friends; they all had built their boats and had sailed. His friends had departed; they knew the secret.

The next morning, without making a conscious decision, Inga sharpened the tools and felled two fine makara trees. He was not precisely building a boat—so he assured himself, but it did no harm for wood to season.

Nevertheless the following day he trimmed the trees, cut the trunk to length, and the next day assembled all the young men to help carry the trunks to the platform. No one seemed surprised; everyone knew that Rona ta Inga was building his boat. Mai-Mio had now frankly taken up with Ama ta Lalau and as Inga worked on his boat he watched them play in the water, not without a lump of bitterness in his throat. Yes, he told himself, it would be pleasure indeed to join his true friends—the youths and maidens he had known since he dropped his milk-name, who he had sported with, who now were departed, and for whom he felt an aching loneliness. Diligently he hollowed the hulls, burning, scraping, chiseling.

Then the platform was secured, the little shelter woven and thatched to protect him from rain. He scraped a mast from a flawless pa-siao-tui sapling, stepped and stayed it. He gathered bast, wove a coarse but sturdy sail, hung it to stretch and season. Then he began to provision the boat. He gathered nutmeats, dried fruits, smoked fish wrapped in sipi-leaf. He filled blowfish bladders with water. How long was the trip to the west? No one knew. Best not to go hungry, best to stock the boat well: once down the wind there was no turning back.

One day he was ready. It was a day much like all the other days of his life. The sun shone warm and bright, the lagoon glittered and rippled up and down the beach in little gushes of play-surf. Rona ta Inga's throat felt tense and stiff; he could hardly trust his voice. The young folk came to the beach; all blessed the boat with water. Inga gazed into each face, then along the line of huts, the trees, the beaches, the scenes he loved with such intensity. . . . Already they seemed remote. Tears were coursing his cheeks. He held up his hand, turned away. He felt the boat leave the beach, float free on the water. Swimmers thrust him out into the ocean. For the last time he turned to look back at the village, fighting a sudden maddening urge to jump from the boat, to swim back to the village. He hoisted the sail, the wind thrust deep into the hollow. Water surged under the hulls and he was coasting west, with the island astern.

Up the blue swells, down into the long troughs, the wake gurgling, the bow raising and falling. The long afternoon waned and became golden; sunset burned and ebbed and became a halcyon dusk. The stars appeared, and Inga sitting silently by his rudder held the sail full to the wind. At midnight he lowered the sail and slept, the boat drifting quietly.

In the morning he was completely alone, the horizons blank. He raised the sail and scudded west, and so passed the day, and the next, and others. And Inga became thankful that he had provisioned the boat with generosity. On the sixth day he seemed to notice that a chill had come into the wind; on the eighth day he sailed under a high overcast, the like of which he had never seen before. The ocean changed from blue to a gray which presently took on a tinge of green, and now the water was cold. The wind blew with great force, bellying his bast sail, and Inga huddled in the shelter to avoid the harsh spray. On the morning of the ninth day he thought

THE SECRET

to see a dim dark shape loom ahead, which at noon became a line of tall cliffs with surf beating against jagged rocks, roaring back and forth across coarse shingle. In mid-afternoon he ran his boat up on one of the shingle beaches, jumped gingerly ashore. Shivering in the whooping gusts, he took stock of the situation. There was no living thing to be seen along the foreshore but three or four gray gulls. A hundred yards to his right lay a battered hulk of another boat, and beyond was a tangle of wood and fiber which might have been still another.

Inga carried ashore what provisions remained, bundled them together, and by a faint trail climbed the cliffs. He came out on an expanse of rolling gray-green downs. Two or three miles inland rose a line of low hills, toward which the trail seemed to lead.

Inga looked right and left; again there was no living creature in sight other than the gulls. Shouldering his bundle he set forth along the trail.

Nearing the hills he came upon a hut of turf and stone, beside a patch of cultivated soil. A man and a woman worked in the field. Inga peered closer. What manner of creatures were these? They resembled human beings; they had arms and legs and faces—but how seamed and seared and gray they were! How shrunken were their hands, how bent and hobbled as they worked! He walked quickly by, and they did not appear to notice him.

Now Inga hastened, as the end of the day was drawing on and the hills loomed before him. The trail led along a valley grown with gnarled oak and low purple-green shrubs, then slanted up the hillside through a stony gap, where the wind generated whistling musical sounds. From the gap Inga looked out over a flat valley. He saw copses of low trees, plots of tilled land, a group of huts. Slowly he walked down the trail. In a nearby field a man raised his head. Inga paused, thinking to recognize him. Was this not Akara ta Oma who had sailed west ten or twelve seasons back? It seemed impossible. This man was fat, the hair had almost departed his head, his cheeks hung loose at the jawline. No, this could not be lithe Akara ta Oma! Hurriedly Inga turned away, and presently entered the village. Before a nearby hut stood one whom he recognized with joy. "Takti-Tai!"

Takti-Tai nodded. "Rona ta Inga. I knew you'd be coming soon."

"I'm delighted to see you. But let us leave this terrible place; let us return to the island."

Takti-Tai smiled a little, shook his head.

Inga protested heatedly, "Don't tell me you prefer this dismal land? Come! My boat is still seaworthy. If somehow we can back it off the beach, gain the open sea. . . ."

The wind sang down over the mountains, strummed through the trees, Inga's words died in his throat. It was clearly impossible to work the boat off the foreshore.

"Not only the wind," said Takti-Tai. "We could not go back now. We know the secret."

Inga stared in wonderment. "The secret? Not I."

"Come. Now you will learn."

Takti Tai took him through the village to a structure of stone with a high-gabled roof shingled with slate. "Enter, and you will know the secret."

Hesitantly Rona ta Inga entered the stone structure. On a stone table lay a still figure surrounded by six tall candles. Inga stared at the shrunken white face, at the white sheet which lay motionless over the narrow chest. "Who is this? A man? How thin he is. Does he sleep? Why do you show me such a thing?"

"This is the secret," said Takti-Tai. "It is called 'death.'"

HEAR ME NOW, MY SWEET ABBEY ROSE

Charles L. Grant

In a mere handful of years, Charles Grant has established himself as one of the most reliable performers around with successful story after successful story of both horror and science fiction (and his sf shows a marked tendency toward horror, for that matter). He's written sf novels such as *Ascension*, and edited an anthology of contemporary horror stories called *Shadows*. He is the author of several others novels, among them *The Hour of the Oxrun Dead* and *The Sound of Midnight*, which a cowardly publisher has tried to foist off as those sorts of bastard gothics called "occult" or "supernatural suspense" stories; but be not deceived, astute reader, they are bona fide masterworks of sheer horror. In person, Charlie Grant is a mild-mannered fellow with a quick (and often unmildly devastating) wit and easy-going manner, tempered somewhat by a nervous shyness. The story below, like those two "occult suspense" novels, is set in the fictitious New England town, Oxrun Station, where it does not pay anyone to be nervous.

I

Dusk; a haze of drifting light that keeps the eye from resting too long on a single tree, a faint star, a leaf that bumps over disused furrows poking out weeds. It drops a lace curtain over the farmhouse and blinds the windows, stills the dog, stirs the cat, makes the kitchen seem far warmer than it is. It takes the freshness from the daylight and returns the evening to the memory of winter. And summons the rolling black that follows a breeze from the surrounding hills. And by the time nightfall is full, and heavy, the only sound is a flock of geese invisible, calling, guiding, sweeping over the land and the house and the hills and the breeze.

Nels leaned against the kitchen door frame and shivered when he heard the birds. Beautiful in the bask of the sun, they were unpleasantly lonely in the hours past nine. Too lonely by far, and he slapped a hand to his thigh, closed the door and moved to sit at the table in front of the iron-black stove. Kelly turned from the refrigerator and held out a bottle of ginger ale. He nodded and pushed back in the hard wooden chair, swallowing at air, idly scratching at the traces of wattle at his throat. He said nothing. He liked to watch his wife move from place to place, within or without the confines of the house, knowing that other men envied him without reservation. Knowing that he envied himself in his fear of losing her. She filled a glass, waited for the bubbles to settle, topped it and set it in front of him. Then, and only then, did she sit opposite him with a cup of tea protected by her palms.

"They're late," she said, blowing upward to fend off a strand of black hair drifting down toward her right eye. "I told them before dark."

"The place is still new," he answered, wrinkling his nose at the carbonation splashing into his face while he drank. "If they get lost, they'll call."

"Grace will," she said with a smile, "but not Abbey or Bess. They've got dollar signs in their eyes already, or didn't you notice."

He laughed and swept a plate of shortbread toward him, picked up one of the flour-and-butter cakes and bit into it. "They take after me. Grace is all yours." Then, with a frown: "Are you worried?"

She shrugged. "Not really, I guess. I just don't want them to have all their fun before the vacation is over, that's all. To get it all out on the first big night in town will make everything else seem . . . well, quiet."

"Dull," he said. "What you mean is, dull."

It was her turn to laugh, lightly, mocking the sigh of the breeze now turned to wind.

Ten o'clock, and the muttering of a car coughing into silence. Nels hustled Kelly into the front room, grabbed at a magazine and switched on the television. Then he thumped at the cushions on the dark quilted sofa, waved his wife to an armchair, and snapped open the first page before the front door swung in and his daughters arrived.

Physically, they were Kelly; from the black hair and eyes to the dark lips and slender figures to the nearly sickly pale complexions made disturbingly erotic by the nips of pink at their cheeks. Twenty, nineteen, eighteen, all in college, all with glasses, all standing with hands on hips staring in at their parents. Grace tsked, Abbey sighed, and Bess walked deliberately over to her father and turned the magazine right side up. "You're impossible," she said, kissing him on the cheek. Nels shrugged and asked how it went.

Grace and Abbey slumped to the braided rug by the raised brick hearth and pulled their heavy sweaters over their heads, shook their hair back into place, and folded the sweaters neatly in their laps.

"They may be rich," Grace finally said, "but you cannot believe how incredibly dull they are."

"God, Pop," Abbey said, pulling at her lower lip, "we went to some place called the Chancellor Inn. There's a restaurant upstairs—it's an old farmhouse, see, I think—and there's a poor excuse for a disco on the first floor. Lots of noise. No action."

"They thought we were rubes or something," Bess said, knocking his legs away so she could sit on the couch with him. "Hicks. I think they think we're going to move in here forever. Raise chickens or ducks, or whatever they do on a place like this."

Kelly looked up from her knitting—a sweater for Nels in muted blues and grays—and smiled sympathetically. Then she looked to her husband, frowned when he lit a cigarette, but said nothing when he studiously avoided her glare.

"Did you guys have a good time?" Abbey said, looking to her father.

"We watched the sun set over that tree in the field."

"Great," Bess said. "That's really . . . great."

"We heard some geese, too."

"Oh my God," Grace said. "I don't think I can stand any more. I'm tired, folks. I think I'll go to bed."

"Me, too," Bess said quickly. "It's the country air, or something."

Abbey alone stayed behind when the footsteps on the stairs

faded into running bath water and the shouts of who gets in first and who uses what towel. She picked up a long splinter of kindling and drew roads between the bricks, connected them, drew them again.

"What's the matter, Abbey?" Nels said softly. "Aren't you tired?"

"Nope," she answered without taking her eyes from the hearth. "Just . . . I don't know. I guess I was expecting something different."

Nels stretched out on the couch again and pillowed his hands behind his head, stared at the dark-beamed ceiling and the shadows that lurked there from the lamp next to Kelly. The vacation in May had been his idea, what with all his daughters' schools ending early and he and Kelly climbing the walls from a particularly harsh winter. The farm had been a quick-growing inspiration, sparked by a friend at the office who had lived in this same house once and remembered—so he claimed—the great times he and his own family had had. Rediscovering the land, roots, the whole mystique of a Nature without city. Not to mention, it had been added slyly, the preponderance of wealth in Oxrun Station and the young men who were attached to it. Kelly thought that part of the argument crass and almost unforgivable; Nels didn't think of it at all. His daughters were, in temperament, much like himself—what came, came, and if it didn't— whatever it was—well, there was no use crying. Time never cried for a flower that died. But Abbey was his special flower, hence her middle name, and it disturbed him that she should be disappointed, that the unusual vacation had turned sour for her already. Normally, she was prepared for anything, to try anything, at least to give everything half a chance to prove itself worthy of her attention. But this, he thought, had somehow killed her enthusiasm before she had given it that one half-chance.

"What?" he said finally, as she knelt on the hearth and arranged the logs to start a fire. "Come on, girl, what's up?"

"They told us there was a lynching here, back before the Civil War. Some abolitionists were hanged from the tree in the field out back. Four of them, I think. I didn't know they did stuff like that in Connecticut."

"You think the farm is haunted, then?" Kelly said, her disbelief evident and marked with the nail of her practicality.

"No, Mother, of course not."

HEAR ME NOW, MY SWEET ABBEY ROSE 107

Kelly looked at Nels, set her knitting in the carpetbag by her side and folded her hands in her lap. "Then what, dear?"

"I don't know, I told you! Let's just say the place doesn't feel right, okay?"

She rose then and hurried from the room, up the stairs and into the giggling storm that erupted when she opened a bedroom door. Nels listened to the laughter for a while and allowed himself a drop of sweet reminiscence, when they had lived in another house in another state, when the girls were younger and going to bed meant only another opportunity to invent new games and friends and create chaos from careful order. And now they were drifting away. It made no difference that he understood the inevitability of it, that young ladies and fledglings soon enough stretched their legs and their wings and discovered that the horizon moved when you approached it. That didn't make any difference at all when the sun had set and his girls were asleep and he could remember pajamas with feet, and dolls with calico dresses, carriages and plastic tea sets and braces and boys.

Maudlin, Nels, he told himself; watch it, or you'll next be thinking how close to fifty you are, and that would crimp this week faster than you can sneeze.

Nels, it doesn't feel right, Kelly said with her hands roaming gently over her swollen stomach.

Nonsense.

A mother knows these things, Nels.

All right then, we'll call Dr. Falbo and see what's what.

It's not that kind of feel.

Then it's the Irish in you and the Norse in me. A combination of fey not seen since the world's creation. Don't worry about it, love, he'll be fine.

And what makes you so sure it'll be a he?

Fey. I told you. I have the sight, in case you didn't know.

And what if it's another girl?

Two girls? Are you kidding? How the hell can I possibly afford two weddings? But . . . if it's a girl, we'll name her Kelly Rose, after you and your mother.

Abbey Rose, she said with a grin. After my mother and the theater in Dublin.

If it is a girl, I'll want another shot at it.

You'll keep your distance, Nels Anderson, or you'll be singing soprano in some damned fey choir.

Early the following morning, Grace and Bess took the car into Oxrun to see, as they explained, what was so special about all the fancy jewelry stores clustered there. Kelly ensconced herself in the kitchen to test the reputation of homemade bread. Alone, then, Nels wandered across the fallow field, jumping at startled grey mice, watching a pair of hawks riding the wind beneath a softly blue sky. He stopped every few yards to overturn a rock, dig around a burrow, marvel at the life no city ever maintained, marveling more that such continual amazements could become so mundane that the previous owners of the farm had given it up and moved to Los Angeles. At last, at noon and in no hurry, he reached the tree he had claimed for his own. It was a chestnut squat with age and broad with a crown that was flecked with new green. Weeds and grass grew up to its bole, surrounded knees of roots that nudged through the rocky soil. He had never seen anything quite like it, and as he grabbed at a twig dangling in front of him, wondered if even the yard of their suburban home would ever seem the same.

"Gruesome," a voice said behind him, and he jumped, a hand to his chest, his mouth open.

Abbey laughed delightedly, clutching at her stomach, stepped backward and fell, her legs splayed and her hands behind her to prop her up. Nels shook his head in rapidly diminishing anger, somewhat embarrassed, and pleased that she had come. He sat where he stood, crossed his legs and rested his palms on his knees. "Now that you've assured me ten years less of a magnificent life, kid," he said. "you can tell me what was really bothering you last night."

She had been having dreams of dying the past few months, each one sending her screaming into her parents' bed; in the last one, she had risen from her coffin at the church to sit beside her father.

Nels prayed they hadn't started again.

"Come on," he said gently, leaning forward slightly. "Come on, Abbey. You can tell me and the tree. We're old friends, the three of us."

Abbey puffed her cheeks. She was ready to deny him, then sagged and began pulling at green blades by her thighs. "They thought we were hicks," she said. "Kind of a reverse snobbery, I guess. Dumb country folk from the city, if you know what I mean. First they tried to get us drunk. Then they tried a few old-fashioned wrestling holds. We'd left the car at one of their houses . . . Frank's . . . he's the one who came out and introduced himself so nicely, remember? We left the car at his house. By the time we got back there, we were a mess. But . . ." and she grinned broadly, suddenly, "our virtue was, for the moment, ladies and gentlemen, still intact. Speaking for myself, that is." And her grin became a laugh.

Nels felt the warmth rising from below his collar, saw that she'd recognized his protective anger and coughed to keep himself calm. He reached blindly over his head, caught at a thin branch and pulled until his fingers had stripped a handful of leaves into his palm. He rolled them into a cylinder, pressed, rolled, and felt the moisture released and rubbed into his skin. It was a good feeling and an uncommon one. When he looked up, he saw his daughter staring at him.

"You're all right, though," he said awkwardly.

"If you're asking if you have to buy a shotgun, the answer is no." She twisted until she was kneeling, took the crushed leaves from his hand and laid them to her cheek, her neck, across her forehead with her eyes closed. Then she stared at the tree and back to him. "Dad," she said, "if you only knew how natural you looked, sitting there."

"Ah," he said. "The primeval in me, that's what it is. One with the land and all that."

"No," she said, frowning as she puzzled it out. "Not quite. But it feels right for you to be here."

"Like it doesn't feel right to be in the house?"

She nodded, quickly shook her head and rose. "It's more like my room back home. I belong there more than anyplace else. You, though . . . I think you belong here."

"So I'll quit my job and we can play farmer for the rest of our lives."

She grinned, brushed at her jeans and smoothed her plaid shirt over her breasts. "Dad, what would you do if I got married?"

"I'd cry a lot and wish the boy luck. Lots of it."

"You'd let me? You'd let me go?"

He swallowed quickly the wisecrack that rose, sniffed and spread his hands helplessly. "I'd have to," he said quietly. "But I sure wouldn't want to."

"Neither would I," she whispered, knelt and kissed him on the cheek. "I love you, Dad. I don't say it enough. I know, but I love you."

Nels watched her leave. And the sadness that suddenly cloaked him grew when his hand absently touched at his close-cropped hair, blond turning white. That, he thought, is what New England does for you, pal; autumn in the spring. He knew there was a tear in his left eye, but he refused to acknowledge it by wiping it away. Soon enough, too soon, far too soon, it was gone, and he turned on his buttocks to stare at the bole, to follow its winding configurations and ease his mind into a state of near-trance. And it wasn't until a shout floated across the field that he came out of it, pushed himself to his feet stiffly and trotted back toward the farmhouse. He saw Grace standing on the back porch, waving her arms, and the trot became a run, the run a dash when his eldest leapt from the steps and raced toward him. She was crying as she dropped into his arms, sobbing out a garbled story of the three men they had met the night before; they had cornered her and Bess in a luncheonette, pressing until the girls had become frightened, following them to the turnoff from the main road and sitting there in their convertible waiting.

"I'll have a look," he said as he led her back into the house. Kelly was not in the kitchen, but he heard soft sounds from upstairs and knew she was busily comforting the youngest. Grace sniffed loudly and borrowed his handkerchief. Ordinarily, had it been Abbey and Bess, he would have fallen instantly into the comforting father role he played for skinned knees and elbows, nightmares and thunderstorms. But Grace was twenty, a woman, and not easily shaken. Those men must have been more than simply crude, more than only playfully threatening. He set his daughter in the living room's armchair and slipped into his windbreaker.

"Stay there," he said. "Get yourself a brandy and light a fire. It'll be cold tonight. A Connecticut May is more like March."

He waited until she had reached for the decanter on the sideboard, then unhurriedly stepped outside and slid in behind the wheel of the car. The keys were still in the ignition and he fired the engine, turned around the oval drive marked with a birch in its center, and drove the half-mile in its center, and drove the half mile to the stone pillars that flanked the farm road's entrance. He braked, got out and walked to the main road that led in a direct line back to the village. There were no cars, no trucks, nothing at all that he could see save another field across the way and the faint rise of the low hill that marked the village park. Not a hill, really, he thought incongruously; more like a bump that the trees came to like.

He waited for nearly half an hour, leaning against one of the low brown pillars and smoking. When the twilight chill finally numbed his hands, he gave it up and drove back to the house, went inside and found all his women in front of Grace's fire. They were playing a word game found in the bookcase built into the back wall, and when they noticed him, they laughed, waved, and ordered him into the kitchen to make a sandwich supper.

"Done," he said, shucking his coat and tossing it to the couch. "Just don't complain if I'm not as good as Bess."

So she isn't the smartest in the world, Kelly, so what? She's got brains enough to make it through any decent college, and that's all that counts.

Suppose Abbey doesn't want to go to college?

All right, so she doesn't go. It's her choice, isn't it. It's her life, not mine, for crying out loud.

Nels, sometimes I think you love her too much.

Kelly! Are you . . . are you saying that I spoil the girl? God forbid, no, dope. I just mean . . . well, sometimes I think she's closer to you than any of us are, that's all.

Good Lord, Kelly, do the other girls . . . do they resent it? I mean, have I—

Failed them? Nels, you're beautiful when you're worried. No, you haven't failed any of us at all. You worry too much. That's your problem, you know, you worry too much. Especially about Abbey. It's fine to say it's her life, not yours, but whenever she's out, more so than with Grace or Bess, you lose more sleep than anyone I know.

I hate to admit it, but you're right. God, that's frightening, you know it? But sooner or later, she'll leave us. She'll grow up and the ties will be gone before we know it. It'll happen so slowly we won't even notice.

Maybe. I hope so. I hope it is slow.

It always is, isn't it?

I suppose so. Anyway, she'll probably be the first to get married, and then it'll be her husband's problem.

Maybe, but I'd hate to be the man to try her out.

Now why did you say that?

I don't know. I really don't know.

They were carrying no weapons that he could see, but the fact didn't make him any less nervous. He had heard the tires on the dirt road long before anyone else, had excused himself from the game to walk out onto the porch for an ostensible breath of fresh air. He refrained from lighting a cigarette, leaned against a post and waited until the car, a low black convertible, had glided without headlights around the birch and parked in front of his own. Three men climbed out, one of them giggling into a fist, and he knew instantly they were drunk and therefore too dangerous to reason with, unless he was lucky.

They arranged themselves at the foot of the porch steps. Steady, not weaving, but the stench of beer was as strong as their obvious sense of masculine outrage.

"Gentlemen," he said, more to hear his own voice than to make them aware he was there, "I don't recall any invitations being sent out for a party tonight."

"Want to see Gracie," said a stocky sweatered man. It was too dark to make out their features; they stood just beyond the diffused glow of the living room lights, were irregular black holes against the black of the evening. "I want to tell her something."

"Grace," he said evenly, "is busy right at the moment. I'll give her the message. Who shall I say is calling?"

"Oh, my, who shall I say is calling," mimicked the one in the middle. "You're very polite, aren't you? Well, I can be polite too, you know. That's Brett over there, and I'm Frank. See? I can be polite if I want to."

"Thank you," Nels said.

The one on the right, the unnamed one, stepped toward him, a man Grace's age but without the lines that would give him age and personality. He raised a fist. "Abbey has a date with me, old man, and I want her out here."

"My goodness," Nels said, pushing away from the post. "I don't think she remembers. And since she doesn't remember, perhaps you ought to find another place to play, all right, boys?"

Brett laughed, then lunged and tripped over the bottom step as Nels whipped a shoe up into his chest, spilling him back into the unnamed one. They sprawled, cursing, and took a long time getting up. Frank just stood there, glaring, until Nels took a step down, and another. Then he swung a wild fist that Nels easily trapped with his hand, flung it aside contemptuously and pushed the man's face back sharply with his palm. He kicked out again to catch Brett between his legs, grinning at the anguished howl while he spun toward Frank, who was trying to dash past him. He caught the man's jacket, spun him back and into the side of their car, grabbed his legs and dumped him into the back seat. Brett, on his knees and retching, was hauled up by his collar and spilled into the passenger side. The third man turned to run when Nels faced him, shrugged and slid in behind the wheel. When Frank rose from the car floor and glared, Nels smiled at him politely.

"Don't say it," he said. "If you're going to come back and teach me a lesson, just come back. But don't say it, all right? It's much too corny."

He was back in the house before the car thundered away, surrounded by his wife and children whose amazement at his reaction was only slightly less than his own. He quickly dropped onto the couch, gladly took hold of an offered brandy and sipped at it until his hands stopped their trembling. When the tale was told, then, the girls preened proudly and Kelly clucked in admiration. Only Abbey, however, stood to one side, staring at him as though he were a stranger, yet not a stranger but rather someone she had known and had not recognized before. Her expression bothered him, but he thought nothing of it until he was in bed and Kelly was tracing promises across his chest.

"Scared?" he said into the darkness, feeling the cold of her hands.

"A little."

"Maybe we should leave in the morning. I asked for trouble and they'll probably give it to me. And I don't want you girls hurt, Kel."

"You did all right out there, Viking."

"They were drunk. A boy could have done it. Bess could have, for that matter."

"That's sexist."

He laughed dutifully, fell silent, a moment later sat straight up and leaned against the headboard.

"What?" Kelly said, her fear too soon open to hide. "What is it?"

"We will go on a picnic tomorrow," he said. "A regular old-fashioned picnic in the field beneath the tree. Complete with mice and ants and flies and all that good jazz."

"For God's sake, Nels, go to sleep."

"But damnit, I'm a hero! Don't I deserve some kind of a reward?"

Her quiet laughter infuriated him until she yanked him down by the hair to kiss him.

He said nothing at all about the look on Abbey's face, the look that was part fear, part question, a large part astonishment: you really *won't* let me go, will you, Daddy?

He said nothing.

He only shuddered.

For crying out loud, Kelly, I don't see any real problem.

But, Nels, she won't go. She's been accepted and she won't go!

All right, so she won't go, so what? If she wants to stay home and go to the community college, that's fine with me. In fact, I'd rather have it that way. I don't think she's ready to leave just yet.

But what if she—

Kelly, will you please leave her alone?

No, Nels, you leave her alone!

The brown and blue blanket still smelled of the attic, but no one seemed to mind, and he sat with his back against the tree and watched them struggling with the lumps in the ground as they set out the food, the bottles of wine, the paper plates Kelly had bought in the village that morning. The air was slightly hazed with uncaring clouds that occasionally blinded the sun, but the day stayed warm and the breeze kept the light from baking too hot. They had discovered a battered soft tennis ball in a closet and had played run-the-bases, man-in-the-middle, and anything else they could remember or devise for the best part of three hours before their hunger rebelled and forced them to eat. The wine spilled freely, then, and Nels felt expansively patriarchal as he fed and was fed, joked and was laughed at, listened for the hundredth time to the stories, the gossip, a vivid reenactment by his three daughters of his protection of the fortress the evening, the century, the lifetime before. Then they made solemn plans for Grace's birthday at the end of the coming week, for Bess' sophomore year, for Kelly's new furniture in their bedroom at home.

Then Abbey announced it was wild flower time, and the girls rushed off in a scattering while Nels brought his wife to his lap and nuzzled her hair, stroked her arm and watched as a black-bottomed cloud threatened the sky.

"Let's go for a walk," he said suddenly; and they did, wandering away from the three and the house until the latter was gone and the former a shadow.

"Abbey had another nightmare last night," Kelly said.

"It was those men," he said quickly. "They'd be enough—"

"No," she said, stopping, turning in the circle of his arms and looking into his eyes. "She dreamt she was dead, again."

He shook his head. "She would have come to see me, like always."

"I heard her crying, Nels. She didn't want to, and she did. There's something wrong, Nels. She's . . . she's afraid of you."

"She's had the dreams before," he said, ignoring her.

"Nels, this is serious, and you know it."

"It's the Irish in her."

"Dammit, Nels!" And she slapped his arms down and away, stalked back toward the picnic. He watched her go, his fists clenched, then hurried to catch up, saying nothing but remaining at her side. He would have tried an epigram or two, something appropriate or entirely non sequitur, but a sudden *crack* made him glance up at the sky. The wind had risen, cold and sifting through the trees at their back like some stalking beast at midnight. He hunched his shoulders and rubbed the back of the neck. Another *crack,* and Kelly stopped, her eyes wide and staring toward the tree. He followed and saw his daughters huddled around the bole, clutching at each other, heard then their screams in atonal harmony and . . . was running.

Kelly shouted behind him.

He ran, nevertheless.

A burrow snagged at his ankle and he fell, barely getting his hands into position in time, feeling his cheeks scrape across the rough ground to let out the blood.

Kelly was past him by the time he had regained his feet, and the shooting continued, the screaming continued, and as the tree grew closer than a hundred yards, he realized that no strike was meant, no killing . . . only a scare; and he began looking for the three men who had been beaten and were now sniping back. It was possible, he thought, that they were still behind the treeline at the edge of the field, hidden and laughing, but he only ran faster, toward the tree and his children. Kelly's arms were waving them down when they rose to greet her and then ... she was stopped.

She fell as though tripped, but Nels saw the spurt of blood at her left shoulder and fell beside her, shouting to Grace to keep the others down.

"Don't die, Kel, for God's sake don't die," he whispered repeatedly as he tore at her sweater, his jacket, his shirt, to ball up cloth and jam it against the wound. It came from a fair distance away, some part of him noted or the shell would have gone through. As it was, she was too stunned to do more than whimper, too astonished yet to feel the pain. When he was done, he lifted her in his arms and carried her awkwardly, suddenly shouting in angered panic when Abbey stood to help him.

And was stopped.

With a scream.

She stood motionless for a second that lasted much longer, toppled with one hand grasping at a branch for support. Her fingers closed on a leaf. It held. Tore. She was face down on the blanket.

Bess broke and ran for the house, but there was no more firing.

There were images, then, of no certain continuity: of red flashing lights and white-coated men and men in blue uniform and men in dark suits and a man intoning and a man moaning and a sling for an arm and a bandage for a face, and a printed sympathy card from the real estate agent in town.

Abbey was buried in the cemetery in Oxrun.

Grace took Bess back to their home, to clean and wait for their parents and school.

Kelly wandered the house.

Nels wandered the fields. The three men had had alibis, and none were arrested. Revenge gave way to sorrow to rage to a feeling that something ... something was not right, not right.

"Nels, we have to go home. Your job—"

"I can't, Kelly. Don't ask me why. But I ... can't."

Nels wandered, sat beneath his tree and wondered.

"Nels, they're giving your job away. I ... we have to go back now. Grace and Bess need us. Dammit, Nels, it's been almost a month!"

He wanted to tell her to pack, that it was over at last, he

wanted to say that life must go on, though, with Millay, he wondered just why. He wanted to. He could not. Kelly left the next day on the first morning train.

And he sat in the kitchen until the sun went down, drinking coffee, drinking tea, shaking his head and waiting for the tears, until just before ten he stiffened.

Oh, Jesus, no, he thought.

He pushed away from the table and stumbled to the door, opened it, crossed the porch and walked to the field. He was frightened. More frightened than when he had heard the first shot and knew what it was, more frightened then when he had stood on the porch and faced three drunken men. He looked back over his shoulder and saw the single light in the kitchen, warm, slightly blurred, and fading.

He told himself to stop. He did not, and could not, until he had reached the tree.

There was no wind.

The branches stirred.

"Abbey?" he whispered.

Stirred, and scratched.

"Abbey, I have a family still. They need me. You've got to let me go."

Leaves trembled.

"Abbey, please, I'm your father!"

Trembled, and curled.

He expected a voice on the wind that did not blow, a young girl's voice that would touch his mind with melancholy and a final good-bye.

What he did not expect was the muttering of anger, and finally the voice that hissed *turnabout, Father, is not always fair*.

DIVERS HANDS

Darrell Schweitzer

> For a number of years, Darrell Schweitzer has been filling the small press magazines with short stories, most of them patterned after the works of Lord Dunsany. They've been good of their type, but they've merely hinted at what this fine young writer might accomplish on his own. His stories of the Knight Julian, however, exhibit his rather remarkable talents more admirably. These stories have been appearing for the most part in an Australian magazine, but one of them found its way into *Heroic Fantasy*, an anthology of original fiction that DAW published earlier, and now here's another one that sees its first publication in an American anthology: this one. When Schweitzer isn't producing short stories, articles and interviews, you can find him working as an assistant editor on *Isaac Asimov's Science Fiction Magazine*.

"In what battle was it, Sir Knight, and to what foe did you lose your hand? Did you slay him who maimed you thus?"

The speaker was seated before me, a short, hooded man with a copious gray beard. I could not see his face in the fading twilight. He was the last one to come that day into my tent, at the crossroads fair in the mountain country beyond the empire of the Greeks, which is called Byzantium. The circumstance was a strange one: I, Julian, of various names and titles, long since lost to chivalry and my God, was reduced to beggary, shunned by the folk of every land. Who would trust this grim, hook-handed knight in tarnished mail, whose shield and surcoat bore not the emblem of the cross? What is he doing here? Is he really a man, they would ask, or some creature out of the darkness? Why goes he not with his comrades, to the east to fight the pagans? At the fairground, in that tent in a strange land near a strange city, and speaking a tongue I knew but rudely, I seemed to fit in, at least for the moment. I could not admit to myself that mere existence had become an end in itself, and each hour of peace a worthy goal for a long quest.

To make a living I told tales of my travels and of the adventures of others, and sometimes when these failed I invented, but no one could tell when I lied and when I didn't. Ever popular was my sojourn in the land of darkness, where dwell folk marvelously transfigured, so that their heads grow beneath their shoulders, and their ears, appended to their arms, stretch wide like the wings of bats, enabling them to fly. Also there were the salt maidens of Antioch, whose tears filled up their entire forms, so that they were left pillars of salt, like Lot's wife, when they mourned a blasphemer struck dead by the Apostle Peter. As each tale concluded, the listener would drop a coin in the bowl I had set out—and the telling was rewarding in another way too.

Being a storyteller is like confessing to a priest—nay—more like the fool in the fable who buried his head among the reeds and whispered *King Midas has asses' ears*. Everyone knows, but it is a fanciful thing. Who believes what is said by the wind in the reeds? Thus one can be unburdened of truth. So I told the questioner the true answer:

"Long and long ago it seems, but not very long ago in fact, there was a knight who met the Devil face to face in a ruined hall deep in the forest, and there he gave himself to him, to ransom a maiden who had been wronged. This was, by his faith, and his faith was a terror to him thereafter, the only chivalrous thing he had done in his entire life, for all his ideals, all his training, all his deeds. And for this he was damned, so that the Devil did not take his soul just then, so sure a thing it was, but instead commanded him, *'Go wander the world which shall this day be made anew, and forever be a stranger, until at last you come to me.'* And in his travels he met an evil thing, which in the guise of a lady comforted him, but in truth drank away his blood and his years. When the thing was slain, as needs it must be, the knight woke from a blissful dream in those false arms, and was confused, and in misguided wrath killed his deliverer, and for this was again damned. Then, on one of the occasions when he wished his life would end, but knew it could not, lest the Devil have him at once, he sought the Vale of Mistorak in the farthest East, and there conversed with a spirit, but bought those words with his own flesh, and that is how he lost his hand."

"And was the bargain well made?" asked the listener. "Was the answer satisfactory?"

"If it were, would I be here in this tent telling such wild tales?"

The hooded one wheezed what was supposed to be a laugh.

"I have no coin for you," he said, "but in exchange, a tale of my own. There was a king, whose name was Tikos, who ruled over a very ancient land. To the castle of his fathers came all the great lords of the world at one time or other. Alexander came there as a boy, and saw the wonder of it, and when he grew older turned his armies away from it, toward the east. But at long last, through treachery wrought by the priests of a new god, against whom the old gods were powerless, the people seized the king and mutilated him according to their custom, cutting off his right hand so that he might never again raise a sword, cutting off his left so he could hold no scepter. Thus was the king reduced to misery and scorn, until he found a way to gain his revenge. He swore himself to a new master. He became *Nekatu*."

"*Nekatu?*"

"As such he had vast powers, including prophecy. It has been prophesied that the knight of your story will come to the castle of the king of mine, and learn what that word means."

With that, he rose and left the tent. The flap waved like a flag with his passing.

"Wait!" I sprang up and went after him, bursting out into the evening air. It was intensely cold already, as it gets so quickly in the mountains. Beyond the peaks, the sun had set in a splash of gold. Overhead, the stars were already out, and I was sure the chill wind I felt came from between them, from beyond the mortal earth, where winged demons freely traffic. Such a demon my listener must have been to get away so fast. There was no sign of him anywhere.

Nekatu, he had said. That was the first time I ever heard the term.

That night as I slept I was haunted by evil dreams, at first, a recurring vision of a meadow strewn with the newly slain, all of them rising up as I approached, their wounds unhealed, to fight again in hopeless misery. Their cries at last drove me from the dream, and I awoke, bewildered for an instant, finding my tent an unfamiliar place. Then I listened to the night noises, tethered horses stamping in the cold, the crackle of campfires, a dog barking, someone singing. Beyond all that, an owl hooted.

I slept again, and this time I was riding through a dark wood, where every tree seemed to lean low with the weight of monstrous menace crouched in the branches, and inhuman faces peered fleetingly between the trunks. I had seldom known such terror in the waking world. My horse wanted to rear up and bolt, and only with utmost effort could I retain control. I gave in to the animal's instincts some, letting it speed up to a trot, then a canter, and finally a full gallop, as its panic and mine were one, and we thundered through the forest in a rain of great clods of mud thrown up by the hooves, and still there were the feeling of suffocating dread, and the half-glimpsed forms between the trees. Then I turned around in the saddle and looked behind me, and saw that I was indeed pursued, by another knight clad all in black mail and a black surcoat, mounted on a black steed, with his visor raised and a bare skull for a face. Then I screamed, and awoke again into the tent, and there was absolute silence in the camp, with every ear turned my way. Was the strange knight wrestling with a demon in his bed? I knew I would have to leave in the morning, before the tale grew in the retelling and reached the ears of a priest, and too many questions were asked.

Just before dawn I dozed off again. I was still riding through the forest, the apparition just behind me, and I was exhausted, as if my dream self had been fleeing on the foam-flecked dream horse all the while I had been awake. The terror was still there, and every instant seemed my last, until finally the forest broke into an open plain where two rivers joined. Where they joined stood a walled town, and beyond it, with a river girding it on either side, was a lone mountain. Three of its sides were sheer cliffs, but on a fourth a road wound down, crossed a bridge, and entered the far side of the town. Atop the mountain perched a castle of black stone. As soon as I spied this place it seemed a great weight was lifted from me, and another glance over my shoulder revealed that my nemesis had vanished. I let my horse slow to a walk, and as I approached the town and castle, the sun rose behind me, out of the forest, banishing all evil.

The last thing I saw—and I don't know if I imagined or truly dreamed it—was the hooded stranger rising from where he sat over a steaming cauldron, stretching his cramped legs, while within all the things in my dreams, the knight, the horse, the forest, the castle, and even myself, sank slowly through the broth to the bottom and there dissolved away.

I had no more visions that night.

There were people milling about when I awoke the third time. When I emerged from my tent they steadfastly refused to look directly at me or speak a word, even if questioned. And I knew not to persist in questioning. Some were breaking camp, piling unsold goods into carts, making ready to go even before the fair was over. I didn't have to ask the reason. An ill omen. There would be no luck in this place, and perhaps a curse for those who lingered. Next year the fair would doubtless be held somewhere else.

I didn't linger either, but instead packed what supplies and money I had into saddle pouches and rode away, leaving my tent where it stood. I couldn't take it with me in any case. For all I cared, the old bread-seller from whom I'd bought it could have it back. He might want to wrestle a devil in there sometime.

I knew that in such dreams, from wherever sent, something of import had been revealed, if a little vaguely, as is the manner of dreams. But such things cannot be without meaning. Indeed, as had been prophesied, I rode west, and that very afternoon came to the forest I had seen. It was not as sinister as its dream self, but always in the periphery of my sight there was a suggestion of a shape that set me ill at ease. I glanced back now and again to see if I was followed. I was alone, but my steed was as nervous as I, and difficult to control.

Beyond the wood was a plain, as I had foreseen, and two rivers met, and a mountain reared above all. One could only reach the castle atop it by passing through the town, as if the castle were the innermost keep of a larger fortress surrounding it.

Soon I came upon peasants bringing their crops to market.

The folk on this side of the forest seldom dared venture to the other, so they were not the same who had been at the fair, or so I hoped. There were all sorts going the same way: two priests—and I recoiled unconsciously at the sight of them—a boy with a mandolin slung over his shoulder, obviously a minstrel, and every variety of low-born person, afoot, astride mules and plow horses, or in carts.

As the traffic increased there were even a few of the wealthy in their ponderous, solid-wheeled carriages, surrounded by troops of men at arms. It occurred to me to seek employment as one such, but first I knew I must discharge whatever supernatural obligation had been laid on me, the dreams would continue, the skeletal rider overtake me as I slept, and at the very least I would awaken mad.

There was a soldier at the town's gate leaning lazily on a pike, asking each man what his business was. A farmer would drive up with a load of cabbages, announce that he'd come to sell cabbages, and be passed through with a bored wave. The nobles in their carriages would be known by the signs of their houses, inevitably on a banner carried by one of their horsemen, and not challenged at all.

In my case, it was not that simple.

"What do you want here?" Seeing that I wore a mail coat under my cloak and a steel cap on my head, and carried a sword, and eyeing the plain black shield that hung by my saddle, and all the while knowing by the most cursory glance that I was a foreigner, the guard stood up attentively, and raised his pike to block my way.

An equally cursory glance on my part revealed no other guards nearby, and none of the men at arms attending the carriages were close enough to come immediately to his assistance, or even ascertain at once what was going on.

So I reached up with my right hand—my only hand, the hook being hidden beneath the cloak—and pushed the pike away. At the same time I feigned a rage and glared at him.

"You filthy churl! How dare you question your betters?" My Greek was rough, but I was understood. The pike dropped limply away, and the fellow's mouth hung agape. He didn't know what to do, and alone he dared do nothing. So I took rein again in hand and spurred my horse quickly into the city before he could recover his wits. Almost as quickly I wondered if I had done the right thing. Would the guard brave his master's wrath and report his incompetence? Well, the die was cast, as Caesar had once remarked, and I had done what I had done. If my strange saga were known, I surely would not be welcomed here, but first I wanted to know what sort of place this was before seeking out its lord and making my way to the castle.

In the main square something was going on which wasn't standard trading or entertainment.

A large crowd had gathered and there was much excitement. I stood up in my stirrups to see more clearly. It was an execution. A man was being drawn and quartered between four separately harnessed oxen. Even over the yells of the mob I could hear his shrieks. As he hung there above the ground, and hooded executioners stood by with switches ready to prod the animals on, another, presumably the Master Executioner, had slit his belly open, yanked out an end of intestine, and begun coiling it around a stick. With every firm, jerking turn came another scream. Then one of the prisoner's arms slipped from the ropes and I saw why—he had no hand, so the wrist slid right out of the knot. Gesticulating furiously, the master rose from the disembowelling, kicked one of his assistants aside, and retied the rope, below the elbow this time.

As if this sight reminded them of something, the crowd began to shout with one voice a single word: *"Nekatu! Nekatu!"*

I sat down, startled. That was the second time I had heard the name, or term, or whatever it was, and I liked the circumstance even less well than I had the first. I took care that my own lack of a hand was concealed. I doubted this was the criminal's offense, but instinct counseled caution.

Disgusted, I rode around the edge of the square and along a narrow street filled with booths. Behind me the shouts of the crowd came to a crescendo, then stopped.

Now, most cities I have seen are vast caverns of wood and stone, and this one was no exception. Night begins early in a city. Even the great capital of Constantinople is lighted only around the palace and guard houses, and in a few principal squares. The common people grope like the blind through muddy, treacherous streets. In this place the upper storeys of the houses leaned over the back streets, the all but touching roofs shutting out all but the light of noontide. As I rode it was well into the evening, the fading sunset reflected only from those high gables and rooftops which caught the glow.

DIVERS HANDS

I came to a gap in the buildings, where I could get a full view of the castle on the hill beyond the town. Now it was silhouetted starkly against the western sky. Even as time passed, and the light faded even more, the place remained dark. Not a torch was lit in a tower; not a lantern glowed from any window. It seemed simply impossible that it could be deserted with a thriving town at its feet.

"Hist!" someone whispered. "Don't be staring at that! Ye'll bring a curse down on yer head."

I looked down, astonished that anyone would speak to me in such a manner. It was an old woman, her hair a tangled white explosion, with a bundle of sticks on her shoulder.

"And what ill can come from looking at the house of your lord? Woman, do you speak treason against him?"

Her face all but split apart with an irregularly toothed grin.

"Our *lord*? Ha! Our mortal lord lives here in the town. Only the wicked call *him* lord!" To make herself more clear, she pointed at the castle with her free hand.

"Does Satan himself roost up there then?" I laughed back at her.

"'Tis no subject for a jest, good sir. That one they quartered today—that's what happens to people who take too much interest in evil places." She crossed herself hastily.

"For merely looking at it?"

She grinned again. Now I was sure she took me for a fool, for all my higher birth.

"He *went* there. He was *Nekatu!*"

As soon as she uttered that word, the exchange was no longer a joke. I leaned over in the saddle and faced her intently. Despite the gloom I could see her eyes well enough to tell she was suddenly frightened of me.

"I have heard of this *Nekatu* many times. Twice since I came here. Old woman, there is gold in this for you if you will kindly tell me what—may the saints preserve us—everyone is talking about. What is *Nekatu?*"

She put her hand to her mouth and said nothing. Ah, I thought. Her tongue is suddenly tied in knots. Thinking to loosen it, I reached into my purse for one of my few coins. But the leather thong was too tightly drawn. I couldn't get it open with one hand. So without giving it any thought, I slipped the tip of my hook between the thong and the bag to work it loose.

And the woman screamed. At the sight of the hook she dropped her bundle and ran down the street shrieking "Nekatu! Help! Help! Another one! Nekatu!"

Instantly what seemed an empty alley filled with people. Some grabbed at my horses' reins. I drew my sword and slashed, and there was a howl of pain, but by then dozens of others had swarmed all around. Hands were pulling me from the saddle. My horse reared up in terror, which only helped them, even if a few skulls were split beneath the hooves. I tumbled over backwards out of the saddle and into the muddy street, striking furiously with sword and hook.

This had a temporary effect. No one was holding me when I hit the ground. I struggled to my feet. Whirling steel kept my foes temporarily at bay. None of them were armed with anything more fearsome than some of the old woman's firewood.

This changed almost at once. Nearby mail clinked, and I glanced quickly in the direction the crone had run. The pikes and steel helmets of the city guard were working their way through the jostling crowd.

With renewed fury I cut my way through the wall of my assailants. My horse had run off. I would have to escape on foot. An iron shoe in the groin, a chop at an upraised arm, a raking slash across the face with my metal hook, and I was no longer surrounded. A shout went up from the guards, and all the people regained their courage and surged after me. The chase went along that street into a narrower one, splashing through the mud, pushing passersby roughly aside until they understood what was happening, and joined in. The cry of *"Nekatu!"* seemed to be a kind of universal alarm, and every citizen stopped what he or she was doing and united against the common enemy.

My mail and my iron-covered shoes weighed me down, and I surely would have been overtaken before long had the chaotic fray not spilled into a lane so narrow that there was barely enough room to squeeze a cart along it—and there was a cart heading straight toward us.

Some of my pursuers hesitated, but I lunged forward with desperate speed. The cart driver drew rein, unsure of what was going on. Before he knew it I was alongside him. I flattened myself against a wall, then gave his horse a long, shallow swipe on the rump with my sword. Of course the enraged animal charged forward, completely out of control, right into

DIVERS HANDS

the mass of my foes. As it clattered past, the protruding axles of the cart missed me by scarcely a span.

Breathing heavily, but still maintaining the strength which had brought me through countless battles, I came at last to the far end of the town, where a gate led to the bridge over the river, then to the winding road up the one less than utterly sheer side of the mountain. This gate was barred from the inside. Now the bridge itself was fortified, and a small number of soldiers thereon could surely prevent an enemy from climbing up onto it from barges. This side was otherwise completely inaccessible. The thick, slippery wall of the town dropped straight to the water's edge, leaving no more than a foot or two of muddy bank. In any case, I'd seen no indication that this was a time of war.

Not hesitating to ponder this idiocy of siege design in a town that seemed completely crazy anyway, I placed both shoulders beneath the massive wooden bar, and with all my strength forced it up until it rose free of its supports and fell to the ground with a thud. The gate swung outward and I staggered backwards through it, onto the bridge.

By now those who hadn't been trampled by the runaway cart had found me again. With long strides I ran across the bridge and part way up the mountain. Then I turned to look. They weren't following. The crowd now filled the gateway, but none would venture forth. A tangle of faces stared up at me, sullen and quiet. It only seemed fitting that people who so irrationally feared men who were missing hands, and who so shunned the castle around which their town was built that they condemned to death anyone who went there, should behave in so ridiculous a way. I was sure they were all lunatics. With a contemptuous snort, I turned and made my way up the mountain at a leisurely pace.

It was only after I had gone a ways and the castle loomed huge above me, blotting out the stars, that it occurred to me that the people might have been sensible after all. Could there be some danger lurking among those towers such that one going the way I was would be insured a more frightful doom than anything the executioner could contrive?

If so, I was in a terrible situation, like a man who cannot swim trapped on a burning ship. I could not return to the town. There was no way to go but up, into the castle I had first glimpsed in a dream. In that dream it had been a place of relief and refuge, but now I was not so sure.

There was a little door beside the main gate of the castle, with a heavy metal iron for a knocker. I clanged the thing until the sound must surely have echoed throughout the whole land.
There was a stirring within.
"*Nekatu*," I said.
A bolt slid aside and the door opened.
That is how I found refuge among the *Nekatu*.

II

"The phrase '*nekatu*' literally means 'messenger,' not in Greek, but in the older language of these people. As you see, I have made good my promise. As soon as you arrived here, you learned the definition."

The same hooded stranger who had come to my tent the night before now led me up a winding flight of stairs, and into a large room. I couldn't tell how large. He carried only a small oil lamp, and nothing was lighted. The castle was clearly in a state of considerable disrepair. I could dimly make out fallen beams, stones, and tattered draperies scattered about.

He put the lamp down on a bare wooden table, pulled out a high-backed chair, and indicated that I should sit. The only sounds were the scraping of the chair, the clank of my shoes, and the soft pad of his slippers. He stood and I sat absolutely still for a moment, and the only sound was a slight fizzling from the lamp. Then there was something else: a faint pattering, like the scurrying of rats. At first I thought it to be that, but there wasn't enough scratching. Too soft, without claws. More like many people drumming their fingers nervously on wood.

I watched my host's every move with utmost suspicion. All this had been his contrivance. He wanted something. I was being brought here as surely as a fish on a hook. To make the point that I was not utterly helpless, I did not sheathe my sword, which I had carried in hand all the way up the mountain, but placed it in clear view in front of me. It clattered,

DIVERS HANDS

and for an instant the tapping sound in the background stopped. Then it resumed, somewhat closer.

The hood fell back, and a thin, bearded, ageless face was revealed. Atop silvery hair rested the thin band of a golden crown.

"King Tikos, I presume."

"The unhappy knight of the tale, I presume." Another chair was dragged, and he sat down across from me. "But let us set aside all pretense. Look at this."

He leaned forward into the light, pushed up both sleeves, and held his wrists up to the lamp, so I could plainly see.

"Look very closely," he said.

I let out an inadvertent grunt of astonishment. There was a thin line across both wrists, and he turned both hands over to show that these lines went all the way around. No one could have scars like that. They were *seams*.

"Sorcery! Not even the greatest doctors of physic...."

"Most not-so-noble knight, if your tale is as true as I think it is, you are not wholly godly yourself."

"That is ... true. But how?"

"This is one of the many powers of the *Nekatu*."

"Messengers?"

"A kind of brotherhood, set apart from the rest of mankind. This is why I have brought you here, why I sought you out when I saw you in the fair and noticed that your left hand was missing."

"Are you some kind of ghoul that you are fascinated by mutilation? Go to the wars in the east, and you'll get your fill."

"No! No! You fail to understand! I offer you a great gift. Look again!"

He reached under the table and drew from someplace a wooden box. The hinged lid came open. Inside there was a left hand carven out of a single piece of crystal, glittering with a thousand facets. It was a stunning piece of work, something with which to ransom empires.

I was not at all sure that it was a trick of the poor lighting that the thing seemed to move. Had the fingers been entirely outstretched? Now they seemed somewhat curled.

"By a most secret art," he said, "I have learned to make these. Contrary to what the philosophers will tell you, that which glitters has substance. Each ray of light captured within the crystal is a living thing, giving the hand itself life.

This hand I have exposed to the stars for a hundred nights, giving it the life of the *Nekatu*. When joined to a wrist it becomes as living flesh in all ways."

"Joined? How so?"

"It naturally adheres, as you shall see. Take off that hook and bronze cap, and be healed and whole again."

The intensity of his gaze, my exhaustion, and the perils I had passed through must have bewitched me, for I thought of little else but having a living hand again, even if there would be a seam around it. I forgot the treacherous, extreme outrageousness of my situation, the childishly obvious fact that the King was not doing this out of charitable commiseration over my wound.

Hardly realizing what I was doing, I pulled the hook and cap off my left wrist, exposing the healed stump. Tikos took the arm in his hand—I did not resist—and joined it to the crystal hand over the flame of the lamp.

I felt no pain. First there was a numbness, then a tingling, a sort of melting, as the flame licked over the wrist and hand, and the substance flowed like hot wax. Even as I watched the crystal lost its lustre, the facets smoothing over, the color fading. It was turning into flesh. I seemed far away from everything, drifting in abstraction. I wondered in bemusement if this were tried on a Negro. Would the hue be right?

When the King let go, the hand seemed as if it had grown there. Thrilling at the sensation, I flexed the fingers, then made a fist and banged with all my might on the table. The sword and the lamp bounced.

"A miracle! I am restored!"

"Yes, miraculous. By the way, are you hungry? I doubt you've eaten."

I made no answer. It seemed such a silly question, like the hues of Negroes. Who could care about food now?

King Tikos snapped his fingers and a tray was set before me. My heart skipped a beat when I saw that it was placed there by *hands*, but nothing more. They floated in the air as if creatures were reaching through from some invisible world into our own.

"*Christ and Satan!*"

"Swear by whomever you like," laughed the King. "Why not Jupiter, Thor, Mithra, and Ahura-Mazda also? It'll do you as much good. Those hands, I can safely tell you now, are simply *Nekatu*, like yourself, only in a far more advanced stage of development. The body withers away—it is unimportant—and is absorbed entirely into the hand. Why has this not happened to me? I remain whole because the Master, whom we all serve—yes, even you now—wills it. I recruit new slaves for him, even if sometimes, like that fool in the town today, a few are lost. He tried to run away."

With a howl of rage and despair, and every curse I could think of garbled together, I grabbed my sword and lunged across the table at the laughing monster, bent on total dismemberment. But before I could even get to my feet a frigid shock ran up my left arm and through my body. I staggered numbly for a second, the sword dropping from senseless fingers, then collapsed forward onto the table, smothering the lamp. That was the last thing I remembered.

For a second night then I was tossed like a cork on a sea of nightmares. At first there was complete darkness, and a feeling of being long dead and very *soft*, trapped far underground, and clawing my way to the surface, until all the putrid flesh of my body had been sloughed off, and only my diamond-hard *hands* emerged from the earth. Then the scene changed and I saw myself lying where I had fallen on the table, my left arm, with that accursed hand, dangling over the edge. Again came a numbness at the wrist, and a sensation of melting.

The thing dropped off, landing on the floor upright on its fingers, like a cat dropped from a rooftop. It stood there like a living thing—which indeed it was—and there was an instant of confusion and disorientation: I was wrenched from where I lay, drifting, falling, floating upward into warmth; and then I was looking up into the gloom at an enormous table with an unconscious giant sprawled over it, and the stump of a left wrist hanging over me.

My soul, my self, was now a prisoner in the hand. I was not in control. Another mind was at work. Following a way the fingers knew, I was carried away from the table and my body, into utter blackness as the hand passed through a tiny crevice in the wall. I could "see" nothing else until I/we/it emerged on the outside of the castle. All the while the sensations of fingertips on damp stone were intense, very real. Then there was the vast panorama of the town and surrounding countryside viewed from a height, and a brilliant full moon in the sky.

The hand wanted to avoid the light. It stayed in the shadows as much as possible as it climbed down the outside of the castle wall, each finger seeking and finding holds sufficient to sustain the weight of the thing. Like a monstrous spider it crept over the stone until it was just above the door through which I had first entered the castle. There followed a sickening, terrifying drop through space as the grip was released, then a jolt as the hand landed upright, as it had done beneath the table.

It crawled down that road up which I had come, scurrying as fast as a rat. For all the distance and its small size, it was at the barred gate of the town very quickly. The closed gate posed no obstacle. The rough outcroppings of the city wall were as sure as the rungs of a ladder. Up and over we went with practiced skill, and once more there was a drop, and the fingers sank the second joint in mud. Still the hand was not stopped. The fingers spread out, then curled, squeezing mud, then spread out in a kind of swimming motion until the fingertips reached more solid ground. This gave way to a paved street, and the filthy fingers paddled silently along the cobblestones, remaining always in the deepest shadows.

"Sight" was a confusing thing. At times I seemed to view the five fingers working, as if I were a tiny observer seated on the back, just behind the knuckles, and at other times the hand would stop, raise the index finger like an eyestalk, and I would get a sweeping view through that.

My waking self, Julian, the man who had been duped, had no idea where we/the hand intended to go, but there was a definite mission in the motion of the fingers. The hand came to certain intersections, and the index finger would scout about, then I would be going down a particular street, to a specific destination.

At last there was a wretched hovel propped between two brick buildings. A board was missing from the door, so the hand could enter without difficulty.

Within, the pattering which was definitely not a rat crossed the floor, steering a wide curve around the glowing coals of the firepit in the middle of the floor. Moonlight streamed through the smoke hole in the roof, and I could clearly discern a person asleep on a heap of straw on the far side of the room. It was the old woman who had carried the sticks.

Stealthily the hand made its way through the straw then began to climb the tattered blanket she had wrapped herself in. The hand began to climb the blanket onto her shoulder. The index finger stood straight up, again the "eye" of the creature, while the second and third fingers pinched cloth between them, as did the little finger and thumb. With these two grips the hand inched its way on top of her, then crept across her rising and falling body. I could feel her heartbeat beneath my fingertips as I moved down onto her breast, over the collarbone—

It was obvious what was intended. I desperately wanted to stop, to curl the fingers into a fist and drop into the straw, to shout a warning with all my breath. But I had no breath. My voice and lungs were back at the castle. I had no will, no control as the fingers slipped around the helpless crone's thin throat. Blood throbbed in her neck, but the skin felt like parchment.

Suddenly, with furious strength, the hand closed on her windpipe. She awoke, sat up wide-eyed in terror, let out a single gurgling cry, and then could utter nothing more. For a minute she writhed in the straw, flailing wildly after her unseen assailant and meeting only empty air, and then she lay still. The horror of the thing was not merely the death, or even my inability to prevent it, but that *I had done the deed*. As the hand strangled her I felt the muscles of a phantom arm, my arm, the arm of my body back at the castle, straining with the work. I felt the weight of my whole body pressed on the woman, pushing her down untill her neck snapped like one of the sticks she had been carrying.

Someone stirred in another part of the room.

"Grandmother? Is that you?" Bare footsteps moved near the firepit, and a handful of rushes was lighted, then carried in my direction. I could see the face of a young girl as she bent over her grandmother, and the contortions of revulsion and mad terror at the sight of the thing still perched on the corpse. The light went out again as the rushes were dropped to the floor. The granddaughter screamed and was answered by shouts from without.

Instantly the hand knew what to do. With unbelievable agility it scrambled up the wall and was out another hole in the rotted wood. Then followed a drop into the muddy back street, and a scramble across to another house, and up a wall. From atop the neighboring roof it watched and gloated—yes, there was a definite feeling of that emotion in the second mind, joined to my own, which I could not escape.

"It has happened again! Grandmother!" the girl tried to explain to others through hysterical tears. *"Nekatu!"*

It was then that I came to understand some of the peculiar things about this town.

III

It was no surprise, but a dreadful, sickening certainty when I awoke the next morning on the table and there was mud on my left hand.

Revenge the King had said. In this way he wrought revenge on those who had overthrown him. No wonder there were no men-at-arms on his battlements. He had an army of *Nekatu* which was far more deadly.

I lurched to my feet and instantly fell. My legs would not support me. I was sick, exhausted, as if I had just completed a vast labor, and I realized that, as the King had said, the hand was beginning to absorb my vitality into itself. I dropped to my knees, grasping the edge of the table with my right hand. I left the other arm hanging limp. The thing seemed asleep. Now, by daylight, my body was my own.

Apparently there were limits. I had to stay alive long enough for the thing to steal my life away. It would take a while. I would have to be kept for a long time. The tray set down by the hands the night before was still there. On it were cold meat, bread, and cheese. A cup of wine stood beside it. This had *not* been there before.

My breakfast was laid out for me.

I spent the day exploring the castle. I could not go into the town, where I would be killed on sight. If I fled over the countryside, making my way down one of the cliffs with only one hand I could trust, I had no doubt the hand could bring me back, or at the very least deal with me the same way it had with the old woman. I could, at last resort, cast myself from the walls, or simply refuse to eat until I starved, but these were indeed last resorts. It is not like a warrior, *any* warrior, be he Christian knight or pagan savage, to surrender before the battle is joined. The enemy must be met, no matter how hopeless the odds.

So all day I wandered through the ruined halls of the castle. I found a library filled with books written in strange scripts. There were also a few in Latin, and these I glanced through. Most were treatises on magic, of vast age. One was dedicated: *To my Lord Nero, who taught me how to begin.* The same Nero who reigned shortly after Christ, and slew the apostles Peter and Paul. How long had it been since King Tikos lost his natural hands? Surely the folk of this town were not his subjects, but their remote descendants.

When twilight was drawing near, I knew my efforts were over for the day. Another night of helpless horror was to follow. But before anything happened I dragged an iron brazier I had found into the room where the wooden table was, then gathered up some dry rushes, bits of wood, and scraps of the fallen tapestries. I meant to keep the place lighted so I could see Tikos when he came to put the spell on me, and slay him if I could. I still had my sword.

Supper had been set in my absence. I ate while the familiar pattering passed back and forth behind the walls. Long shadows crossed the floor.

There was a footstep behind me.

"Ah, now that you've dined, it's time for another errand," said King Tikos.

Before I could even turn around, the cold blast overwhelmed me.

Many more died that night, but not in the town below. The mission was far stranger. I was in the company of a whole brigade of *Nekatu*, perhaps as many as fifty. Together we climbed *up* the outside of the castle, to the top of a tower. There a flock of black hawks were waiting, as still as carven gargoyles. Each hand climbed on the back of a bird, the thumb and forefinger hooked around the neck, the rest grasping the body. The feel was very familiar. I've handled falcons often.

There was a more terrifying drop than before as the bird I was riding fell into the abyss, heavy with its burden, struggling for flight. It flapped desperately, then caught the air and rose clumsily to join the others, all of them lurching in an equally heavy manner. Below, the fields and hills rolled. Moonlight gleamed on the two rivers. We followed one of them to its source in the mountains beyond a forest, then over the mountains until we came to the manor of some lord. The birds waited patiently on walls and window ledges while the passengers dismounted and went about their business. The hands worked in pairs this time, not necessarily left and right, but always in pairs. I was with a huge black member—answering my question about Negroes. Together we came to a chamber in which a man and a woman slept. Now the black hand did something which I had witnessed the first night, but had never been able to imitate. It floated in the air, as if attached to an invisible body, as those bringing the tray had done. It slid a sword from the scabbard which hung from the bedpost. All this while my own hand was climbing up the side of the bed, inching up a blanket. "A more advanced stage," the King had said. A *Nekatu* which still had a human body, a newcomer like myself, had not yet all the powers given to that fiendish brotherhood. I could not yet rise and float. I had to crawl.

The murder was done. I/the hand in which my self was trapped crept to the face of the man, then clamped tightly over his mouth while the black hand slit his throat from ear to ear with the sword. The lady slept through the whole deed, so swiftly and silently was it performed. Again I felt the weight of my whole body leaning over the bed, gagging my victim while my accomplice slew him.

The sword was placed gently on the floor and the two of us returned to the windowsill, there mounting our bewitched steeds. As if at a signal, the whole flock took off at once, bearing the army of *Nekatu* back to the castle of King Tikos. I was not told, but I knew that what I had participated in was not unique that night. In twenty-five rooms wives would wake up, soaked with blood, and scream as they found themselves sharing beds with still warm corpses. Could King Tikos hear the screams? Was he somehow nourished by the terror and death?

Once more I found myself in that room by the table, and a breakfast had been prepared for me. Where did he get the food? No stores could keep fresh all that time. Did he send *Nekatu* to rob butchers and bakers? Well, that was the most innocuous thing they would ever do.

I hated myself as I ate. It was all I could do not to vomit as I remembered what had happened. It was time, I told myself, to leap to an easy death, before more innocents perished. *I* was not innocent. I had many times longed for death. But then the familiar terror came. . . . After death—damnation, the eternal torments I could escape only for that brief time I

DIVERS HANDS

lived. Like all men, I am ultimately selfish. I would sacrifice the whole world to escape Hell even for a short while. I could kill myself only on a sudden, saving impulse swifter than thought. If I reasoned what was right, just, and the moral thing to do, I would forget all about rightness, justice, and morality, and be paralyzed.

That day I continued to search the castle, hoping to find some secret thing by which I could justify myself.

And I was rewarded. There was a small door beneath what had once been a long bench. I made a torch out of wood, weeds from a courtyard garden, and scraps of cloth, lit it with flint and steel from the pouch on my belt, and descended into a vault. There I found twelve stone coffins, each of them with, curiously, an opening of about a span cut into the top.

No, not curious at all. A span is measured by the spread of a man's fingers.

Within were *Nekatu* of "a more advanced stage of development." When I slid the lid off the first coffin, I grew faint at the sight, but quickly gathered my courage. There lay an ancient, withered corpse, little more than skin stretched tight over bones, save that on one of the arms the shrunken skin blossomed out into a perfect living hand.

The fury of loathing gave me strength. I hacked at the thing with my sword, severing the hand, cutting again and again until the fingers were scattered and the whole body was a ruin. The skull splintered; the ribcage collapsed into slivers and chips. Only when nothing remained recognizable did I stop, sweat-covered for all the dampness of the vault, breathing heavily from my labor. After a pause I went on to the next one and destroyed it as thoroughly, but more methodically.

I was encouraged that my left hand was *my* left hand as I did this work. It did as my muscles commanded, and aided me in my task.

That night, however, the King again appeared from nowhere—I still had no idea how he did it—and more evil work was done. The army of *Nekatu* was abroad once more, and I noticed, and despaired as I saw, that some of them were crisscrossed with imperfectly healed scars. One or two even "limped" as they crawled on broken fingers. But they did what their master bade them. This time we came to a monastery, and, after stealing candles from the chapel altar, each of the *Nekatu* crept into a cell and burned out the eyes of the monk therein.

IV

When next I awoke, my vital essence was so drained I could not rise. I was getting rapidly weaker. My flesh was wasting away. Already I was as gaunt as a starving beggar, increasingly like the shrivelled corpse of the *Nekatu* in the coffins. Doubtless before long I would be unable to move at all, and many hands would carry me to those same or similar coffins, and place me in one of them. Only with utmost effort could I crawl to the chair, eat, and live for another day. Now I knew I could never fling myself from a parapet. I'd never reach the wall. So I sat there throughout the day, as sunlight shifted from window to window along the south side of the room.

I was very cold. Somehow I found the strength to rise after a while and light the brazier. I could think of nothing but warmth. For warmth, in my wretched condition, I would sell my soul. But my soul was already spoken for, so I had to provide for myself.

Thus I sat as evening fell, leaning against the back of the chair, my sword before me on the table, both hands in my lap, right on top of left in vain hope of restraining it. Beside me, the brazier sputtled and crackled. The smell of smoke was comforting, my single tie to earthly things? Whenever the flames burned low I fed them bits of straw, cloth, and splinters of rotten wood. A heap of fuel was within arm's reach.

King Tikos arrived. He did not come into the room; he was merely *there*. I thought the white spot in the air was a trick on my tired eyes, but it grew and took shape, and he was in the room with me. His slippers padded softly on the floor as he walked. All but soundless, a horde of *Nekatu* kept pace with him on extended fingers. There were more of them than I had ever imagined. They poured from the cracks and holes until the floor was covered. There were easily a thousand of them. How foolish to think my tiny group made up the whole army!

"It is time," said the King, "that our brother be brought

fully into our fellowship. No waiting in the vaults for him. The Master is coming this night to claim and transform him."

He was speaking to the hands, not to me. I was merely an object to be dealt with. He paced back and forth as he spoke, the *Nekatu* scurrying this way and that after him like thousands of crabs come out of the sea just long enough to devour a drowned sailor the waves had washed up.

"We must wait, brothers. Have patience. The Master will come when the Master feels it is time. In the Master's world, beyond our own, time is not as we know it. I have been there as none of you have, and have seen, so believe me. Shapes and sounds and colors are all wondrously transformed, unrecognizably different. Senses are confused. One *hears* the color white, tastes the sweet tang of terror. A scream is like a soft caress *within* the body. Space, and time, and distance? These do not exist where the Master dwells, any more than depths exist in the world of a drawing on a page of parchment. Can one of those figures stand up, and walk out of the book? The Master can. You and I shall be able to also, in the end, when this world likewise belongs to the Master. That is why I worship him. That is why he is greater even than the God who created this universe. The Master walks between many universes. *Whence comest thou? From walking to and fro in the sum of cosmoses, and up and down in it, between the planes and angles.* That is why the Master is the Master.

"And yet," said the King, pacing back and forth in the semi-darkness amid the thousand disembodied hands, "and yet I do not fear the Master where I now stand, for he needs me, to become material in our world. To take on solid substance. *And the word was made flesh, and screamed among us.* He is not as powerful here as he is in the void between the voids."

I listened to all this with the dull incomprehension of a pig in the slaughterhouse overhearing the talk of two butchers. Surely Tikos was mad to talk of anything beyond the sphere of the Earth, the moon and sun moving around it, and the fixed stars in the spheres of the firmament beyond, but then I was surely mad to be dreaming this nightmare in which I now existed, and the whole world was mad to allow such thoughts to come to be, and God was mad, as I knew well, for having created it that way. *And the Earth was without*

shape and form, and darkness was on the face of the deep.
Ah! If only the Father had been truly wise, and not meddled!

"The Master comes!" There was a rippling of the air, like foam on the sea an instant before a great whale leaps from the depths. For the first time Tikos spoke to me: "Watch! Watch, Sir Knight, and listen, and observe the last thing you shall ever observe with mortal eyes and ears. Tonight on this night of nights, the last of the harvest moon, the Master comes into this chamber, and you will be within our grip. *Ours.* I am part of the Master. This is the ultimate secret. Now, as I have promised, you truly know the meaning of the word *Nekatu*. A messenger, a servant of the Master, a finger of his hand."

Literally. As I watched the whiteness in the air returned and surrounded the King. He stood still. A thousand hands paused on five thousand fingertips. Four columns of whiteness began to materialize around him, and as they did he lost his own shape. He was flowing together, arms melting into his body, his two legs become one. Like wax. A candle. *Lighted.* Fire. Dimly the association anchored in my mind.

A finger of the Master. Exactly. That was what he had become. The four other fingers appeared beside him, and he—the index finger—was lifted off the floor as the Master reared up. The Master was a huge hand, that of a giant as tall as the castle if any body had been present. Something reaching through the air out of an invisible world coexistent with our own.

The hand climbed up on the table. It was the size of a horse. The wood creaked under its weight.

All time seemed suspended, and in my abstraction, I noticed a curious thing. The finger which had been King Tikos had a red welt around it. Was the Master a kind of *Nekatu* of a larger world, not complete without the animate finger which was the king, or which he had become? Was this the ultimate bargain to which the maimed and outcast king had agreed so long ago, through which he gained his continual revenge?

Joined together, a voice in the back of my mind chanted. Candle. Wax. Welting. Fire. Wax. *Fire.*

Now my left hand, that which was *Nekatu*, had come alive. The rest of my body was too weak to obey any commands, so the hand was on the table, crawling toward the far end where the Master stood on fingertips a foot across, dragging me with it. Now my awareness was entirely in my head. The hand didn't need me, and moved of itself.

So I was pulled forward, across the table, toward the grasp of the Master.

I leaned forward. My chin touched the hilt of my sword, which was still on the table in front of me. With impossible strength the *Nekatu* hand was dragging me up out of the chair, onto the table. It passed the overturned oil lamp from the first night.

Fire. Wax. Melting.

In the remote regions of my mind, where thoughts were still my own, the idea came. I laughed at the brilliance of it. I was completely detached, my awareness floating. What was happening was not *really* happening. It was an intellectual exercise. I had always been good at things like chess. There was all the time in the world to carefully consider. Soon, someday, I would try—

I lost myself wholly for an instant, and *was* in the *Nekatu* hand, unheeded, but feeling the attraction of the Master, the call to union, a kind of lust—

—and was again myself, and in less than a split second the thoughts, the little voices, melted and turned and twisted upon themselves: Fire. Wax. Fire. Candle. Fire. Fire. *Fire.* . . .

The unexpected: a convoluted stratagem—again I slipped into blackness, was in hand for a longer interval, and the call was far, far stronger—and flashed back, perhaps for the last time, into the body and mind of the man Julian—the convoluted stratagem: while all attention was on my left hand, the *Nekatu*, the right hand was doing something.

In the realm of philosophical abstraction, detached from time and space, as an interesting exercise, the fingers of my *right* hand, my human hand, curled around the hilt of my sword as it lay there on the table.

With a sudden *thwunk!* the right hand brought the sword up and around and down, crashing into the tabletop, aimed at the *Nekatu* hand, but clumsily. It missed by less than the width of the blade.

The hand stopped, startled. The master stood there impassively. The thousand *Nekatu* on the floor remained motionless.

The grip on my left arm was relaxed for an instant. I was

free. My body fell backwards into the chair, and with desperate effort I thrust the left hand into the flaming brazier.

The *Nekatu* hand recoiled. The Master stumbled backwards, and toppled off the end of the table, landing with a heavy thud on the floor, crushing those beneath him. Now a lifeless hand hacked apart during the day feels nothing, but a living one at night is different—and the Master directs all his hands, feeling as they feel.

Feeling as I feel. The hand did not go for my throat. The Master now writhed with the agonies of those he had crushed in his fall, and I, linked to them as a *Nekatu*, felt the same. It was in the fury of this pain that I was able to put my left hand back on the tabletop, then with my right, with the sword I still held, strike the mightiest blow ever struck in all the battles of mankind. I could have felled whole cities with it. The blade crashed down, through the wrist, just above the place where it joined the *Nekatu* hand. Honest agony followed. I was severed from the Master—it was mortal blood that flowed now from the stump. Only my own body.

I screamed, and in screaming woke fully into myself. Thick in the midst of the fight, instinct took over. The Master stood up once more, trembling on his pale, flabby fingers and began to crawl back up onto the table. I hurled the brazier at him, and again he retreated from the flames. I lifted the table with my bleeding stump, and the hand that still held the sword, and flipped it over on top of him. I sheathed the sword, and hurled handfuls of kindling onto the heap. There was some oil left in the lamp which now poured out and kept the fire going until it could catch on the wood.

All this while the *Nekatu* stood motionless on the floor, waiting for commands. I trampled them with my iron shoes.

All this while blood was gushing from my left arm. It was only as I fell forward, to the very edge of the flames now licking over the upside-down table that I realized my death was moments away. To this day I am amazed that I was able to do anything as rational as reaching forward with the bleeding arm, forcing the wound into the fire, and closing the wound. This new pain somehow gave me strength enough to rise from my feet and stagger down the winding stair, through the door, and out of the castle.

I was mad. I screamed. I howled. I laughed. I was as far from myself as I had been on the midnight missions of the *Nekatu*. There was that remote part of me which knew what was going on, but the rest raged in a frenzy of pain, fear, and sub-bestial fury.

Do you believe in miracles? *Speak not!* Any words are lies! *You know!*

Was it not a miracle that when I came to the bottom of the mountain road, with the castle burning fiercely behind me, the people of the town opened their gates and let me pass? "He is dead," I said, not knowing if the Master even *could* die. I think they feared me more than King Tikos. I think they took me for some new demon more terrible than the old. They opened the gate before I could blast it with a thunderbolt. They brought my horse to me. To appease my wrath? To get rid of a dread savior delicately before his unknown will be known? They saw my wounded wrist and knew I was no longer *Nekatu,* and they saw the glare from the castle above. Was this not a miracle?

Was it not a miracle that I found myself, when for the first time in a very long while I could think coherently, riding across a meadow far to the west of the city, beyond the mountains, a place I had once spied from the air, it seemed, in a dream?

And what else could it have been but a miracle, which brought me at last to a monastery of blind monks, who discovered by feel the wound on my arm, and said, "Look brothers, he is afflicted even as us," while carrying me to a bed and stumbling to fetch medicines?

Later, when again I was reduced to beggary, I refrained from telling stories, lest I somehow forget myself and accidentally relate how I lost my left hand twice.

HEADING HOME

Ramsey Campbell

> Ramsey Campbell's first collection of short stories, *The Inhabitant of the Lake*, appeared while he was still in his teens. As if that wasn't shock enough to his competitors, his achievements since then, including story collections like *The Height of the Scream*, novels like *The Doll Who Ate His Mother*, and anthologies like *Superhorror*, have set him up as one of the unchallenged leaders of the field. "Heading Home" is the shortest story in this anthology, but it delivers some gargantuan chills . . .

Somewhere above you can hear your wife and the young man talking. You strain yourself upward, your muscles trembling like water, and manage to shift your unsteady balance onto the next stair.

They must think he finished you. They haven't even bothered to close the cellar door, and it's the trickle of flickering light through the crack that you're striving toward. Anyone else but you would be dead. He must have carried you from the laboratory and thrown you down the stairs into the cellar, where you regained consciousness on the dusty stone. Your left cheek still feels like a rigid plate slipped into your flesh where it struck the floor. You rest on the stair you've reached and listen.

They're silent now. It must be night, since they've lit the hall lamp whose flame is peeking into the cellar. They can't intend to leave the house until tomorrow, if at all. You can only guess what they're doing now, thinking themselves alone in the house. Your numb lips crack again as you grin. Let them enjoy themselves while they can.

He didn't leave you many muscles you can use; it was a thorough job. No wonder they feel safe. Now you have to concentrate yourself in those muscles that still function. Swaying, you manage to raise yourself momentarily to a position from which you can grip the next higher stair. You clench on your advantage. Then, pushing with muscles you'd almost forgotten you had, you manage to lever yourself one step higher.

You maneuver yourself until you're sitting upright. There's less risk that way of your losing your balance for a moment and rolling all the way down to the cellar floor where, hours ago, you began climbing. Then you rest. Only six more stairs.

You wonder again how they met. Of course you should have known that it was going on, but your work was your wife and you couldn't spare the time to watch over the woman you'd married. You should have realized that when she went to the village she would meet people and mightn't be as silent as at home. But her room might well have been as far from yours as the village is from the house; you gave little thought to the people in either.

Not that you blame yourself. When you met her—in the town where you attended the University—you'd thought she understood the importance of your work. It wasn't as if you'd intended to trick her. It was only when she tried to seduce you from your work, both for her own gratification and because she was afraid of it, that you barred her from your companionship by silence.

You can hear their voices again. They're on the first floor. You don't known whether they're celebrating or comforting each other as guilt settles on them. It doesn't matter. So long as he didn't close the laboratory door when he returned from the cellar. If it's closed you'll never be able to open it. And if you can't get into the laboratory he has killed you after all. You raise yourself, muscles shuddering with the effort, your cheek chafing against the wood of the stair. You won't relax until you can see the laboratory door.

You're reaching for the top stair when you slip. Your chin comes down on it, and slides back. You grip the wooden stair with your jaws, feeling splinters lodge between your teeth. Your neck scraped the lower stair, but it has lost all feeling save an ache fading slowly into dullness. Only your jaws prevent you from falling back where you started, and they're throbbing as if nails are being driven through their hinges with measured strokes. You close them tighter, pounding with pain, then you overbalance yourself onto the top stair. You teeter for a moment, then you're secure.

But you don't rest yet. You edge yourself forward and sit up so that you can peer out of the cellar. The outline of the laboratory door billows slightly as the lamp flickers. It occurs to you that they've lit the lamp because she's terrified of you, lying dead beyond the main staircase—as she thinks. You laugh silently. You can afford to. When the flame steadies you can see darkness gaping for inches around the laboratory door.

You listen to their voices upstairs and rest. You know he's a butcher, because once he helped one of the servants to carry the meat from the village. In any case, you could have told his profession from what he has done to you. You're still astonished that she should have taken up with him. From the little you knew of the village people you were delighted that they always avoided the house.

You remember the day the new priest visited the house. You could tell he'd heard all the wildest village tales about your experiments; you were surprised he didn't try to ward you off with a cross. When he found you could argue his theology into a corner he left, a twitch pulling his smile awry. He'd tried to persuade you both to attend the church, but your wife had sat silent throughout. It had been then that you decided to trust her to go to the village. You'd dismissed the servants, but you told yourself she would be less likely to talk. You grin fiercely. If you'd been as inaccurate in your experiments you would be dead.

Upstairs they're still talking. You rock forward and try to wedge yourself between the cellar door and its frame. With your limited control it's difficult, and you find yourself leaning in the crack with no purchase on the wood. Your weight hasn't moved the door, which is heavier than you have ever before had cause to realize. Eventually you manage to wedge yourself in the crack, gripping the frame with all your strength. The door rests on you, and you nudge your weight clumsily against it.

It creaks away from you a little, then swings back, crushing you. It has always hung unevenly and persisted in standing ajar; it never troubled you before. Now the strength he left you, even focused like light through a burning-glass, seems unequal to shifting the door. Trapped in the crack, you relax for a moment. Then, as if to take it unawares, you close your grip on the frame and shove against the door, pushing yourself forward as it swings away. It returns, answering the force of your shove, and you aren't clear. But you're still falling into the hall, and as the door chops into the frame you fall on your back, beyond the sweep of the door.

You're free of the cellar, but on your back you're helpless. The slowing door is more mobile than you. All the muscles you've been using can only work aimlessly and loll in the air. You're laid out on the hall floor like a laboratory subject, beneath the steadying flame.

Then you hear the butcher call to your wife "I'll see," and start downstairs.

You begin to twitch all the muscles on your right side frantically. You roll a little toward that side, then your wild twitching rocks you back. About you the light shakes, making your shadow play the cruel trick of achieving the roll you're struggling for. He's at the halfway landing now. You work your right side again and hold your muscles still as you begin to turn that way. Suddenly you've swung over your point of equilibrium and are lying on your right side. You strain your aching muscles to inch you forward, but the laboratory is feet away, and you are by no means moving in a straight line. His footsteps resound. You hear your wife's terrified voice, entreating him to return to her. There's a long pondering silence. Then he hurries back upstairs.

You don't let yourself rest until you're inside the laboratory, although by then your ache feels like a cold stiff surface within your flesh, and your mouth like a dusty hole in stone. Once beyond the door you sit still, gazing about. Moonlight is spread from the window to the door. Your gaze seeks the bench where you were working when he found you. He hasn't cleared up any of the material that was thrown to the floor by your convulsion. Glinting on the floor you see a needle, and nearby the surgical thread which you never had occasion to use. You relax to prepare for the next concerted effort, remembering.

You recall the day you perfected the solution. As soon as you'd quaffed it you felt your brain achieve a piercing alertness, become precisely and continually aware of the messages of each nerve and preside over them, making minute adjustments at the first hint of danger. You knew this was what you'd worked for, but you couldn't prove it to yourself until the day you felt the stirrings of cancer. Then your brain seemed to condense into a keen strand of energy that stretched down and burned the cancer out. That was proof. You were immortal.

Not that some of the research hadn't been unpleasant. It had taken you a great deal of furtive expenditure at the mortuaries to discover that some of the extracts you needed for the solution had to be taken from the living brain. The villagers thought the children had drowned, for their clothes were found on the river bank. Medical progress, you told yourself, had always involved suffering.

Perhaps your wife suspected something of this stage of your work or perhaps they'd simply decided to rid themselves of you. You were working at your bench, trying to synthesize your discovery when you heard him enter. He must have rushed at you, for before you could turn you felt a blazing slash gape at the back of your neck. Then you awoke on the cellar floor.

You edge yourself forward across the laboratory. Your greatest exertion is past, but this is the most exacting part. When you're nearly touching your prone body you have to turn around. You move yourself with your jaws and steer with your tongue. It's difficult, but less so than tonguing yourself upright on your neck to rest on the stairs. Then you fit yourself to your shoulders, groping with your perfected mind until you feel the nerves linking again.

Now you'll have to hold yourself unflinching or you'll roll apart. With your mind you can do it. Gingerly, so as not to part yourself, you stretch out your arm and touch the surgical needle and thread.

IN THE ARCADE

Lisa Tuttle

In a mere half dozen years, as I write this introduction, 1984 will be past. It will be the property of historians, statisticians and trivialists: the fodder of nostalgia. We'll know the titles of its best-selling books, its financially successful movies, the most popular of its television series. It will have been the year of a Presidential election in America, and we'll know who won that election and who lost, just as we'll know the winners and losers of that year's Olympic games; and the triumphs and failures of the year's various sports seasons. The fads of 1984 will either have vanished or shown a remarkable longevity. Its popular music will be fading from our ears and memories . . . with the exception of that fortunate small group that will become called "golden oldies." The year, once the bugbear and frightwig of the dystopic fantasist, will be gone and its reality will have joined the fantasy with, we suspect, more than a little irony. It will be the tyranny of our nightmares against that more common and familiar tyranny we live with day to day and barely notice. Lisa Tuttle writes crisp little short stories that deal pointedly with that day to day tyranny, and we offer one of them here for your interest. Tuttle is from Texas, by the way, and although the fact that she is less than nine feet tall might appear to belie the legends about that state, don't you believe it. Her talent is genuinely gigantic.

Eula Mae woke. She peeled the sheet away from her perspiring body and sat up. Man, she was hot. The moon shone directly into the room through the uncurtained window, falling in a pool on the bed and giving the white sheets an almost phosphorescent glow against her dark skin.

She swung her legs over the side of the bed. It was strange to be awake so late at night. Everything was so still. Her husband slept silently in his half of the old, spring-shot bed. Eula Mae wondered what, in all this silence, could have awakened her.

It was odd, to be awake while everyone slept. She didn't think it had ever happened to her before. To go back to sleep seemed the only reasonable thing to do now, but she wasn't the least bit sleepy. She got up and walked to the window. That moon certainly was big and bright and low in the sky.

She put her palms flat on the rough, paint-peeling window sill, ducked her head beneath the sash and leaned out into the night. No lights gleamed from any of the crumbling tenements that lined the street, and only two street lamps shone—the rest stood darkly useless, bulbs shattered by children or angry drunks. Nothing moved. There was no sound. Eula Mae frowned slightly, and listened. The quiet wasn't natural—there should have been *some* sound, if only the faraway monster of traffic making itself heard. Did everyone and everything sleep without dreams? It was not natural; it was the stillness of a machine at rest, not the restless sleep of a city. She strained to hear the sounds she knew she should hear.

There! Was that. . . ? But now Eula Mae could not be certain. Had she heard that faint humming noise, or had she only felt the blood and breath traversing the highways of her own body?

Eula Mae sighed deeply and wondered how close to morning it was. She would not sleep again this night. She shifted her weight from one foot to the other and raised her eyes to the moon.

The sight of it shocked her, and shook the center of things. The known world, her world, ceased to be. The moon had always been there, she'd looked at it almost every night of her life. And now she looked up and saw not the familiar moon at all but a simulacrum, a falsehood, a stage moon: a light. Nor was that the night sky it shone in—attached to an invisible ceiling, the light shone down through swaths of deep blue drapery. The familiar horizons became limited and strange. If that was not her moon, this could not be her city. Where was she?

"Howard," she said unhappily, turning back into the room. A cry for help. "Oh, Howard, wake up."

The still form did not stir. Eula Mae sat on the edge of the bed, which sagged still more under her weight, and put her hand on her husband's bare shoulder. His skin was smooth and cool.

Her lips formed his name again, but she did not speak. She had suddenly comprehended just what was so unnatural about his stillness. He was not breathing.

She moaned and began to shake him, trying to shake him back into life, to get him started again, knowing it was hopeless.

Oh, Howard. Howard. Howard.

He lay there like a doll, like a bolster on the bed, still and sleek and cool. He was somewhere very far away from the close heat of the room.

Eula Mae sat with her hands resting on her husband's body. Tears ran down her cheeks. She did not move. Perhaps, if she were still enough, she would go where Howard was. But the sobs forced themselves up from her gut, wrenched her body, made her shake.

Then the fear prevailed. The fear made her get up off the bed (slowly, trying not to jar the body), the fear made her stop crying. She had to go somewhere, she had to be with someone. She fumbled about in the big metal wardrobe, seeking her clean housedress, but it took too long, and the sagging, hanging door on the locker kept swinging inward, bumping her, and the fear overruled all. She had to get out. She thought of her children, sleeping in the next room. She would take them and go to her sister's place.

The front room was dominated by the big bed where the children slept. Eula Mae noticed the wrongness as soon as she stepped through the door. There was no sound. Taddie's usual adenoidal snore didn't ripple the air—none of them, in fact, were breathing. She forced herself to go close to the bed, but she couldn't make herself touch them. If she touched them, felt them lifeless beneath her fingers, they would be turned into strangers for sure.

The facts were almost too stark to question. She wondered only why she, out of them all, had been permitted to awaken.

Her mind searched restlessly, almost without her volition, for a prayer that would mean something.

Friends lived downstairs. She could go to them. The latch on the front door was stubborn, as always, but tonight it seemed a sinister stubbornness, locking her in deliberately in a room where everything once familiar had been changed to evil. The door finally, groaning querulously, opened to her, and she ran down stairs which tore with splintery mouths at her bare feet.

"Annie! George!" She pounded at their door. Her voice bounced from wall to wall in the ill-lit corridor and came back to her ears, thin and strange, frightening her so that she shut her mouth and used only her fists to call for help.

Nothing. Eula Mae was afraid to go out into the unnatural night, lit by the make-believe moon—this building was, at least, a known shelter—but she could not stay here among the dead. Her sister Rose Marie lived just up the street, in an identical tenement house, in a nearly identical two-room apartment. Her sister Rose Marie would take her in.

Eula Mae heard a scuttling sound. Roaches. Oddly, the sound was reassuring. It was familiar; it meant life here in this deathly still place.

She went into the street, not looking up. Her head was beginning to ache. She put her hand to her forehead, where the pain seemed to be centered, and felt the familiar imprint of the six-pointed star. She pulled her fingers away hastily, for their touch seemed to acerbate her headache. She remembered a radio program she'd heard once, about a woman who had fallen and bumped her head and then forgotten everything—who she was and where she lived. Could something like that have happened to her? But what could she possibly have forgotten that would make sense of all these changes in her world?

The door of Rose Marie's building always hung open, and Eula Mae entered the narrow little hallway nervously. The mailboxes on the right wall had been smashed into useless metal, and she was afraid every time she came here that someday whoever had smashed those boxes would be waiting to smash *her*.

As always, reprieved once more from a smashing, Eula Mae scurried up the creaking stairs as rapidly as she could without stumbling.

No one answered her calls or her poundings. No one in

her sister's apartment, and no one up and down the hallway, although the sound must have been heard throughout the thin-walled building. Were they all gone? Frightened? Deaf? Could everyone be dead?

Finally, Eula Mae broke in the door of her sister's apartment. It was not difficult: Eula Mae was a powerfully built woman, although she did not think of herself as physically strong.

The front room was littered with children. One narrow cot held two, and the rest were on pallets on the floor. Eula Mae picked her way among them. She could hear no breathing, but did not want to investigate more closely.

A curtain separated the front room from Rose Marie and Jimmy's bedroom. Eula Mae pushed through the curtain and heard the welcome sound of soft snoring.

Her heart leaped with gratitude. "Rose Marie? Jimmy? Wake up!"

The slight, sibilant snore continued undisturbed. Eula Mae approached the bed. "Hey, get up!" she said loudly, and bent over her sister.

But no breath came from Rose Marie's nostrils, and no heartbeat disturbed the pink nylon ruffles of her negligee. Jimmy was snoring: he slept beside his dead wife. Eula Mae was outraged by this, and she leaned across the body of her sister and shook Jimmy's arm vigorously.

"You! Wake up! Quit that snoring and listen to me! Hear me? Wake up!"

Not even the rhythm of his snores altered. He slept on, as unreachable as Rose Marie.

Eula Mae straightened up and let her arms fall to her sides, realizing that she was quite alone. She was accustomed to making decisions, to running both her own life and the lives of other people, but she'd never been alone, and in a situation she flatly did not know how to handle.

She went back down the hall that reeked of long-forgotten meals, and down the treacherous stairs, and back into the deserted street. She would try to find someone, anyone, any friend or stranger to assure her that she was not the last person left alive; then they would decide what to do.

As she walked silent streets she remembered something her youngest brother had said. It might have been just another of the stories he loved to make up—just another of his innumerable horror stories about the omnipresent Whitney—or it might have been true.

"They've got a gas," he said. "They pipe it into rooms and kill everyone there. They tell us something like, 'this way to the showers' or, 'wait in this room till the doctor gets here' and then," his eyes glittered, "then they slip a tube under the door, or pump gas in through pipes in the vents and . . . a few little coughs, a choke or two you hardly notice and . . . zap . . . everybody's wiped out. Snuffed."

Eula Mae had been a little bit afraid of him when he told her that: he'd enjoyed the telling so much; he had looked gloating and sly, not much at all like her beloved little brother.

"That's the way the Man solves the nigger problem," he'd said cheerfully. "He just puts 'em all to sleep, like dogs with rabies."

When she came out of her reverie, Eula Mae saw that she had walked much farther than she would have thought possible. She had walked straight out of the city and into the countryside. She stepped from concrete onto a dirt road, and looked around in wonder. The sudden transition was mysterious; Eula Mae *knew* she could not have come so far in such a short time—true, she had been preoccupied, but she doubted she had walked even a mile yet. By all that was logical, she should still be in the heart of the city. Yet she looked around, and her eyes gave her evidence of a cotton field, a watermelon patch just across the road, and some tumbledown wooden shanties a bit farther away.

She walked on toward the shanties, and went right up to one. But then she hesitated before mounting the steps to the dilapidated porch. A dog slept there, nose between his paws. Or did he sleep? The dog did not stir, nor give any sign that it knew she was there, staring at it. Had it indeed been a gas? Some mysterious gas, sprayed over all the areas where blacks lived? But if that were true, why had she lived on?

She walked past the shanty, continuing down the road, although her head hurt more with every step and she wanted to lie down somewhere, to rest, to be free of the pain that was knocking about inside her skull, burning a hole in her forehead. But she feared that if she rested she would never rise again.

So she walked on, she walked on—she walked quite suddenly into an invisible wall.

She backed off, staring stupidly at the horizon, at the moonlit dusty road which stretched before her. Then she tentatively stretched out a hand, and the hand went right through everything—the sky, the grass, the road, the distant shacks—and touched a hard, flat, smooth, invisible wall.

Eula Mae began to walk slowly alongside the wall, one hand outstretched and touching it to assure herself of its presence. She walked that way, following it, for some distance. It was eerie, seeing her hand pass through the landscape and touch something solid she could not see. But she did not have strength to spare for wondering. Her headache was almost overwhelming, and she had to fix all her attention upon moving, just moving. Reasons and answers would have to come later, if they ever came, just as rest would come later. For now she would have to move, because she was afraid to stop or turn back.

Once, Eula Mae looked to her right, away from the wall, and was startled to see that she was walking along a street only four blocks from where she lived. Why had she never tried to walk through the wall, toward the buildings that seemed to be there? Or had she? She could not remember. Perhaps it was not important to know if her universe had always been circumscribed by this wall, or if this was a recent change.

Abruptly the wall ended, projection merging with reality in a solid building. It was just another broken, dying tenement, like so many others in the neighborhood. This one was scarred with "Condemned" signs, and a door gaped blackly open.

Eula Mae hesitated a moment, the pain in her head holding her back like a brutal fist. She gasped slightly, and pushed herself through the doorway.

The hall it opened on was short and dark with a door closed at the opposite end. Eula Mae fumbled with the knob, and the door opened onto a blaze of light.

When she opened her eyes—slowly, against the pain of the headache and the glaring brightness—Eula Mae saw that she had opened a door leading into a wide, white-walled corridor lit by fluorescent ceiling panels. It was nothing from her world.

Eula Mae looked up and down the hall. White walls, punctuated by doors, stretched in either direction. She saw no one, heard no one, and hesitantly entered the hall. She looked back at her door and saw, in stark black letters at the top of the doorframe, one word: NIGGERTOWN.

The pain in her head, which had become so persistent that she could almost ignore it, suddenly seared and stabbed with a new intensity. Eula Mae gnawed her lip to keep from whimpering. It was foolish to go on; foolish not to go home where she could lie down . . . but she thought of lying next to her dead husband, and knew she could not go back with nothing accomplished. If she was a fool, well, then, she was a fool. She would go on.

She walked away from Niggertown. She came to a door labeled "Little Israel" and hesitated . . . and then walked on. Eula Mae saw that the corridor had a turning just ahead and her pace quickened.

At the turn, the hall opened into a large, circular gallery. It was empty of people. All around the walls projected booths or stalls, similar to those found at fairs and amusement parks of all sizes—the sort where tickets are sold and goods dispensed. And, as at a fair (and seeming to Eula Mae to be very much out of place in this clean, large, empty, well-lit hall) each booth was decorated with garish signs and posters, each proclaiming the particular attraction to be purchased at that booth.

"Niggertown"—the word garish in red and black—caught her eye, and she let herself be drawn to that booth.

Clowns in black-face. It was a depiction Eula Mae was accustomed to. Thick-lipped, pop-eyed, fuzzy-headed darkies. Mammies with their babies, little pickaninnies, young bucks in overalls strumming banjos.

"See," shouted the caption above one picture, "customs held since tribal days in darkest Africa!" Above a cartoon of soulful darkies looking heavenward was the suggestion: "Join the happy darkies in heartwarming 'spirituals' and sing your blues away!"

Centered amid all the garish drawings was a box set in a bold typeface. Eula Mae read it, her lips moving slightly as she grappled with each word.

"Guaranteed Satisfaction! Observe first-hand a vanished way of life. See them tremble before you, the hated 'honky'—OR, for the thrill of a lifetime, never to be forgotten, SEE LIFE THROUGH BLACK EYES! Yes! Our surrogate people are so real, so lifelike, that only a trained expert can tell the difference. Plug right in and instantly you see, hear, smell, taste and feel just as you can in your own body. Walk among them undetected in an android nigger body—they'll accept you as one of the 'tribe,' never suspecting, while you—"

Voices. They cut through her confusion and the pain in her head. Eula Mae was frozen like a rabbit before headlights. Which way to run? People—she had been looking for people, but what if—

Caution won. She stumbled behind the poster-bedecked booth, crouched, and waited.

Clicking footsteps: bootheels. Eula Mae peered around the side of the booth, and terror flowed over her as she saw who was there.

Two white men, fine, blond, strong, Aryan types. The pride of the world. One wore coveralls and carried a tool kit; the other was a guard of some kind, in a gray and black uniform, swastikas shining discretely from his shoulders.

The worker was complaining; the guard listening with a slight smile curling his lips.

"It's just that it's so damn unnecessary. It's an unnecessary expense to maintain real people—the public wouldn't know the difference if we replaced 'em all with androids. It'll have to be done eventually, when they die out, so why not replace 'em all right now? The surrogates wouldn't give us this kind of trouble."

"You're probably right," said the guard. "The public wouldn't know—the public is very gullible. But the Old Man himself sometimes comes around here . . . he'd know . . . he likes . . ."

"He comes here?" asked the other in awe.

The guard frowned at being interrupted. He had stopped walking in order to speak his piece, and he expected the other to be properly respectful of his words.

"Yes. This is one of the last places you can see such things . . . most other arcades are composed entirely of surrogates. Some of them very fine, true, but not the real thing. And to some, like the Old Man, having the real thing is very important. It makes him very proud, to be able to come here, to see a way of life he's wiped from the earth . . ." The guard began to walk again, and the other fell into step beside him.

As they turned the corner out of sight, Eula Mae could still hear the guard's fine, resonant tones going on: "But, of course, even the Old Man will not last forever . . . when he finally goes then you can have all your replacements, and you'll only have to maintain your surrogate people."

Voice and footsteps faded out. Eula Mae got to her feet, slowly and painfully. Her head hurt too much to think, almost too much to move. She could only wish she'd never awoken, never noticed that there was something wrong with the moon . . . It took her minutes to gain the strength and the will to take a few steps forward, and she was so engrossed in this simple action that she did not hear the returning footsteps until it was much too late.

She heard one voice say quietly, "Ah, there it is."

And then the pain in her head blazed up, she went blank, and she crumpled in a heap in the center of the big arcade.

NEMESIS PLACE

David Drake

Readers of past volumes of *Year's Best Horror* will remember such David Drake stories as "Something Had to Be Done," "Best of Luck," and "Children of the Forest." Drake is an assistant town attorney of Chapel Hill, North Carolina, assistant editor of that remarkable small-press horror magazine *Whispers*, and co-publisher (with Karl Wagner) of the specialty press Carcosa, which has given us recent and important collections of horror fiction by Manly Wade Wellman, E. Hoffmann Price and Hugh B. Cave. Moreover, Drake is well-known as a science fiction writer, especially for his Hammer's Slammers stories. But if there is any aspect of imaginative writing at which Drake must be said to be the leading practitioner, it has to be the historical fantasy. Karl Wagner has said of him that he's a Romanophile who doesn't believe the Empire has fallen. Drake has proven this point again and again, by helping Wagner with the historical research for his Bran Mak Morn novel, *Legion of the Shadow*; by writing historical stories like "Children of the Forest;" and with his stories of Vettius and Dama, which have been appearing in various anthologies and magazines since Drake started selling his fiction. One of them was in *Fantastic* last year, and we snatched it up to include here. You're certain to enjoy it, but look out for that ending: if you aren't careful it just might sneak right past you.

Vettius and his half-section of troops in armor filled the innkeeper's narrow office. "The merchant Dauod of Petra," he said, pointing his finger like a knifeblade at the shocked civilian's throat. "Which room?"

"S-second floor," stuttered the innkeeper, his face gone the color of tallow when the Emperor's soldiers burst in on him. "Nearest the ladder."

"Ulcius, you watch him," nodded the big legate to the nearest of his men. The other soldiers and Dama were already swinging toward the ladder that served as sole means of access to the inn's upper floors. Dama was half the bulk of any of the burly troops, an elfin man of Cappadocian stock whose blond hair was now part silver. He was not visibly armed, but neither had Vettius brought his friend on the raid to fight.

The fat teamster who had started down the ladder had sense enough to change direction as the soldiers came scrambling up. Their hobnailed sandals rasping the tiles were the only sound they made as they formed a semicircle around the indicated doorway. Dulcitius, the Thracian centurion with a godling's face and a weasel's eyes, drew his sword silently. Vettius checked the position of his men, shifted so that his own armored body masked Dama, and kicked in the latched wooden door. All five of them were inside before the room's gray-haired occupant could sit up on his mattress.

"Your name and business, *now!*" Vettius thundered in Aramaic. He had not drawn his own long spatha, but either of his knotted fists was capable of pulping the frail man on the bed.

"Sirs, I'm Dauod son of Hafiz, nothing more than a trader in spices," the old man whined. His hands trembled as they indicated the head-sized spice caskets arrayed beneath the room's barred window.

"You were told right," Dama said with flat assurance. He had traded in more countries than most of the Empire knew existed, and the local dialects were as much a part of his memories as the products the people bartered. "That's not an Arab accent," he went on, "it's pure Persian. He may be a spice trader, but he's not from Petra or anywhere else inside the Empire."

The legate's square face brightened with triumph. "Amazing," he said, irony barbing his words. "I didn't realize there was anybody in Antioch who wasn't too busy listening for treason to bother telling us about a Persian spy."

The old man cowered back against the wall deforming the

billet that served as pillow at the head of his bed. Vettius' practiced eye caught the angular hardness in the cloth. His hand shot out, jerking away the billet and spilling to the floor the dagger within it. Briefly no one moved. The Persian was hunched as though trying to crawl backwards into the plaster.

Dama toed the knife, listening critically to its ring. "Silver," he announced. "I don't think it's meant for a weapon. It's magic paraphernalia, like the robe it was wrapped in."

"Uh?" Vettius glanced at the coarse woolen blanket he had snatched and found that when it unrolled it displayed a garment of gauzy black silk as fine as a spider's weaving. In metal threads on the hem were worked designs that appeared notational but in no script with which the legate was familiar. Vettius kicked the silver dagger, the arthame, into the passageway and tossed the robe after it. He deliberately turned his back on the man who called himself Dauod. Bending, he grasped a handle and snaked out one of the bottom layer of spice caskets. It was of leather like the rest, its tight lid thonged to the barrel; but the workmanship was exceptionally good, and a recent polishing could not hide signs of great age. Vettius fumbled at the knot, then popped the fastening with a quick flexion of his fingers.

The old Persian gave a wordless cry and leaped for the legate's back. Dulcitius' sword darted like pale lightning, licking in at the Persian's jaw hinge and out the opposite temple in a spray of blood. Vettius spun with a bellow and slapped his centurion down with a bear-quick motion. "You idiot, who told you to kill him? Was he going to hurt *me*?"

Dulcitius clanged as he bounced against the wall, his face as white as his tunic except where Vettius' broad handprint glowed on his cheek. His sword was still imbedded in the skull of the dying man thrashing on the floor, but a murderous rage roiled in his eyes. Unseen to the side, Dama freed the small knife concealed in his tunic.

"There was no call to do that," Dulcitius said slowly.

"There wasn't bloody call to kill the man before we even started to question him!" Vettius snarled back. "If you're too stupid to see that, you've got no business with officer rank— and I can see to that mistake very promptly, damn you. Otherwise, get downstairs with Ulcius. Find out from the innkeeper who this Dauod saw, what he did—every damn thing about him since he came to Antioch."

Vettius was by birth a Celtiberian, one of the black-haired, black-hearted race who had slammed a bloody door on the Teutoni and sent them stumbling back into the spears of Rome and Marius. Four and a half centuries had bled neither the courage of his forefathers nor their savagery from the tall legate; Dulcitius stared at him, then turned and left the room with neither a curse nor a backward glance.

"Start looking through his gear," Vettius said mildly to the remaining soldiers. "He's not going to tell us much himself."

The casket in his own hands sucked as he opened it to reveal a scroll and a glass bottle, round and nested in a leather hollow that held it firm. Vettius weighed the sphere in his hand. The silvery mercury that filled it had just enough air trapped with it beneath the seal to tremble.

Dama was already glancing at the scroll. "It's in Greek," he said, frowning, "most of it. 'The record of the researches of Nemesius—'"

"His real name was Nemesius?" the legate interrupted.

"'—of Nemesius of Antioch,'" continued Dama unperturbed, "'in the third year of the reign of the Emperor Valerianus.'"

The line troops had paused from opening chests filled only with spices. Vettius himself had the look of a man uncertain as to who is playing the trick on him. "Valerian," he repeated. "But he was killed...."

"Almost a century ago," the Cappadocian finished for him in agreement. "What was a Persian wizard doing with a parchment written a century ago by a Greek philosopher?"

Vettius' tongue prodded his left cheek. He could command troops or seduce women in eight languages, was truly fluent in five of them; but only in Latin could he claim literacy. "I'll be pretty busy the next few days," he lied unnecessarily. "Why don't you read it yourself and tell me what you think of it?"

"Sestia'll probably be glad that I've found something to do for a few days besides pester her," Dama said with a fond smile. "Sure, it can't hurt for me to take a look at it."

The moon and three triple-wicked oil lamps lighted the pillared courtyard. Servants had cleared away the last of the platters, leaving the two friends to Chian wine and the warm Syrian night.

"I'm sorry Sestia got a headache at the last minute," Dama said. "I'd like the two of you to get better acquainted."

"She got the headache when she heard I was coming for dinner," remarked Vettius, more interested in straightening his tunic than in what he was saying.

"You don't usually have that problem with women," gibed the merchant.

"She knows the kind of guy I am, that's all."

"Nobody who really knows you, Lucius, would think you'd seduce a friend's wife."

"Yeah, that's what I mean."

Dama drew an aimless design in wine lees on the marble tabletop. The legate glanced up, flushed, and gulped down the contents of his own cup. "Mithra," he apologized. "I've drunk too much already." Then, "Look, have you gotten anything out of the scroll? Neither the innkeeper nor anything we found in the room gives us a notion of what this Dauod was up to."

The Cappadocian set the leather case on the table and drew the parchment out of it. "Umm, yes, I've got a notion . . . but it's no more than that and you may want to call me a fool when I tell you."

"You aren't a fool," said Vettius quietly. "Tell me about the scroll."

"Nemesius of Antioch was searching for the secret of life and a way of turning base metals into gold. He wrote an account of his attempts here—" Dama spread the scroll slightly to emphasize it—"after he succeeded in both. Or so he says."

"Even that long ago I'd have heard of him if that was true," the soldier snorted.

"Except," Dama pointed out, "that was the year the Persians sacked Antioch. And Nemesius' villa was outside the walls." He spun the parchment to a passage he had noted. "'. . . leaving in place of the lead a column of living gold, equal to me in height and in diameter some three cubits.' Now, what I suspect is that your Dauod was no spy. He was a wizard himself, not of the ability of Nemesius but able to understand the processes he describes and to believe they might work. He was a scholar, too, enough of one to read this scroll in a casket looted on whim a century ago; and a gambler besides to risk his life on its basis in a hostile empire."

"But for what?" Vettius demanded. "You said the place was sacked."

"Nemesius had an underground laboratory. He describes

the secret entrance to it in this parchment," Dama replied. "It just could be that the Persian who found the chest—and probably Nemesius—above ground missed the passageway below. If so, the gold might still be there."

Vettius' intake of breath was that of a boy seeing for the first time a beautiful woman nude. "That much *gold*," he whispered. He sat up on his couch and leaned forward toward his friend, mind working like a tally board. "Hundreds of talents, maybe thousands. . . . If we could find that, we'd each be as rich as the Emperor's freedmen. What would you do with wealth like that, Dama?"

"I'd leave it to rot in the ground," the merchant said without inflection. Vettius blinked at the violence of the words and the Cappadocian's hard blue eyes. "I read you what Nemesius created," Dama went on. "I didn't read you how he went about it. Neither for eternal life nor for all the gold on earth would I have done half the things he claims to have done. There's an evil to that gold. It's dangerous, the danger reeks all through this parchment, though Nemesius never puts a name to why. Maybe he was afraid to. Let the gold lie for somebody in more need of trouble than you or I are."

Vettius took the bulb of mercury from the casket to occupy his hands while he pondered. The bubble danced through the transparence, a mobile facet in the light of the oil lamps. The cap was of thin, carven gold, but the short neck of the bottle had been sealed with wax before the gold was applied.

"Why two seals, do you suppose?" Vettius asked rather than voice what was really on his mind.

"Quicksilver combines with gold, rots it into a paste," Dama explained. "The wax is the real closure, the metal over it just for show." He paused, continued when he saw the soldier was still not ready to speak. "Nemesius used quicksilver in his searching, both for life and for gold. He says he always carried this bottle with him; why, I don't know. The manuscript doesn't explain."

"You've spent your life gathering gold, trading for gold, haven't you?" the big Spaniard rumbled, slipping the mercury back into the case and then looking at his wine cup.

"Yeah, I have," Dama agreed, his posture a conscious disavowal of the tension lacing the night. "Spices from Taprobane, silks from India. Once I went all the way to the Serian lands for silk, but the extra profit wasn't worth the danger."

"All your life looking for gold and you tell *me* not to dig an emperor's ransom out of the ground when it's right here waiting. I don't understand it, Dama." Vettius raised his voice and his eyes together. "You're playing a game of some sort and I don't know what it is!"

"No game at all," said Dama, still quietly. He faced his friend as he had once faced a gut-shot bear. The merchant had seen other men suddenly besotted with an idea—a cavalryman hammered into fanaticism by the majesty of his Arian God, a shipmaster so certain that a fourth continent lay west of Ireland that he convinced a full crew to disappear with him in search of it. A jest, even a misspoken word, would send such men into murderous frenzies. "Sure, I love gold, but I know it. I'm not joking at all, Lucius, when I say there's a wrong feel to this hoard. I'll help you any way I can to see that you find it, but I'll have no portion of what Nemesius left."

Slowly Vettius reached for the wine bowl and bent a rueful smile onto his face. "That's fair," he said as he poured for both of them. "A good bit too fair, but we'll worry over that when the gold's in our hands, hey?" He paused; then, too eagerly for his pretense of calm, he blurted, "You think there's a real chance of locating Nemesius' cellars after this time?"

Dama nodded. "Let me think about it. There's a way to do most things if you think about them a while."

The soldier sipped, then gulped his unmixed wine to the lees and stood up. The light bronzed his skin and made each bristle of his nascent beard a spearpoint. "I'll be off, then," he said. "I—I really appreciate all you've done, will do, Dama. It isn't for me, not really; but if I had wealth enough to make those idiots in Constantinople listen to what I say about the army. . . ."

Dama clapped him on the arm. "As you said, we'll talk about that when the gold's in your hands."

After his friend had left behind his lamp-carrier, drunken but erect and with a vicious smile on his face that no footpad would dare to trouble, Dama returned to the courtyard. Sestia's room would be locked. From past experience Dama knew to stay out of her wing of the house and not make a fool of himself before her servants, trying to wheedle his wife out of her pique through bolted wood. Instead, he fingered the bulb of mercury, then re-opened the scroll beside it. When dawn began to sear the marble facings of the court he was still at the table dictating notes to the sleepy clerk he had dragged from bed three hours before.

"You're sure that's the place?" said Vettius, a neutral figure in the dusk unless one noted the tip of the scabbard lifting the hem of his long travelling cloak. The mud-brick warren around them scampered with the sounds of furtive life, some of it human, but no one approached the friend.

"I'm not *sure* the sun will rise in the morning," retorted Dama, "but there's plenty of evidence, yes, that Nemesius' villa was here. He disappeared in the first sack, probably burned with his buildings. His heirs sold the tract to a developer to run up a cheap apartment block—land outside the walls wasn't considered a good place for fancy houses right then. Which shows good sense, because when the Persians came back three years later they burned the apartments too."

There had been signs of that during daylight, ancient scorch marks on the rubble still heaped among the rank weeds. "Strange that no one rebuilt since," said Vettius, squinting to sharpen his twilit image of the barren acre before him.

"The site had gotten a reputation." Dama shrugged his own worn cloak loose, shifting his grip on the leathern chest he carried. "That's really what made it possible to find it." He gestured. "There's a lot of people in the city—the dregs who live here, even the ones a few levels removed who associate with them—who know what you mean when you ask about Nemesius' estate that was somewhere off the Sidon road. 'Oh, yeah,' they say, 'Nemesis Place'. Their faces tighten up and they add, 'What do you want with that, anyway? Nobody goes around there.' "

The little merchant flicked his gaze once more around the darkness. "Not quite true, of course. People cut down saplings for firewood here. Probably some of them sleep in the ruins now and again. They don't stay long, though. Nothing in particular, just uneasiness. 'Nemesis Place'."

"Balls," said Vettius, beginning to stride into the clearing. "I don't feel uneasy."

"You didn't look very comfortable when we slipped out the gate this afternoon," commented Dama as he trotted alongside, casket thumping his thigh. "Second thoughts, or you just don't like to sneak by your own men and not be able to scream that their bronze hasn't been polished?"

Vettius slowed and glanced at his friend. Surprise audible in his voice, he said, "You know me too well. I don't like them thinking they can ignore me just because I've told them we'll be gone three days, hunting in the hills. Dulcitius was supposed to command the gate guard today, but because they think I'm gone already he seems to have traded time with Furianus without having cleared it with me."

Dama stumbled, more in anger than from the fragment of stone in the brush. "Dulcitius," he repeated. "I've seen him hanging around my gate. Tell him for me that I'll kill him if I ever catch him there again."

"Don't fool with that one," said Vettius very softly.

"I'm not afraid," Dama snapped.

"Dama, you know about a lot of things I don't," the soldier said. "But take my word about killers. Don't ever think of going up against Dulcitius alone."

"This is far enough," said Dama, changing the subject as a pile of masonry loomed up in front of them. Beside it he knelt to light a thick tallow candle with the slow match he had brought in a terra-cotta jar. "They followed the villa's groundplan when they built the apartments," he explained. "Used the old foundations. I checked yesterday and the cap slab over the hidden stairway is still in place."

"Did you open it?"

Dama ignored the suspicion leaking out in his friend's tones. "I couldn't, not without either you or a team of mules. Finally decided I'd use you."

The air was so still that the candle flame pulsed straight up at the moonless sky. By its light Vettius saw set in what had been a courtyard pavement the mosaic slab beneath which Nemesius had described his stairway as lying. The pattern laid over a counter-weighted bronze plate was of two intertwined dragons, one black and the other white. It was impossible to tell whether the beasts were battling, mating, or—just possibly—fissioning. Their tails were concealed beneath a concrete panel which had skewed across the mosaic when the building collapsed.

"I brought a sledge," said Dama, extracting the tool from the double sling beneath his right arm, "but I'll let you do the work."

"Umm," mumbled Vettius, considering the obstructing concrete. It had been part of a load-bearing wall, hand's-breadth thick and fractured into a width of about three feet. The far end disappeared under a pile of other rubble. Vettius tossed aside his cloak and squatted over the slab, his hands turned backward to grip its irregular edge.

Dama frowned. "Dis, you'll need the hammer."

"Very likely," Vettius agreed, "but that's a lot of racket that I'd like to avoid if we can." He stiffened, his face flushing as tendons sprang out on his neck. The slab quivered. His linen tunic ripped down to his waist. Then his thighs straightened and the slab pivoted on its buried end, sliding back a foot before the off-balance soldier sat down on it.

"After—what? Twenty-six years?—you still have the ability to surprise me, Lucius," said Dama. He knelt and twisted at one of the circular tiles in the border until metal clicked. The mosaic rocked upward at an additional finger's pressure on one end.

Vettius stood, shrugged, and straightened his scabbard. "Let's go," he said, reaching for the candle.

"A moment." Dama folded his cloak, lumpy with hints of further preparations against unknown needs. From his sash he stripped everything but an additional candle and his own sword, a foot shorter than Vettius' spatha but heavy and chisel-sharp on both edges. Drawing it before he lifted the casket in his left hand he said, "All right, I'm ready."

"Are you that worried?" Vettius asked with a grin. "And if you are, why're you lugging that box along?"

"Because I am that worried. Nemesius says he carried it, and he knew a lot more about what he was getting into than you or I do."

The flight of brick steps was steep and narrow, dropping twenty feet to a pavement of living rock. The candle burned brightly although the air had a metallic odor, a hint that was more an aftertaste. The gallery into which the stairwell opened was a series of pilastered vaults whose peaks reached close to the surface. The candle suggested the magnitude it could not illuminate.

"Mithra," Vettius said, raising the light to the full height of his arm, "how can you have a secret vault when it's so big half of Antioch must have been down here swinging picks to excavate it?"

"Yes, I've wondered how he got it excavated too," Dama said. He did not amplify on the question.

The walls were veneered with colored marble. A narrow shelf at shoulder height divided the panels, smooth below but relieved with all manner of symbols and fanciful beasts from ledge to ceiling. The technical craftsmanship was good, but execution of the designs showed a harshness akin to that of battle standards.

"He doesn't seem to have needed all this room," the soldier remarked as they entered the third vault. It held a dozen long racks of equipment and stoppered bottles, but even that was but partial use of its volume.

They circled the racks. The last of the four vaults was not empty either. "Oh, dear Jesus," whispered Dama while his bigger companion muttered, "Mithra, Mithra, Mithra," under his breath. A low stone dais stood in the center of the chamber. Nemesius must have been a tall man. The column of gold he referred to as being as tall as he was would have overtopped even Vettius standing beside it. He must have measured by the long cubit as well, for the diameter of the mass was certainly over five feet. Its surface was irregular, that of waves frozen as they chopped above a rip tide, and bloody streaks shot through the bulk of yellower metal.

"Oh, yes. . . ." Vettius said, drawing his spatha and stepping toward the gold.

"Careful, Lucius," Dama warned. "I don't think we'd better hack off a piece yet. Nemesius gives a formula for 'unbinding' the column. I think I ought to read that first."

Vettius made a moue of irritation but said only, "We haven't found any tricks, but yeah, that doesn't mean that he didn't play some." He held the candle close as Dama opened the casket and unrolled the parchment to the place he needed.

The merchant had sheathed his own sword. Kneeling and drawing a deep breath, he read aloud in Greek, "In the names by which you were bound, Saloë, Pharippa, Phalertos, I unbind you."

Voice gathering strength from the husky whisper with which he had begun, Dama read the next line in Persian, using the old pronunciation: "By the metals in which you were locked in death, lead, sulphur, quicksilver, I free you to life."

There were five more sentences in the spell, each of them in a different tongue; Vettius understood none of them. One reminded him of phrases mumbled by a horseman who rode with a squadron of Sakai irregulars but who came from much farther east. At the climax, Dama's voice was an inhuman thunder explicable only as a trick of the room's acoustics. "Acca!" he shouted, "Acca! Acca!"

The words struck the gold like hammer-blows and it slumped away from them. The column sagged, mushroomed, and began to flow across the dais before resolidifying. A single bright streak zigged from the main mass like a stream across mudflats. "What in the name of Dis did you do?" Vettius cried. The candle in his hand trembled as he held it up.

The metal seemed rigid. It had fallen into an irregular dome over most of the dais and some of the rock beneath it. "As if we'd heated it," Dama said. "But. . . ." He reached up, ignited his other taper from the flame of the first, and set it on the floor beside the leather case. Then he stepped toward the dais while Vettius waited, torn by anger and indecision.

Two rivulets streamed outward to meet the Cappadocian's approach. He paused. Vettius shifted the spatha in his hand and said, "Dama, I—"

Dama sprang back as the golden streamlets froze, then scissored through the air. Hair-fine and rigid as sword edges, they slit the flapping hem of his tunic but missed the flesh. The dome itself lurched toward the men, moving from the dais with the deceptive speed of a millipede crawling across a board set in its path.

Dama scooped at the handle of the leather box. He caught it, missed his footing, and skidded it a dozen feet across the stone. Vettius had turned and run back toward the chamber's entrance. His candle went out at his first loping stride but the one still lighted on the floor caught a glittering movement ahead of him. "Lucius!" Dama shouted, but the big soldier had seen the same tremor and his sword was slashing up and outward to block the golden thread extruded when the column first collapsed. Steel met gold and the softer metal sang as it parted. The severed tip spun to the floor and pooled while the remainder of the thin tentacle wavered, still blocking the only exit. Ruddy streaks rippled through the main bulk as it closed on its victims.

Vettius cut again at the gold before him but it had thickened after its initial injury, forming a bar that only notched on impact. With a python's speed it looped on the blade and snatched it from the Spaniard's grip. Dama had taken two steps and jumped, using his left hand to help boost his whole lithe body up onto the shoulder-high ledge. Vettius saw the leap, spun like a tiger to follow. Nemesius' casket was open on the floor. Dama stared, understood, and cried, "The quicksilver! Break it on—"

Vettius bent and snatched up the glittering bulb of liquid. He raised it high as the fluid mass threw out a sheet which lapped across his ankles. Able but unwilling to act he moaned, "Oh dear Gods, the gold!" and the sheet bulged into a quilt as the whole weight of metal began to flow over him.

Dama leaned forward, judging distance with the cool precision with which he would have weighed a bolt of silk in his warehouse. The swift arc of his sword overbalanced him as he knew it would. He was falling onto the swelling monster below at the instant his point shattered the glass ball in his friend's hand. Droplets of mercury spewed across the mass of gold and fused with it.

The chamber exploded in a flash of red. Momentarily the walls blazed with the staring, shadowless eyes of the beasts limned on the frieze. Slowly, dazzled but not blinded, the two men pulled themselves free of gritty muck while their retinas readapted to the light of the single candle. Where they had been exposed to the flash their skins had the crinkly, prickly feel of sunburn.

"You took a chance there," Vettius said matter-of-factly. Most of the gold seemed to have disintegrated into a powder of grayish metal, lead, to judge by its weight. Where the mercury had actually splashed were clinging pools with an evil, silvery luster. "When I locked up like I did, you could have gotten out along the ledge."

"I've got enough on my conscience without leaving a friend to that," Dama said.

"I knew what had to be done, but I just couldn't . . . destroy it," the soldier explained. He was on his knees, furrowing the edge of the lead dust deeply with his hands. "That gold . . . and I'm damned if I can understand why, now, but that gold was worth more to me than my life was. Guess that's what you need friends for, to do for you what you won't do for yourself."

Dama had retrieved the candle and held it high. "Some other time we'll talk that over with a philosopher. Now let's get out of here before we find some other goody our friend Nemesius left."

"Give me a moment. I want to find my sword."

The merchant snorted. "If you cared as much about some

woman—*one* woman—as you do about the sword, Lucius, you'd be a happier man. You know, right now I feel like I had been gone the three days I told Sestia I would."

"Found it," said Vettius, carefully wiping hilt and blade on his tunic before sheathing the weapon. "Let's go back and greet your wife."

Later that night Dama understood a number of things. As stunned as a hanged man, he gurgled "Sestia!" through the shattered door to his wife's chamber. The centurion's sword and dagger were on a table near the bed, and Dulcitius was very quick; but Vettius had drawn before he kicked in the panel. Nothing would stop the overarm cut of his spatha, certainly not the bedding nor the two squirming bodies upon it.

COLLABORATING

Michael Bishop

Since he began his career as a science fiction writer back in 1970 with "If a Flower Could Eclipse," and "Pinon Fall," Michael Bishop has written some of the most moving stories this field has yet seen: "Death and Designation Among the Asadi," "The Samurai and the Willow," "Old Folks at Home," "The House of Compassionate Sharers," "Stolen Faces," "A Little Knowledge," "Within the Walls of Tyre"—the list would almost be a catalog of his fiction. The quality that has set him apart from the general run of sf and fantasy writers has been a depth of humanity that has enabled him to produce quiet, personal stories that can hold their own when set down among the tales of grandeur and action that seems always destined to be the norm for both science fiction and fantasy, to say nothing of horror. "Collaborating" is really a character study of a person—or persons—others might, in their ignorance, call a monster; and as such, it's a tour de force. Probably no one else could have written it. This is its first appearance in the U.S.

How does it feel to be a two-headed man? Better, how does it feel to be two men with one body? Maybe we can tell you. We're writing this—though it's I, Robert, who is up at the moment—because we've been commissioned to tell you what it's like living inside the same skin another human being inhabits and because we have to have our say.

I'm Robert. My brother's name is James. Our adoptive surname is Self—without contrivance on our part, even if this name seems to mock the circumstances of our life. James and I call our body The Monster. Who owns The Monster is a question that has occupied a good deal of our time, by virtue of a straitjacketing necessity. On more than one occasion The Monster has nearly killed us, but now we have pretty much domesticated it.

James Self. Robert Self. And The Monster.

It's quite late. James, who sits on the right side of our shoulders, has long since nodded away, giving control to me. My brother has subdued The Monster more effectively than I, however. When he's up, we move with a catlike agility I can never manage. Although our muscle tone and stamina are excellent, when I'm up The Monster shudders under my steering, and shambles, and shifts anatomical gears I didn't even know we possessed. At six foot three I am a hulking man, whereas James at six foot four—he's taller through the temples than I—is a graceful one. And we share the same body.

As a result, James often overmasters me during the day: I feel, then, like a sharp-witted invalid going the rounds in the arms of a kindly quarterback. Late at night, though, with James down in sleep and The Monster arranged propitiatingly on a leather lounge chair, even I can savor the animal potential of our limbs, the warmth of a good wine in our maw, the tingle of a privately resolvable sexual stirring. The Monster can be lived with.

But I'm leaping ahead. Let me tell you how we got this way, and what we look forward to, and why we persevere.

James and I were born in a southeastern state in 1951. (Gemini is our birth sign, though neither of us credits astrology.) A breech delivery, we've been told. I suppose we aligned ourselves buttocks first because we didn't know how to determine the precedence at the opposite end. We were taken with forceps, and the emergence of James and Robert together, two perfect infant heads groggy from the general anesthetic they'd given our mother, made the obstetrics team draw back into a white huddle from which it regarded us with fear, skepticism, awe, incredulity. How could anyone have expected this? A two-headed infant has only one heartbeat to measure, and there'd been no x-rays.

We were spirited away from the delivery room before our mother could recover and ask about us. The presiding physician, Dr. Larimer Self, then decreed that she would be told her child was stillborn. Self destroyed hospital records of the birth, swore his staff to silence, and gave my biological father, an itinerant laborer following the peach and cotton crops, a recommendation for a job in Texas. Thus, our obstetrician became our father. And our real parents were lost to us forever.

Larimer Self was an autocrat—but a sentimental one. He raised James and me in virtual isolation in a small community seventeen miles from the tri-county hospital where we'd been born. He gave us into the daytime care of a black woman named Velma Bymer. We grew up in a two-story house surrounded by holly bushes, crape myrtle, nandin, and pecan trees. Two or three months ago, after attaining a notoriety or infamy you may already be aware of, we severed all connections with the outside world and returned to this big, eighty-year-old house. Neither Robert nor I know when we will choose to leave it again; it's the only real home we've ever had.

Velma was too old to wet-nurse us, and a bachelor woman besides, but she bottle-fed us in her arms, careful to alternate feedings between Robert's head and mine since we could not both take formula at once. She was forty-six when we came into her care, and from the beginning she looked upon us not as a snakish curse for her own barrenness, but as a holy charge. A guerdon for her piety. My memories of her focus on her raw-boned, purple hands and a voice like sweet water flowing over rocks. James says he remembers her instead for a smell like damp cotton mixed up with the odor of slowly baking bran rolls. Today Velma drives to Wilson & Cathet's for her groceries in a little blue Fiat and sits evenings in her tiny one-room house with the Bible open on her lap. She won't move from that house—but she does come over on Thursday afternoons to play checkers with James.

Larimer Self taught us how to read, do mathematics, and reconcile our disagreements through rapid, on-the-spot bargaining. Now and again he took a strop to The Monster.

Most children have no real concept of "sharing" until well after three. James and I, with help from our stepfather, reached an earlier accommodation. We had to. If we wanted The Monster to work for us at all we had to subordinate self and cooperate in the manipulation of legs, arms, hands. Otherwise we did a Vitus dance, or spasmed like an epileptic, or crumpled into trembling stillness. Although I wrote earlier that James often "overmasters" me, I didn't mean to imply that his motor control is stronger than mine, merely better, and I sometimes voluntarily give him my up time for activities like walking, lifting, toting, anything primarily physical. As children we were the same. We could neutralize each other's strengths, but we couldn't—except in rare instances of fatigue or inattention—impose our will on the other. And so at six or seven months, maybe even earlier, we began to learn how to share our first toy: the baby animal under our necks. We became that organizational anomaly, a team with two captains.

Let me emphasize this: James and I don't have a psychic link, or a telepathic hookup, or even a wholly trustworthy line to each other's emotions. It's true that when I'm depressed James is frequently depressed, too; that when I'm exhilarated or euphoric James is the same. And why not? A number of feelings have biochemical determinants as well as psychological ones, and the biochemical state of Robert Self is pretty much the biochemical state of James Self. When James drinks, I get drunk. When I take smoke into our lungs, after a moment's delay James may well do the coughing. But we can't read each other's thoughts, and my brother—as I believe he could well say of me, too—can be as unpredictable as an utter stranger. By design or necessity we share many things, but our personalities and our thoughts are our own.

It's probably a little like being married, even down to the matter of sex. Usually our purely physical urges coincide, but one can put himself in a mental frame either welcoming or denying the satisfaction of that urge, whereupon, like husband and wife, James and Robert must negotiate. Of course, in our case the matter can be incredibly more complex than this. Legislation before congress, I suppose you could call some of our floor fights. But on this subject I yield to James, whose province the complexities are.

All right. What does being "up" mean if neither James nor I happen to be strong enough to seize The Monster's instrument panel and march it around to a goose step of our own? It means that whoever's up has almost absolute motor control, that whoever's down has willingly relinquished this power. Both James and I can give up motor control and remain fully aware of the world; we can—and do—engage in cognitive activity and, since our speech centers aren't affected, communicate our ideas. This ability has something

Eastern and yogic about it, I'm sure, but we have developed it without recourse to gurus or meditation.

How, then, do we decide who's to be up, who's to be down? Well, it's a "you first, Alphonse" / "after you, Gaston" matter, I'm afraid, and the only thing to be said in its favor is that it works. Finally, if either of us is sleeping, the other is automatically up.* The Monster gets only three or four hours of uninterrupted rest a night, but that, we have decided, is the price a monster must pay to preserve the sanity of its masters.

Of course there are always those who think that James and I are the monster. Many feel this way. Except for nearly two years in the national limelight, when we didn't know what the hell we were doing, we have spent our life trying to prove these people wrong. We are human beings, James and I, despite the unconscionable trick played on us in our mother's womb, and we want everybody to know it.

Come, Monster. Come under my hand. Goodbrother's asleep, it's seven o'clock in the A.M., and you've had at least three long hours of shut-eye, all four lids fluttering like window shades in gusty May! Three hours! So come under my hand, Monster, and let's see what we can add to this.

There are those who think that James and I are the monster.

O considerate brother, stopping where I can take off with a tail wind, even if The Monster is a little sluggish on the runway this morning. Robert is the man to be up, though; he's the one who taps this typewriter with the most authority, even if I am the high-hurdle man on our team. (He certainly wouldn't be mixing metaphors like this, goodbrother Robert.) Our editor wants both of us to contribute, however, and dissecting our monsterhood might be a good place for James to begin. Just let Robert snooze while you take my dictation, Monster, that's all I ask.

Yes. Many do see us as a monster. And somewhere in his introductory notes my goodbrother puts his hand to his mouth and whispers in an aside, "James is taller than me." Well, that's true—I am. You see, Robert and I aren't identical twins. (I'm better looking than Robert.) (And taller.) This means that a different genetic template was responsible

---

*This state can be complicated however. James dreams with such intensity that The Monster thrashes out with barely restrainable, subterranean vehemence. Not always, but often enough.

for each goodbrother's face and features, and, in the words of a local shopkeeper, "That just don't happen." The chromosomes must have got twisted, the genes multiplied and scrambled, and a monster set loose on the helical stairway of the nucleotides. What we are, I'm afraid, is a sort of double mutant. . . . That's right, you hear me clearly, a mutant.

M.U.T.A.N.T.

I hope you haven't panicked and run off to Bolivia. Mutants are scary, yes—but usually they don't work very well or fit together like they ought. A lot of mutations, whether fruit flies or sheep, are stillborn, dead to begin with. Others die later. The odds don't favor creatures with abbreviated limbs and heads without skull caps. Should your code get bollixed, about the best you can hope for is an aristocratic sixth finger, one more pinky to lift away from your tea cup. And everybody's seen those movies where radiation has turned picnicking ants or happy-go-lucky grasshoppers into ogres as big as frigates. Those are *mutants*, you know.

And two-headed men?

Well, in the popular media they're usually a step below your bonafide mutant, surgical freaks skulking through swamps, axe at the ready, both bottom lips adrool. Or, if the culprit *is* radiation—an after-the-bomb comeuppance for mankind's vanity—one of the heads is a lump capable only of going "la la, la la" and repeating whatever the supposedly normal head says. Or else the two heads are equally dumb and carry on like an Abbott and Costello comedy team, bumping noggins and singing duets. Capital crimes, all these gambits. Ha ha.

No one identifies with a two-headed man.

If you dare suggest that the subject has its serious side, bingo, the word they drop on you is—"morbid." Others in the avoidance arsenal? Try "grotesque." "Diseased." "Gruesome." "Pathological." "Perverse." Or even this "*poly*perverse." But "morbid" is the mortar shell they lob in to break off serious discussion and the fragments corkscrew through you until even you are aghast at your depravity. People wonder why you don't kill yourselves at first awareness of your hideousness. And you can only wince and slink away, a morbid silver trail behind you. Like snail slime.

Can you imagine, then, what it's like being a (so-called) two-headed man in Monocephalic America? Robert and I may well be the ultimate minority. Robert and I and The Monster, the three of us together.

Last year in St. Augustine, Florida, at the Ripley's museum, on tour with an Atlanta publicist, my brother and I saw a two-headed calf.

Stuffed. One head blind and misshapen, lolling away from the sighted head. A mutant, preserved for the delight and edification of tourists to the Oldest City in the U.S.A. Huzza huzza.

In the crowded display room in front of this specimen our party halted. Silence snapped down like a guillotine blade. What were the Selfs going to do now, everyone wondered. Do you suppose we've offended them? Aw, don't worry about it, they knew what they were getting into. Yeah, but—

Say I to brother, "This is a Bolshevik calf, Robert. The calf is undoubtedly no marcher in the procession of natural creatures. It's a Soviet sew-up. They did it to Man's Best Friend and now they've done it to a potential bearer of Nature's Most Perfect Food. Here's the proof of it, goodbrother, right here in America's Oldest City."

"Tsk, tsk," says Robert. He says that rather well.

"And how many Social Security numbers do you suppose our officialdom gave this calf before it succumbed? How many names did they let this moo-cow manqué inscribe in the local voting register?"

"This *commie* calf?"

"Affirmative."

"Oh, two, certainly. If it's a Soviet sew-up, James, it probably weaseled its rights from both the Social Security apparatus and the voting registrar. Whereas we—"

"Upright American citizens."

"Aye," says Robert. "Whereas we are but a single person in the eyes of the State."

"Except for purposes of taxation," say I.

"Except for purposes of taxation," Robert echoes. "Though it is given to us to file a joint return."

We can do Abbott and Costello, too, you see. Larry Blackman, the writer, publicist, and "talent handler," wheezed significantly, moved in, and herded our party to a glass case full of partially addressed envelopes that—believe it or not—had nevertheless been delivered to the Ripley museum. One envelope had arrived safely with only a rip (!) in its cover as a clue to its intended destination.

"From rip to Zip," I say, "and service has gotten worse."

Blackman coughed, chuckled, and tried to keep Robert from glancing over our shoulder at that goddamn calf. I still don't know if he ever understood just how bad he'd screwed up.

That night in our motel room Robert hung his head forward and wept. We were wracked with sobs. Pretty soon The Monster had ole smartass Jamebo doing it, too, just as if we were nine years old again and crying for Velma after burning a strawberry on our knobbly knee. James and Robert Self, in a Howard Johnson's outside St. Augustine, sobbing in an anvil chorus of bafflement. . . . I only bring this up because the episode occurred toward the end of our association with Blackman and because our editor wanted a bit of "psychology" in this collaborative effort.

There it is, then: a little psychology. Make of it what you will.

Up, Monster! Get ye from this desk without awakening Robert and I'll feed ye cold peaches from the Frigidaire. Upon our shared life and my own particular palate, I will.

People wonder why you didn't kill yourselves at first awareness of your hideousness.

(James is reading over our chest as I write, happy that I've begun by quoting him. Quid pro quo, I say: tit for tat.)

Sex and death. Death and sex. Our contract calls upon us to write about these things, but James has merely touched on the one while altogether avoiding the other. Maybe he wishes to leave the harvesting of morbidities to me. Could that possibly be it?

("You've seen right through me, goodbrother," replies James.)

Leaving aside the weighty matter of taxes, then, let's talk about death and sex. . . . No, let's narrow our subject to death. I still have hopes that James will spare me a recounting of a side of our life I've allowed him, by default, to direct. James?

("Okay, Robert. Done.")

Very well. The case is this: When James dies, I will die. When I die, James will die. Coronary thrombosis. Cancer of the lungs. Starvation. Food poisoning. Electrocution. Snakebite. Defenestration. Anything finally injurious to the body does us both in—two personalities are blotted out at one blow. The Monster dies, taking us with it. The last convulsion, the final laugh, belongs to the creature we will have spent our lives training to our wills. Well, maybe we owe it that much.

You may, however, be wondering: Isn't it possible that James or Robert could suffer a lethal blow without causing his brother's death? A tumor? An embolism? An aneurysm? A bullet wound? Yes, that might happen. But the physical shock to The Monster, the poisoning of our bloodstream, the emotional and psychological repercussions for the surviving Self would probably bring about the other's death as a matter of course. We are not Siamese twins, James and I, to be separated with a scalpel or a medical laser and then sent on our individual ways, each of us less a man than before. Our ways have never been separate, and never will be, and yet we don't find ourselves hideous simply because the fact of our interdependence has been cast in an inescapable anatomical metaphor. Just the opposite, perhaps.

At the beginning of our assault on the World of Entertainment two years ago (and, yes, we still receive daily inquiries from carnivals and circuses, both American and European), we made an appearance on *Midnight Chatter*. This was Blackman's doing, a means of introducing us to the public without resorting to loudspeakers and illustrated posters. We were very lucky to get the booking, he told us, and it was easy to see that Blackman felt he'd pulled off a major show-business coup.

James and I came on at the tail end of a Wednesday's evening show, behind segments featuring psychologist Dr. Irving Brothers, the playwright Kentucky Mann, and the actress Victoria Pate. When we finally came out from the backstage dressing-rooms, to no musical accompaniment at all, the audience boggled and then timidly began to applaud. (James says he heard someone exclaim "Holy cow!" over the less than robust clapping, but I can't confirm this.) *Midnight Chatter's* host, Tommy Carver, greeted us with boyish earnestness, as if we were the Pope.

"I know you must, uh, turn heads where you go, Mr. Self," he began, gulping theatrically and tapping an unsharpened pencil on his desk. "Uh, *Misters* Self, that is. But what is it—I mean, what question really disturbs you the most, turns you off to the attention you must attract?"

"That one," James said. "That's the one."

The audience boggled again, not so much at this lame witticism as at the fact that we'd actually spoken. A woman in the front row snickered.

"Okay," Carver said, doing a shaking-off-the-roundhouse bit with his head, "I deserved that. What's your biggest personal worry, then? I mean, is it something common to all of us or something, uh, peculiar to just you?" That *peculiar* drew a few more snickers.

"My biggest worry," James said, "is that Robert will try to murder me by committing suicide."

The audience, catching on, laughed at this. Carver was looking amused and startled at once—the studio monitor had him isolated in a close-up and he kept throwing coy glances at the camera.

"Why would Robert here—that's not a criminal face, after all—want to murder you?"

"He thinks I've been beating his time with his girl."

Over renewed studio laughter Carver continued to play his straight-man's role. "Now is *that* true, Robert?" I must have been looking fidgety or distraught—he wanted to pull me into the exchange.

"Of course it isn't," James said. "If he's got a date, I keep my eyes closed. I don't want to embarrass anybody."

It went like that right up to a commercial for dog food. Larry Blackman had written the routine for us, and James had practiced it so that he could drop in the laugh lines even if the right questions weren't asked. It was all a matter, said Blackman, of manipulating the material. *Midnight Chatter's* booking agent had expected us to be a "people guest" rather than a performer—one whose appeal lies in what he is rather than the image he projects. But Blackman said we could be both, James the comedian, me the sincere human expert on our predicament. Blackman's casting was adequate, I suppose; it was the script that was at heart gangrenous. Each head a half. The audience liked the half it had seen.

("He's coming back to the subject now, folks," James says. "See if he doesn't.")

After the English sheepdog had wolfed down his rations, I said, "Earlier James told you he was afraid I'd murder him by committing suicide—"

"Yeah. That took us all back a bit."

"Well, the truth is, James and I *have* discussed killing ourselves."

"Seriously?" Carver leaned back in his chair and opened his jacket.

"Very seriously. Because it's impossible for us to operate independently of each other. If I were to take an overdose of amphetamines, for instance, it would be *our* stomach they pumped."

Carver gazed over his desk at our midsection. "Yeah. I see what you mean."

"Or if James grew despondent and took advantage of his up time to slash our wrists, it would be both of us who bled to death. One's suicide is the other's murder, you see."

"The perfect crime," offered Victoria Pate.

"No," I replied, "because the act is its own punishment. James and I understand that very well. That's why we've made a pact to the effect that neither of us will attempt suicide until we've made a pact to do it together."

"You've made a pact to make a suicide pact?"

"Right," James said. "We're blood brothers that way. And that's how we expect to die."

Carver buttoned his jacket and ran a finger around the inside of his collar. "Not terribly soon, I hope. I don't believe this crowd is up for that sort of *Midnight Chatter* first."

"Oh, no," I assured him. "We're not expecting to take any action for several more years yet. But who knows? Circumstances will certainly dictate what we do, eventually."

Afterwards viewers inundated the network's switchboard with calls. Negative reaction to our remarks on suicide ran higher than questions about how the cameramen had "done it." Although Blackman congratulated us both heartily, The Monster didn't sleep very well that night.

"He thinks I've been beating his time with his girl."

Well, strange types scuttled after us while Blackman was running interference for Robert and James Self. The Monster devoured them, just as if they were Alpo. When it wasn't exhausted. We gave them stereophonic sweet nothings and the nightmares they couldn't have by themselves. Robert, for my and The Monster's sakes, didn't say nay. He indulged us. He never carped. Which has led to resentments on both sides, the right and the left. We've talked about these.

Before leaving town for parts north, west, and glittering, Robert and I were briefly engaged to be married. And not to each other. She was four years older than us. She worked in the front office of the local power company, at a desk you could reach only be weaving through a staggered lot of electric ranges, dishwashers, and hot-water heaters, most of them white, a few avocado.

We usually mail in our bill payments, or ask Velma to take them if she's going uptown—but this time, since our monthly charges had been fluctuating unpredictably and we couldn't ring through on the phone, I drove us across the two-lane in our business district. (Robert doesn't have a license.) Our future fiancée—I'm going to call her X—was patiently explaining to a group of housewives and day laborers the rate hike recently approved by the Public Service Commission, the consumer rebates ordered by the PSC for the previous year's disallowed fuel tax, and the summer rates soon to go into effect. Her voice was quavering a little. Through the door behind her desk we could see two grown men huddling out of harm's way, the storeroom light off.

(Robert wants to know, "Are you going to turn this into a How-We-Rescued-the-Maiden-from-the-Dragon story?")

("Fuck off," I tell him.)

(Robert would probably like The Monster to shrug his indifference to my rebuke—but I'm the one who's up now and I'm going to finish this blood-sucking reminiscence.)

Our appearance in the power company office had its usual impact. We, uh, turned heads. Three or four people moved away from the payments desk, a couple of others pretended—not very successfully—that we weren't there at all, and an old man in overalls stared. A woman we'd met once in Wilson & Cathet's said, "Good morning, Mr. Self," and dragged a child of indeterminate sex into the street behind her.

X pushed herself up from her chair and stood at her desk with her head hanging between her rigid supporting arms. "Oh, shit," she whispered. "This is too much."

"We'll come back when you're feeling better," a biddy in curlers said stiffly. The whole crew ambled out, even the man in overalls, his cheeks a shiny knot because of the chewing tobacco hidden there. Nobody used the aisle we were standing in to exit by.

The telephone rang. X took it off the hook, hefted it as if it were a truncheon, and looked at Robert and me without a jot of surprise.

"This number isn't working," she said into the receiver. "It's out of order." And she hung up.

On her desk beside the telephone I saw a battered paperback copy of *The Thorn Birds*. But X hadn't been able to read much that morning.

"Don't be alarmed," I said. X didn't look alarmed. "We're a lion tamer," I went on. "That's the head I stick into their mouths."

"Ha ha," Robert said.

A beginning. The game didn't last long, though. After we first invited her, X came over to Larimer Self's old house— *our* old house—nearly every night for a month, and she proved to be interested in us, both Robert and me, in ways that our little freak-show groupies never had any conception of. They came later, though, and maybe Robert and I didn't then recognize what an uncommon woman this hip and straightforward X really was. She regarded us as people, X did.

We would sit in our candle-lit living room listening to the Incredible String Band sing "Douglas Traherne Harding," among others, and talking about old movies. (The candles weren't for romance; they were to spite, with X's full approval, the power company.) In the kitchen, The Monster, mindless, baked us chocolate-chip cookies and gave its burned fingers to Robert or me to suck. Back in the living room, all of us chewing cookies, we talked like a cage full of gibbering monkeys, and laughed giddily, and finally ended up getting serious enough to discuss serious things like jobs and goals and long-dreamt-of tomorrows. But Robert and I let X do most of the talking and watched her in rapt mystification and surrender.

One evening, aware of our silence, she suddenly stopped and came over to us and kissed us both on our foreheads. Then, having led The Monster gently up the stairs, she showed it how to coordinate its untutored mechanical rhythms with those of a different but complementary sort of creature. Until then, it had been a virgin.

And the sentient Selfs? Well, Robert, as he put it, was "charmed, really charmed." Me, I was glazed over and strung out with a whole complex of feelings that most people regard as symptomatic of romantic love. How the hell could Robert be merely—I think I'm going to be sick—"charmed"?

("The bitterness again?")

("Well, goodbrother, we knew it would happen. Didn't we?")

We discussed X rationally and otherwise. She was from Ohio, and she had come to our town by way of a coastal resort where she had worked as a night clerk in a motel. The Arab oil embargo had taken that job away from her, she figured, but she had come inland with true resilience and captured another with our power company—on the basis of a college diploma, a folder of recommendations, and the snow job she'd done on old Grey Bates, her boss. She flattered Robert and me, though, by telling us that we were the only people in town she could be herself with. I think she meant it, too, and I'm pretty certain that Robert also believed her. If he's changed his mind of late, it's only because he has to justify his own subsequent vacillation and sabotage.

("James, damn you—!")

("All right. All right.")

About two weeks after X first started coming to our house in the evenings, Robert and I reached an agreement. We asked her to marry us. Both of us. All three of us. There was no other way.

She didn't say yes. She didn't say no. She said she'd have to think about it, and both Robert and I backed off to keep from crowding her. Later, after she'd somehow managed to get past the awkwardness of the marriage proposal, X leaned forward and asked us how we supported ourselves. It was something we'd never talked about before.

"Why do you ask?" Robert snapped. He began to grind his molars—that kind of sound gets conducted through the bones.

"It's Larimer's money," I interjected. "So much a month from the bank. And the house and grounds are paid for."

"Why do you ask?" Robert again demanded.

"I'm worried about you," X said. "Is Larimer's money going to last forever? Because you two don't *do* anything that I'm aware of, and I've always been uptight about people who don't make their own way. I've always supported myself, you see, and that's how I am. And I don't want to be uptight about my—well, my husbands."

Robert had flushed. It was affecting me, too—I could feel the heat rising in my face. "No," Robert said. "Larimer's legacy to us won't last forever."

X was wearing flowered shorts and a halter. She had her

clean bare feet on the dirty upholstery of our divan. The flesh around her navel was pleated enticingly.

"Do you think I want your money, Rob? I don't want your money. I'm just afraid that you may be regarding marriage to me as a panacea for all your problems. It's not, you know. There's a world that has to be lived in. You have to make your way in it for yourselves, married or not. Otherwise it's impossible to be happy. Don't you see? Marriage isn't just a string of party evenings, fellows."

"We know," I said.

"I suppose you do," X acknowledged readily enough. "Well, I do, too. I was married in Dayton. For six years."

"That doesn't matter to us. Does it, goodbrother?"

Robert swallowed. It was pretty clear he wished that business about Dayton had come out before, if only between the clicks of our record changer. "No," he said gamely. "It doesn't matter."

"One light," the Incredible String Band sang: *"the light that is one though the lamps be many."*

"Listen," X said earnestly. "If you have any idea what I'm talking about, maybe I *will* marry you. And I'll go anywhere you want to go to find the other key to your happiness. I just need a little time to think."

I forget who was up just then, Robert or me. Maybe neither of us. Who cares? The Monster trucked us across the room with the clear intention of devouring X on the dirty divan. The moment seemed sweet, even if the setting wasn't, and I was close to tears thinking that Robert and I were practically *engaged* to this decent and compassionate woman.

But The Monster failed us that night. Even though X received the three of us as her lover, The Monster wasn't able to perform and I knew with absolute certainty that its failure was Robert's fault.

"I'll marry you," X whispered consolingly. "There'll be other nights, other times. Sometimes this happens."

We *were* engaged! This fact, that evening, didn't rouse The Monster to a fever pitch of gentle passion—but me, at least, it greatly comforted. And on several successive evenings, as Robert apparently tried to acquiesce in our mutual good fortune, The Monster was as good as new again. I began to envision a house in the country, a job as a power-company lineman, and, God help me, children in whose childish features it might be possible to see something of all three of us.

("A bevy of bicephalic urchins? Or were you going to shoot for a Cerberus at every single birth?")

("Robert, damn you, *shut up!*")

And, then, without warning, Robert once again began sabotaging The Monster's poignant attempts to make it with X. Although capable of regarding its malfunctioning as a temporary phenomenon, X was also smart enough to realize that something serious underlay it. Sex? For the last week that Robert and I knew her, there wasn't any. I didn't mind that. What I minded was the knowledge that my own brother was using his power—a purely *negative* sort of power—to betray the both of us. I don't really believe that I've gotten over his betrayal yet. Maybe I never will.

So that's the sex part, goodbrother. As far as I'm concerned, that's the sex part. You did the death. I did the sex. And we were both undone by what you did and didn't do in both arenas. At least that's how I see it. . . . I had intended to finish this—but to hell with it, Robert. You finish it. It's your baby. Take it.

All right. We've engaged in so many recriminations over this matter that our every argument and counterargument is annotated. That we didn't marry X is probably my fault. Put aside the wisdom or the folly of our even hoping to marry— for in the end we didn't. We haven't. And the fault is mine.

You can strike that "probably" I use up there.

James once joked—he hasn't joked much about this affair—that I got "cold foot." After all, he was willing, The Monster was amenable, it was only goodbrother Robert who was weak. Perhaps. I only know that after our proposal I could never summon the same enthusiasm for X's visits as I had before. I can remember her saying, "You two don't *do* anything that I'm aware of, and I've always been uptight about people who don't make their own way." I'll always believe there was something smug and condescending—not to say downright insensitive—in this observation. And, in her desire to know how we had managed to support ourselves, something grasping and feral. She had a surface frankness under which her ulteriority bobbed like a tethered mine, and James never could see the danger.

("Bullshit. Utter bullshit.")

("Do you want this back, Mr. Self? It's yours if you want it.")

COLLABORATING

(James stares out the window at our Japanese yew.)

X was alerted to my disenchantment by The Monster's failure to perform. Even though she persevered for a time in the apparent hope that James would eventually win me over, she was as alert as a finch. She knew that I had gone sour on our relationship. Our conversations began to turn on questions like "Want another drink?" and "How'd it go today?" The Monster sweated.

Finally, on the last evening, X looked at me and said: "You don't really want us to marry, do you, Robert? You're afraid of what might happen. Even in the cause of your own possible happiness, you don't want to take any risks."

It was put up or shut up. "No," I told her: "I don't want us to marry. And the only thing I'm afraid of is what you might do to James and me by trying to impose your inequitable love on us in an opportunistic marriage."

"*Opportunistic?*" She made her voice sound properly disbelieving.

"James and I are going to make a great deal of money. We don't have to depend on Larimer's legacy. And you knew that the moment you saw us, didn't you?"

X shook her head. "Do you really think, Rob, that I'd marry—" here she chose her words very carefully—"two-men-with-one-body in order to improve my own financial situation?"

"People have undergone sex changes for no better reason."

"That's speculation," she said. "I don't believe it."

James, his head averted from mine, was absolutely silent. I couldn't even hear him breathing.

X shifted on the divan. She looked at me piercingly, as if conspicuous directness would persuade me of her sincerity: "Rob, aren't you simply afraid that somehow I'll come between you and James?"

"That's impossible," I answered.

"I know it is. That's why you're being unreasonable to even assume it could happen."

"Who assumed such a thing?" I demanded. "But I do know this—you'll never be able to love us both equally, will you? You'll never be able to bestow your heart's affection on me as you bestow it on James."

She looked at the ceiling, exhaled showily, then stood up and crossed to the chair in which The Monster was sitting.

She kissed me on the bridge of my nose, turned immediately to James and favored him with a similar benediction.

"I would have tried," she said. "Bye, fellas."

James kept his head averted, and The Monster shook with a vehemence that would have bewildered me had I not understood how sorely I had disappointed my brother—even in attempting to save us both from a situation that had very nearly exploded in our faces.

X didn't come back again, and I wouldn't let James phone her. Three days after our final good-bye, clouds rolled in from the Gulf and it rained as if in memory of Noah. During the thunderstorm our electricity went out. It didn't come back on all that day. A day later it was still out. The freezer compartment in our refrigerator began to defrost.

James called the power company. X wasn't there, much to my relief. Bates told us that she had given notice the day before and walked out into the rain without her paycheck. He couldn't understand why our power should be off if we had paid our bills as conscientiously as we said. Never mind, though, he'd see to it that we got our lights back. The whole episode was tangible confirmation of X's pettiness.

It wasn't long after she had left that I finally persuaded James to let me write Larry Blackman in Atlanta. We came out of seclusion. As X might have cattily put it, we finally got around to *doing* something. With a hokey comedy routine and the magic of our inborn uniqueness we threw ourselves into the national spotlight and made money hand over fist. James was so clever and cooperative that I allowed him to feed The Monster whenever the opportunity arose, and there were times, I have to admit, when I thought that neither it nor James was capable of being sated. But not once did I fail to indulge them. Not once—

All right. That's enough, goodbrother. I know you have some feelings. I saw you in that Howard Johnson's in St. Augustine. I remember how you cried when Charles Laughton fell off the cathedral of Notre Dame. And when King Kong plummeted from the Empire State Building. And when the creature from 20,000 fathoms was electrocuted under the roller coaster on Coney Island. And when I suggested to you at the end of our last road tour that maybe it was time to make the pact that we had so long ago agreed to make one day. You weren't ready, you said. And I am unable by the rules of both love and decency to make that pact and carry out its articles without your approval. Have I unilaterally rejected your veto? No. No, I haven't.

So have a little pity.

Midnight. James has long since nodded away, giving control to me. Velma called this afternoon. She says she'll be over tomorrow afternoon for checkers. That seemed to perk James up a little. But I'm hoping to get him back on the road before this month is out. Activity's the best thing for him now—the best thing for both of us. I'm sure he'll eventually realize that.

Lights out.

I brush my lips against my brother's sleeping cheek.

MARRIAGE

Robert Aickman

In a recent review of an Aickman story, Joanna Russ confessed in liking it that she could not shake the impression that Aickman is a woman writing under a male pseudonym—although in fairness to her, she did not imply that her impression was more than just that. Robert Fordyce Aickman is a member of a number of boards and organizations in Britain, including London Opera Society Ltd., Northampton Drama Club, and the Inland Waterways Association (which he founded). Outside the horror field, he has written *Know Your Waterways*, and an autobiography, *The Attempted Rescue*. He is the grandson of Richard Marsh, the writer of thrillers who is best remembered, probably, for *The Beetle*. Since 1951, Aickman has been producing horror stories such as "The Trains," "Ringing the Changes," "Pages from a Young Girl's Diary," and "The Real Road to the Church," among a great many others, establishing a body of work noted for a depth of insight that has surpassed that of any other writer in the horror field of that period, with the exception of Fritz Leiber. In short, Robert Aikman may be the most important and skilled writer of horror fiction now practicing, as this powerful story attests.

Helen Black and Ellen Brown: just a simple coincidence, and representative of the very best that life offers most of us by way of comedy and diversion. A dozen harmless accidents of that kind and one could spend a year of one's life laughing and wondering, and ever and anon recur to the topic in the years still to come.

Laming Gatestead met Helen Black in the gallery of the theater. The only thing that mattered much about the play or the production was that Yvonne Arnaud was in it, which resulted in Helen adoring the play, whereas Laming merely liked it. However, the topic gave them something to talk about. This was welcome, because it was only in the second intermission that Laming had plucked up courage (or whatever the relevant quality was) to speak at all.

Helen was a slightly austere-looking girl, with a marked bone structure and pale eyes. Her pale hair was entirely off the face, so that her equally pale ears were conspicuous. She might not have been what Laming would have selected had he been a playboy in Brussels or a casting director with the latest "Spotlight" on his knees; but, in present circumstances, the decisive elements were that Helen was all by herself and still quite young, whereas he was backward, blemished, and impecunious. Helen wore a delightfully simple black dress, very neatly kept. When they rose at the end of the applause, to which Laming had contributed with pleasing vigor, Helen proved to be considerably the taller.

Secretly, Laming was very surprised when she agreed to come with him for coffee and even more surprised when, after a second cup, she accepted his invitation to another gallery, this time with Marie Tempest as the attraction. A night was firmly settled upon for the following week. They were to find one another inside. Helen had appreciated how little money Laming might have, and being entertained to coffee was quite enough at that stage of their acquaintanceship.

He took her hand, only to shake it, of course, but even that was something. It was, however, a dry, bony hand, more neutral, he felt, than his own.

"Oh," he said, as if he had been speaking quite casually. "I don't know your name."

"Helen Black."

"Perhaps I'd better have your address? I might get a sore throat."

"42 Washwood Court, N.W.6."

Of course his Chessman's Diary for that year had been carefully though unobtrusively at the ready: an annual gift from his Aunty Antoinette.

"I'm Laming Gatestead."

"Like the place in the North?"

"Not Gatestead. Gatestead."

"So sorry." Her eyes seemed to warm a little in the ill-lit back street, on to which the gallery exit romantically debouched.

"Everyone gets it wrong."

"And what an unusual Christian name!"

"My father was keen on Sir Laming Worthington-Evans. He used to be secretary of state for war. He's dead now."

"Which of them is?"

"Both are, I'm afraid."

"I *am* sorry. Was your father a soldier?"

"No, he just liked to follow political form, as he called it."

They parted without Laming's address in Drayton Park having had to be prematurely divulged.

After that, they saw Leslie Banks and Edith Evans in *The Taming of the Shrew*, and before they had even stirred their coffee, Helen said, "My roommate and I would like you to come to supper one of these evenings. Not before eight o'clock, please, and don't expect too much."

Roommates were not always joined in such invitations, but Laming realized that, after all, Helen knew virtually nothing about him and might well have been advised not necessarily to believe a word men actually said.

"My roommate will be doing most of the cooking," said Helen.

Ah!

"What's her name?"

"Ellen Brown."

"What an extraordinary coincidence!"

"Isn't it? How about next Wednesday? Ellen comes home early on Wednesdays and will have more time."

"What does Ellen do?"

"She advises on baby clothes."

"Not exactly my world. Well, not yet."

"Ellen's very nice," said Helen firmly.

Helen's face offered much expression, Laming reflected. Within her own limits, she seemed to do perfectly well without it.

And, indeed, Ellen *was* nice. In fact, she was just about the nicest girl that Laming had ever encountered (if that was the word). Her handshake was soft, lingering, and very slightly moist, and the deep V of her striped jumper implied a trustfulness that went straight to Laming's heart. She had large brown eyes, a gentle nose, and thick, short hair, very dark, into which one longed to plunge first one's fingers and then one's mouth. Laming found himself offering her the box of White Magic peppermint creams he had brought with him, before realizing that of course he should have proffered it first to Helen.

In fact, Ellen, herself so like a soft round peppermint cream, immediately passed the unopened box to Helen, which hardly made an ideal start to what was bound to be a tricky evening.

Ellen looked much younger than Helen. Fifteen years? Laming wondered. But he was no good at such assessments and had several times in his life made slightly embarrassing errors.

"I'm quite ready when you both are," said Ellen, as if Helen had contributed nothing to the repast. There was no smell of cooking and no sign of a teacloth. Everything was calm and controlled.

"Laming would like a glass of sherry first," said Helen. She wore a simple dark-blue dress.

Again Laming had difficulty in not raising his glass primarily to Ellen.

There was a little soup and then a cutlet each, with a few runner beans and pommes a la Suisse.

Helen sat at the head of the small rectangular table, with Laming on her left and Ellen on her right.

Laming was unable to meet Ellen's lustrous eyes for more than a second at a time, but there was no particular difficulty in gazing for longer periods at the glimpses of Ellen's slip, peony in color. Ellen's hand movements were beautiful too.

Helen was talking about how much she adored Leslie Banks. She would go absolutely anywhere to see him, do absolutely anything. She said such things without a trace of gush or even any particular animation. It was possibly a manner she had acquired in the civil service. (She was concerned in some way with poultry statistics.)

"I often *dream* of that mark on his face," said Helen calmly.

"Is it a birthmark?" asked Ellen. Her very voice was like sweet chestnut puree at Christmas and, in the same way, offered only sparingly. She had said only five things since Laming had been in the room. Laming knew because he had counted them. He also remembered them, word perfect.

"I think it's a war wound," said Laming, speaking toward his cutlet.

"Ellen wouldn't know," said Helen. "She doesn't follow the stage very much. We *must* go and see Raymond Massey some time, Laming. I adore him too, though not as much as Leslie Banks."

"Raymond Massey is a Canadian," offered Laming.

"But with hardly a trace of an accent."

"I once saw Fred Terry when I was a kid," said Laming. "In *Sweet Nell of Old Drury*."

"I was brought up in Sidmouth, and Ellen in Church Winshull," said Helen.

"Only North London," said Laming, with exaggerated modesty. "But I saw Fred Terry and Julia Neilson at the King's Hammersmith when visiting my aunty."

"I simply long to go to Stratford-on-Avon," said Helen. "I believe Fabia Drake's doing frightfully well there."

"Yes, it would be lovely," said Laming.

"I adore opera too. I long to go to Bayreuth."

Laming was too unsure of the details to make an effective reply to that; so he concentrated on paring away the hard narrow strip from the upward edge of his cutlet.

Later there were orange segments and cream; while Helen spoke of life in South Devon, where she had lived as a child and Laming had twice been on farmhouse holidays.

Ellen brought them coffee, while they sat on the settee. Her eyes were reflected in the fluid. No odalisque could have made slighter movements to more effect.

The peppermint creams came partially into their own.

"I don't eat many sweet things," said Helen. "You *must* remember, Laming?"

The worst part was that now he *did* remember. She had submitted quite a list of such items in the cafe after Marie Tempest. What she liked most was chicken perfectly plain. What she liked least was anything rich. What a crashing mistake he had made in the selection of his gift! But what else would have been practicable?

Ellen, however, was making up for her roommate. She was eating cream after cream, and without even asking before taking another, which made it all the more intimate.

"I long to visit Japan and see the Noh." said Helen.

Laming did not know about that at all and could only suppose it was a relative of the mikado, about whom there was something unusual. Or perhaps it was a huge stone thing, like the Sphinx.

"When I get my certificate, I'm going on a real bust," said Laming, then blushed at the word. "*If* I get my certificate, that is."

"Surely you will, Laming?"

"No one can ever be quite sure."

Ellen was twisting about in the armchair, arranging herself better.

Laming told a rather detailed story about the older colleague in the firm who had left no stone unturned but still lacked a certificate. "It's held up his marriage for more than eight years. He was there long before I was."

"I'm sure that won't happen to you, Laming. Shall we ask Ellen to give us some more coffee? Don't you adore coffee? I drink it all night to keep me awake."

Laming assumed that it was her statistics. Increasingly, civil servants were having to take work home, as if they had been in real business. Laming had read about it in the evening paper, more than once, in fact.

"Not too full, Ellen! I shall slop it over myself."

"Would you like to see my old programs, Laming? Ellen won't mind, I'm sure."

But Laming had managed to glimpse a meaning look in Ellen's soft features. It contrasted noticeably with Helen's habitual inexpressiveness.

"*I* should like it, but I think we should do something that Ellen can join in."

He was quite surprised at himself and did not dare to look at Helen that time.

"Shall we play three-handed Rocket?"

"I'm afraid I don't know the rules."

"I'm nothing like clever enough for them," said Ellen, her sixth or seventh remark.

Laming had ceased to count. He knew he could not carry any more remarks faithfully enough in his mind.

"Well, then, we'll just talk," said Helen. "What are we going to do next, Laming?"

"There's that thing at the Apollo."

"Yes, I long to see that."

"I can't remember a single thing that's been said about it."

"We mustn't always allow our minds to be made up for us."

They had all become quite chummy, Laming realized; nor could it be the passing effect of alcohol. At that moment he felt that he had been really accepted into the household. Instinctively, his manners fell to pieces a little.

At the end of the evening, Helen said, "You must come again often. We like having company, don't we, Ellen?"

Ellen simply nodded, but with her lovely, almost elfin, smile. She was fiddling with the bottom edge of her jumper, using both hands. The narrow horizontal stripes were in a sort of gray, a sort of blue, a sort of pink. Her skirt was fawn.

"I should very much like to, Helen," replied Laming, in a public-school manner, though the place he had been to was pretty near the bottom of any realistic list.

"Well, do. Now, Laming, we meet a week from today at the Apollo."

She imparted her dry grip. Laming could not but remember that only three or four weeks ago it had all but thrilled him. When in bed, he must look at his Chessman's Diary to see *exactly* how long ago it had been.

Ellen merely stood smiling, but with her hands locked together behind her skirt, a posture that moved Laming considerably.

On the way home, however, he was wrestling with a problem more familiar: the problem of how to attempt reciprocation in these cases, when one could not at all afford it; these cases in which hospitality could hardly be rejected if one were to remain a social being at all. The complaint against life might be that even if one expended one's every mite, which would be both unwise and impracticable, the social level accomplished did not really justify the sacrifice. Most urgently one needed to start at a higher level: *ab initio, ab ovo*. And, if one hadn't, what really was the use?

But after business came pleasure, and Laming, awake in bed, spent a long, long time musing on Ellen, and twisting about restlessly. It was gray dawn before, in a sudden panic, he fell asleep.

In fact, *was* thinking about Ellen a pleasure? Apart from the inner turmoil caused by her very existence, there was the certainty that she was quite other than she seemed, and the extreme uncertainty about what to do next in order to advance with her.

When his mother brought him his cup of tea, he looked at her with sad eyes, then quickly turned away, lest she notice.

However, for the first time in Laming's life, something extraordinary happened, something that a third party might have marveled at for months and drawn new hope from.

Only two days later a crisis had arisen in the office: one of the partners required a parcel to be delivered at an address "down Fulham way," as the partner put it; and Laming had been the first to volunteer for the job—or perhaps, as he subsequently reflected, the junior who could best be spared.

"You can take a No. 14 most of the distance," the partner had said. "If you get stuck, ask someone. But do take care, old chap. That thing's fragile." Whereupon he had guffawed and returned to his den.

Laming had clambered off the bus at more or less the spot the partner had indicated and had looked around for someone to guide him further. At such times, so few people look as if they could possibly know; so few are people one could care or dare to address at all. In the end, and without having to put down the heavy parcel, Laming had obtained directions from a middle-aged district nurse, though she had proved considerably less informed than Laming had taken for granted. In no time at all, Laming had been virtually lost, and the parcel twice or thrice its former weight.

And now he had come to a small park or municipal garden, with mongrels running about the kids in one corner, breaking things up. He was very nearly in tears. At the outset, it had seemed likely that offering to perform a small service would stand well for him in his career, but that notion had gone into reverse and japed at him within five minutes of his starting to wait for the bus. He could hardly carry the parcel much farther. Ought he to spend money of his own on a taxi? If one were to appear?

And then he saw Ellen. The road was on his left, the dark-green park railings were on his right, and there were very few people on the pavement. Ellen was walking toward him. He nearly fainted, but responsibility for the parcel somehow saved him.

"Hullo, Laming!"

It was as if they were the most tender and long-standing of friends, for whom all formality was quite unnecessary.

"Hullo, Ellen!"

He too spoke very low, though really they were almost alone in the world.

"Come and sit down."

He followed her along the length of railing and through the gate. In a sense, it was quite a distance, but she said nothing more. He had heard that, in circumstances such as these, burdens became instantly and enduringly lighter, but he was not finding that with the parcel.

She was wearing a sweater divided into diamonds of different colors, but with nothing garish about it; and the same fawn skirt.

Once or twice she looked back with an encouraging smile. Laming almost melted away, but again the parcel helped to stabilize him.

He had naturally supposed that they would sit on a seat. There were many seats, made years ago of wooden beams set in green cast iron frames, some almost perpendicular, some sloping lasciviously backward. Many had been smashed up by children, and none at that moment seemed in any way occupied.

But Ellen sat down at the foot of a low grassy bank, even though there was an empty seat standing almost intact at the top of the rise. Laming, after a moment for surprise and hesitation, quite naturally sat down beside her. It was early May and the grass seemed dry enough, though the sky was overcast and depressing. He deposited the parcel as carefully as he could. It was a duty to keep close to it.

"I want you," said Ellen. "Please take me." She lifted his left hand and laid it on her right thigh, but under her skirt. He felt her rayon panties. It was the most wonderful moment in his life.

He knew perfectly well also that with the right person such things as this normally do not happen, but only infrequently with the wrong person.

He twisted around and, inserting his right hand under her jumper until it reached up to her sweetly silken breast, kissed her with passion. He had never kissed anyone with passion before.

"Please take me," said Ellen again.

One trouble was of course that he never had, and scarcely

knew how. Chaff from the chaps really tells one very little. Another trouble was "lack of privacy," as he had heard it termed. He doubted very much whether most people—even most men—started in such an environment, whatever they might do later.

He glanced around as best he could. It was true that the park, quite small though it was, now seemed also quite empty. The children must be wrecking pastures new. And the visibility was low and typical.

"Not the light for cricket," said Laming. As a matter of fact, there were whitish things at the other end, which he took to be sight screens.

"Please," said Ellen, in her low, urgent voice. Her entire conversational method showed how futile most words really are. She began to range around him with her hand.

"But what about—?"

"It's *all right*. Please."

Still, it really was the sticking point, the pons asinorum, the gilt off the gingerbread, as everyone knew.

"Please," said Ellen.

She kicked off her shoes, partly gray, partly black; and he began to drag down her panties. The panties were in the most beautiful, dark-rose color: her secret, hidden from the world.

It was all over much more quickly than anyone would have supposed. But it was wrong that it should have been so. He knew that. If it were ever to become a regular thing for him, he must learn to think much more of others, much less of himself. He knew that perfectly well.

Fortunately the heavy parcel seemed still to be where he had placed it. The grass had, however, proved to be damp after all.

He could hardly restrain a cry. Ellen was streaked and spattered with muddy moisture, her fawn skirt, one would say, almost ruined; and he realized that he was spattered also. It would be impossible for him to return to the office that day. He would have to explain some fiction on the telephone, and then again to his mother, who, however, he knew, could be depended upon with the cleaners—if, this time, cleaning could do any good. He and Ellen must have drawn the moisture from the ground with the heat of their bodies.

Ellen seemed calm enough, nonetheless, though she was not precisely smiling. For a moment, Laming regretted that she spoke so little. He would have liked to know what she was thinking. Then he realized that it would be useless anyway. Men never know what girls are thinking, and least of all at moments such as this. Well, obviously.

He smiled at her uneasily.

The two of them were staring across what might later in the year become the pitch. At present, the gray-greenness of everything was oddly meaningless. In mercy, there was still almost no one within the park railings; that is, no one visible, for it was inconceivable that in so publicly available a place, only a few miles from Oxford Circus and Cambridge Circus, there should at so waking an hour be no one absolutely. Without shifting himself from where he was seated, Laming began to glance around more systematically. Already he was frightened, but then he was almost always more frightened than not. In the end, he looked over his shoulder.

He froze.

On the seat almost behind them, the cast-iron and wood seat that Ellen had silently disdained, Helen was now seated. She wore the neat and simple black dress she had worn in the first place. Her expression was as expressionless as ever.

Possibly Laming even cried out.

He turned back and sank his head between his knees.

Ellen put her soft hand on his forearm. "Don't *worry*, Laming," she said.

She drew him back against her bosom. It seemed to him best not to struggle. There must be an answer of some kind, conceivably, even, one that was not wholly bad.

"*Please* don't worry, Laming," said Ellen cooingly.

And when the time came for them to rise up finally, the seat was empty. Truly, it was by then more overcast than ever: Stygian might be the very word.

"Don't forget your parcel," said Ellen, not merely conventionally but with genuine solicitude.

She linked her arm affectionately through his and uttered no further word as they drew away.

He was quite surprised that the gate was still open.

"Where shall we meet next?" asked Ellen.

"I have my job," said Laming, torn about.

"Where is it?"

"We usually call it Bloomsbury."

She looked at him. Her eyes were wise and perhaps mocking.

"Where do you live?"

"Near Finsbury Park."

"I'll be there on Saturday. In the park. Three o'clock in the American Garden."

She reached up and kissed him most tenderly with her kissing lips. She was, of course, far, far shorter than Helen.

"What about Helen?" he asked.

"You're going to the Apollo with Helen on Wednesday," she replied unanswerably.

And, curiously enough, he had then found the address for the parcel almost immediately. He had just drifted on in a thoroughly confused state of mind, and there the house obviously was, though the maid looked very sniffy indeed about the state of his suit in the light from the hall, not to speak of his countenance and hands; and from below a dog had growled deeply as he slouched down the steps.

Soon, the long-threatened rain began.

Of course, had he been a free agent, Laming was so frightened that he would not have seen Ellen again. But he was far from a free agent. If he had refused, Ellen might have caused trouble with Helen, whom he had to meet on Wednesday: women were far, far closer to other women in such matters, than men were to men. Alternatively, he could never just leave Ellen standing about indefinitely in the American Garden; he was simply not made that way; and if he were to attempt a deferment with her, all her sweetness would turn to gall. There was very little scope for a deferment, in any case: the telephone was not at all a suitable instrument, in the exact circumstances, and with his nervous temperament. And there was something else, of course: Laming now had a girl, and such an easygoing one, so cozy, so gorgeous in every way; and he knew that he would be certain to suffer within himself later if he did not do what he could to hold on to her—at least to the extent of walking up to the American Garden and giving it one more try. Helen or no Helen. It is always dangerous to put anything second to the need we all feel for love.

It was colder that day, and she was wearing a little coat. It was in simple midbrown and had square buttons, somewhere between bone and pearl in appearance. She was dodging about among the shrubs, perhaps in order to keep warm. Laming had wondered about that on the way up.

"Hullo, stranger!"

"Hullo, Ellen!"

She kissed her inimitable kiss, disregarding the retired railwaymen sitting about in greatcoats and mufflers, waiting for the park cafe to open.

"We're going somewhere," said Ellen.

"Just as well," said Laming, with a shiver, partly nerves, partly sex, partly cool, damp treacherous weather. But of course he had struck entirely the wrong and unromantic note. "Where are we going?" he asked.

"You'll see," said Ellen, and took his arm in her affectionate way, entirely real.

The railwaymen glowered motionlessly, awaiting strong tea, awaiting death, seeing death before them, not interfering.

Ellen and Laming tramped silently off, weaving around bushes, circumventing crowded baby carriages.

Orsino, Endymion, Adonis: the very roads were named after lovers. Laming had never noticed that before. He had always approached the park from the south, and usually with his mother, who did not walk fast and often gasped painfully. Once in the park she had downed a whole bottle of Tizer. How they had all laughed about that, forever and a day!

Around this turn and that, in the queer streets north of the park, Ellen and Laming stole, tightly locked together; until, within the shake of a lamb's tail as it seemed, they were ascending a narrow flight of steep black stairs. Ellen had unlocked the front door, as if to the manner born, and of course she was going up first. She unlocked another door and they were home and dry.

"Did it work out all right about your clothes? The mud, I mean?"

She merely smiled at him.

"Who lives here?"

"My sister."

"Not Helen!"

Of course not Helen. What a silly thing to say! How stupidly impulsive! Ellen said nothing.

There were little drawings on the walls by imitators of Peter Scott and Mabel Lucie Attwell, but all much faded by years of summer sun while the tenant was out at work.

Or tenants. Most of the floor space was occupied by an extremely double divan, even a triple divan, Laming idiotically speculated, squarer than square. It hardly left room for the little round white table, with pansies and mignonette round the edge. All seemed clean, trim, self-respecting. The frail white chairs for dinner parties were neatly tucked in.

"Is your sister married?"

Ellen continued silent. She stood in front of him, smiling, abiding.

He took off her coat and placed it on the hanger on the door. There was a housecoat hanging there already, sprayed with faded yellow Chinamen and faded blue pagodas and faded pink dragons with one dot in each eye.

"She won't barge in on us suddenly?"

Ellen threw back her head. Her neck was beautifully shaped, her skin so radiant, that it seemed all wrong to touch it. She was wearing a little mauve dress, fastening up the back, and with a pleated skirt.

Laming put his hands gently on her breasts, but she did not raise her head.

When he lifted it for her, it fell forward on her front, in renewed token of uninterest in sociable conventionalities, in the accepted tensions.

Laming unfastened her dress and drew it over her head. Unskillfully though he had done it, her hair looked almost the same, and, in what slight disorder had arisen, even more alluring.

She was wearing nothing but a plum-colored garter belt and lovely, lovely stockings.

Laming wished there was somewhere where he himself could undress alone. There were various doors. The kitchenette. The bath and toilet. A cupboard or two for rainwear and evening dresses and ironing boards. It would look silly to open so many doors, one after the other. Laming drew the curtain across the window, as if that made any difference. In any case, and owing to mechanical difficulties, he had drawn it only half across the window.

He undressed with his back to her, as if that made any difference either.

She would be naked by now, and half laughing at him, half fractious, because he had never before knowingly seen a naked adult woman.

When, lumpishly, he turned to her, she had removed her garter belt, but still wore her stockings, now secured by garters. She had brought them out from somewhere. They were bunched up in pink, violet, and black lace. She was no longer smiling. She looked as serious and ethereal as an angel on a card.

"What about—?" There was that, and everyone knew it.

"Come in," said Ellen, climbing in herself.

The immense divan was as the sea. Clinging together, he and she were drowning in it, down, drown, down, drown. As they dropped, all the way, she showed him small, wonderful things, which tied him in fetters, clogged him with weights.

Hours later, as it seemed, it was over; and until who could tell when? It had continued for so long that he was afraid to look at his watch. *Post coitum omne animal triste est,* as the boozy classics and history master had pointed out to the middle fifth, Laming's highest form in the school.

However, it was still daylight. Could it be the next day, Sunday? Had his mother been left alone in the house all night? Of course not, but the real trouble was the utter and total irreconcilability between this life, real life perhaps, and daily life. Laming apprehended this with a lurch like a broken leg or arm: a fracture that could never mend.

Ellen was pottering about, doing things to herself, making tea.

It occurred to Laming that exactly at the point where this life, real life, and daily life were at right angles, stood Helen, or, rather, sat on a park bench. Laming, naked in some almost unknown person's bed, actually found himself looking around the room for her, and with small starts of terror, as when jabbed by a schoolfriend's penknife.

Ellen emerged from the kitchenette with two cups of tea on a small tray. It had been a gift offer and was covered with eider ducks, the name of the firm scrupulously omitted. Ellen had straightened both her stockings and her tight, frilly garters. Laming could still feel the latter tickling his thighs when it had all begun.

Tea was just what he wanted; Ellen had somehow known that, as his mother always knew it. Ellen was drinking it only for company's sake and making eyes at him over the rim of the cup. God, the illusion there can be in a single cup of hot tea! In the first cup, anyway. But it would be quite like Helen to materialize ever so faintly, just when he was relaxing, though it would have been difficult for her to find anywhere suitable to sit in the bijou flatlet. The only armchair was filled with copies of *The Natural World,* so that Ellen was sitting

MARRIAGE

on the foot of the divan, with her legs pressed together in the most ladylike degree. Her breasts were firm as cockleshells.

She rose chastely and came for his empty cup.

"More?"

He faintly shook his head. Normally, he would have accepted and probably gone on accepting, but now he felt unequal even to drinking tea. He was a haunted man.

Ellen took the cups back into the kitchenette, and he could hear her tidily washing them up. She put the milk back in the refrigerator, and what was presumably the ingredient itself back into a little cabinet which shut with a click and was probably marked *Tea*. She returned to the living room and, standing before a small octagonal looking glass in which the reproduction of "The Childhood of John the Baptist" had previously been reflected, began to comb her silky but sturdy hair.

Laming assumed from this that they were about to depart and felt most disinclined. It was as when at last one reaches Bexhill or Gognor Regis and the beach is calling, but never before has one felt more promise to lie in mere musing in and upon one's new bed and, thus, half slumbering one's life away.

Ellen combed and combed; then she tied a wide cherry-colored sash around her breasts and reentered the divan with him. He could smell the scent she had sprayed on her neck and shoulders in the bathroom. Even her eyes were brighter than ever under the influence of some ointment. Her hand began once more to explore Laming. To his surprise, he roused up immediately, and was bemused no more. It might have been the brief and partial breaking in of daily life that had half stupefied him. He tied Ellen's sash tighter than ever with the strength that is supposedly male; so that her bright eyes clouded like pools.

Hours later once more; it was not merely dark but black as blindfold, and they were both lying on the floor, relishing its hardness through the carpet, which stretched from wall to wall, though that was but a short way, however one measured it. Ellen's body was hard too, now that there was resistance. Their legs tangled like rubbery plants. She showed him things that can only be done in the dark, however clumsily, things he would never be able quite to evade or reject.

Laming felt an agonizing, sciatic pain and writhed upwards, though Ellen's arms were still around his waist.

He saw that from what must have been the ceiling, or at least very near the ceiling, a pair of pale eyes were looking expressionlessly down on him, on the two of them. He could even see some hint of the bone structure surrounding the eyes. Then there was another pain, like a gutting knife ripping out his tendon.

He yelled out, from the pain and from the vision. Instantly, Ellen was all softness and tenderness, a minstering angel of the midnight. He clenched his eyes shut, as he had so often done in childhood and at school, however foolish it might seem to do it when all was dark anyway.

Midnight! Or could it be even later? He had no idea what had become of his watch. He only knew that his mother must have started worrying long since. Her dependence on him was complete, so that much of the time he quite forgot about her.

He was lying on his back with Ellen on top of him, embracing him, enveloping him, enchanting him. Her released bosom pressed tenderly down on him, and her mouth rested softly on his chin. In the end, she had reconciled him to reopening his screwed up eyes, which were about the level of her head. He had to give himself a mental jerk in order to perform the operation, but he really knew quite well that the other eyes, or face, would have gone. They never remained for very long.

When they had the light on and were walking about again, he still felt the sciatic stress, very much so. He was positively limping, though Ellen could not have been nicer about it, more sympathetic. It proved not to be midnight at all, let alone later. It was only about quarter to eleven.

"Doesn't your sister want to come home sometimes?"

"Not when *we* want the flat, silly."

They walked, arm in arm, to Major House station. Even the jazz on the radio had mostly stopped.

"I'm seeing Helen on Wednesday," he remarked idiotically.

"And me on Saturday," she responded. "Same time and place. OK?"

There was a kind of pause.

"OK, Laming?"

"OK," said Laming.

She kissed him softly and disappeared down the station steps with complete composure, utter serenity.

It was only just after quarter past when Laming put his

key in his mother's front door. Though his mother was pale, she was so glad to see him that it was quite easy to explain that another chap had suggested that he and Laming go to the movies and that the picture had proved much longer than they had thought, and so forth. The film had been about climbing in the High Andes, Laming said, and there were wonderful shots of llamas.

"I thought they were in the Himalayas, Laming."

"These were llamas with two l's, Mumsey dear. As if they were Welsh llamas. They have almond eyes and they spit."

The explanations were practicable because he had in fact seen the film, without having bothered to tell her. It had been shown some weeks ago in the canteen next door to the office, where many of the men found their way for lunch. It was being circulated to such places by some adult educational organization. The oddest things prove in the end to have a use of some kind, Laming reflected. He had often noticed that.

"What's the matter with your leg, Laming?"

"I think I've twisted it somehow."

"Better see Dr. Pokorna on Monday before you go to work."

"It'll be quite well by Monday, I promise, Mumsey."

She still looked doubtful, as well as pale.

"I promise."

What he could never decide about her was whether she really took it for granted that girls were a matter of indifference to him.

"Something wrong with your leg, Laming?"

"I seem to have twisted it, Helen. I've no idea where."

"What have you been doing with yourself since our little party?"

"Same old grind." Really, he could not bring himself to meet her eyes. He did not see how he ever again could meet them, look right into their paleness. What was he to do?

"Not many people here," he said.

"We mustn't let ourselves be affected by numbers. We must behave and react exactly as we should if the theater were packed."

"Yes, of course," said Laming, though he did not know how he was going to do that either.

Furthermore, the curtain simply would not go up. Even

though no one new had come in for ten minutes by Laming's watch, the watch that had been lost in the big bed.

"Did you enjoy our party?" asked Helen.

"You know I did, Helen."

"Ellen said she thought you didn't like her."

"Of course I liked her, Helen."

"Don't you think she's very attractive in her own way?"

"I'm sure she is."

"I sometimes feel quite a shadow when I'm with her, even though I may be that much cleverer."

"She doesn't seem to speak very much."

"Ellen's a very nice person, but she happens to be the exact opposite to me in almost every way," explained Helen. "I should adore to change places with her once in a while. Don't you think that would be great fun?"

A man in a dinner jacket had come onto the front of the stage and was reading from a piece of paper, having first assumed a pair of spectacles, while they watched it. It appeared that one of the company had a sudden attack of gastric flu; time had passed while his understudy had been sought for on the telephone; and it had now been decided that someone else's understudy should come on in the proper costume and read the part from the script.

"I thought that understudies were always waiting about in the wings," said Laming.

"I expect there isn't much money with this production," said Helen. "It's a shame about the poor fellow being ill, isn't it?"

"I've never heard of him."

"It might have been his big chance," said Helen, "and now it's gone, because the play might be off before he's better."

"We mustn't think about that," said Laming, following her earlier and more sanguine cue.

How on earth was he to entertain her at the end? After that party? What exactly would she expect? The problem had been worrying him all day. He had become involved with two girls when he could not afford even one, never had been able to and probably never would.

Descending the many steps to ground level, Helen summed up excellently: the rest of the cast had naturally been affected by the zombie in their midst, and it would be unfair to judge the play, as a play, by this single overcast representation. "I adore blank verse, anyway," Helen concluded.

Laming hadn't even realized.

"Especially this new kind," said Helen. "It can be terribly exciting, don't you think?"

Of course she gave no sign of being excited in the least, because she never did.

"Would you like a Welsh rarebit tonight, Helen? By way of a little change?"

"Oh, no, I can't eat things like cheese. Our usual cup of coffee is absolutely all I need. Besides, it makes a kind of tradition for us, don't you think?"

At the end, she suggested that next time they go to *Reunion in Vienna*, with the Lunts.

He really could not suggest that there might be difficulty in finding a free evening, and he doubted whether she could suggest it either, even in quite other circumstances.

"The Lunts are very popular," he pointed out. "We might not get in."

"Let's try. If we fail, we can always go to something else. We shall be in the middle of Theaterland. What about a week from today?"

"Could we make it Thursday?"

They agreed to meet in the queue that time.

They still shook hands each time they parted, though, by now, only in a token way. Advance in intimacy was marked by her omission to remove her glove for such a trifling, though symbolic, contact.

"You tie me up nicely and then you can do what you like with me. Afterwards, I'll tie you up and do things with *you*." For Ellen it was a quite long speech, the longest, he thought, he had ever heard her make. They had already been in the flatlet a good couple of hours.

It had become much warmer, as befitted the later part of May, and she had been wearing a short-sleeved blouse, instead of a sweater; a beach skirt instead of the fawn one. The blouse was in narrow honey and petunia stripes, with a still narrower white stripe at intervals. Ellen had left most of the buttons unfastened. The retired railwaymen, some without their jackets, had just stared and then began talking with self-conscious absorption, to their fellow workers, willing her to go, to be burnt up, while they diverted attention. Ellen was also wearing little-girl knee socks. Laming was desiring her far past the point of embarrassment all the way to the flatlet.

He could not even touch her, let alone take her half-bare arm.

But when, at that later point, he acted upon her suggestion, he had to admit to himself that he lost initiative: he did not really know what he *could* do, what would be far enough out of the ordinary to please her. And when he appealed to her for suggestions, she began to display that all too familiar female amalgam of mockery and fury.

It was when he struck out at her with the first thing that came to hand that he saw Helen standing in the window with her back to the room. She too wore a lighter dress, one that Laming had not seen before; cornflower-colored. Previously, he had himself had the window behind him, or at his feet, but of course she could not have been there or she would have cast a shadow, and right across Ellen's body. Or was that true of whatever was in the room with him and Ellen?

The figure in the window was all too manifestly sunk in trouble and despair. One could almost hear the sobs and see the bitter tears falling on the new dress. Even the hair was obviously disordered across the face.

Laming threw away the object he had snatched up, totally unromatic and unsuitable in any case.

"What's the matter now?" inquired Ellen.

"Look!" This time Laming actually pointed a shaking finger. "Look!" he cried again.

"What at?"

On the previous occasions he was unsure whether or not Ellen had seen what he saw. He also realized quite well, then and now, that it would probably remain uncertain, no matter what she said or did.

"Look at *me* instead," said Ellen quietly. "Do something nice to me, Laming!"

He looked back at the window, but of course the two of them were once more along, or seemingly so.

"Oh, my God," cried Laming.

"Do something nice to me, Laming," said Ellen again. "Please, Laming."

She was becoming ever more talkative, it would seem; and he had realized that there were things one could do, which involved talk, very much so. The popular antithesis between talk and action is frequently false, but in no case more so than after meeting a girl in the American Garden.

MARRIAGE

Laming liked *Reunion in Vienna* better than any other play he could remember. He could identify almost completely with the archduke in white tunic and scarlet trousers, for whom Haydn's stirring anthem was played whenever he appeared, and for whom ladies wore lovely evening dresses almost all the time. There was sadness in it too, though; if there was no hope at all of ever living like that (because nowadays no one did), what point was there to living at all? Laming was so carried away by the finale to Act One that he momentarily forgot all about Helen, and when the intermission came, he could think of nothing to say to her. She might perhaps like the play, at least up to a point; but it could not conceivably mean as much to her as it meant to him.

What Helen proved really to like was Lynne Fontanne. "I should adore to look as elegant as that," she said.

"You often do," responded Laming, though it cost him an effort, and she actually took his hand for a moment as they sat there.

How strange life is! Laming reflected. If he had somehow been richer, he could obviously have been a Lothario. As things were, Helen's hand frightened him. Also she was wearing the cornflower dress he had first seen the previous Saturday in the flatlet.

"I love coming here with you," she said later, when they were in the cafe. "It's an adventure for me." If only she could have *looked* more adventurous! Laming supposed it was that which was wrong.

Moreover, the three girls who served in the place, all obtrusively married, had long ago come to recognize Helen and Laming when they entered and to take them more and more for granted. Helen quite probably liked that, but Laming did not. Also they solicited with increasing cheekiness for more substantial orders than single cups of coffee. Laming was perfectly well aware that the three girls were laughing at him every minute he was in the place and probably for much of the rest of their time together too.

"What about *Careless Rapture* next week?"

"We shall never get in to *that*."

"The gallery's *enormous*."

He had not known, because he had never entered the Theatre Royal, Drury Lane.

Again they agreed to meet in the queue. That evening, Helen had continued to insist upon paying for herself, most honorably.

"I adore Ivor Novello's way of speaking," said Helen. "It gives me the shivers."

"Isn't he—?"

"What does *that* matter, Laming? We must be open-minded, though of course I wouldn't actually *marry* Ivor."

Laming could think of no rejoinder.

In any case he needed no reminding that he was a man marked down.

And to think that he had started all this himself, taken the initiative quite voluntarily! At least, he supposed he had. In what unpredictable ways just about everything worked out! Most things, in fact, went into full reverse, just as was always happening at school! If you want peace, prepare for war, as the classics and history master had admonished them.

"I can't *wait* till next time," said Helen unexpectedly, as they parted.

Not that even then her eyes lighted up, or anything like that.

Laming realized that work with poultry statistics in the civil service was hardly calculated to put a light in anyone's eyes. He quite appreciated the need to be fair. It was simply so difficult to act upon it.

Laming thought of Ellen's eyes.

But apparently the immediate trouble was to be that Helen's inability to wait until next time had to be taken literally. Laming began to see her all over the place.

The first occasion was the very next morning, Thursday. He had been sent out by the office manager to buy sponge cakes to go with everyone's midmorning coffee, and he had glimpsed her back view on the other side of the street, still in that same dress, purchased or brought out for the summer that was now upon them all.

He was very upset.

Nonetheless, the second occasion proved to be that same afternoon. Laming had been dispatched by the partner who was in charge of buying to an address in E.1., almost Whitechapel, Laming thought; and, in that unlikely region, he saw Helen in her dress climbing aboard a No. 25 bus, not ten yards in front of him. She was having difficulty with what appeared to be a heavy black bundle. Indeed, on account of it, she might well have spotted Laming, and perhaps had. Of course it would have been unreasonable to suppose that in the course of a single day she would have had time or reason to change her dress. Still, Laming was now not merely ordinarily frightened, but for the time almost deprived of thought, so that he could not for the life of him recall what he had been told to seek in E.1. The buying partner spoke very sharply to him when he crept into the office empty-handed (he had managed to lose even his library book) and ashen.

And after Laming had been totally unable to explain himself to his mother, and had then passed one of his utterly sleepless nights, came, on Friday morning, the third occasion; and, this third time, he walked straight into Helen, head-on. Things had begun to move faster.

He had left the office quite voluntarily, saying that he needed to be in the fresh air for a few minutes, and had walked into Helen within a bare two hundred yards from the outer door, where Tod sat, the one-eyed custodian. It was before Laming had even reached the appliance place on the corner, about which everyone joked.

What was more, he could have sworn that not for a second had he seen her coming, even though there were very few people on the pavement, far, far fewer, he would have said, than usual at that hour. If he had detected her, if there had been even the slightest tremor of warning, he would have shown the swiftest possible pair of heels the street had ever seen, convention or no convention, bad leg or no bad leg; and if he had been run over in the process, would it have mattered very much?

Helen was wearing another neat summer dress (after all, a whole sleepless night had passed), this one white creeping foliage on a brick wall background, as Laming could see quite well; and she was again carrying something weighty, this time slung over her left shoulder, which gave her an utterly absurd resemblance to the cod-carrying fisherman in the Scott's Emulsion advertisement. There was no advertisement that Laming knew better than that one; standing, as it did, for *mens sana in corpore sano*.

"Hullo," said Laming, in a very low, very shivery voice, audible to no one but her.

She simply trudged past him in her white court shoes, very simple in design. She showed no sign of even seeing him, let alone of hearing his greeting. Under other circumstances, it might have been difficult to decide whether she looked alive or dead. Her burden duly took the shape of a long, gray anonymous object. It seemed to be heavier than ever, as Helen was staggering a little, deviating from a perfectly straight course.

Laming clung sickly to the railings until a middle-aged woman with hair made metallic by curlers came halfway up the area steps and asked if he was all right.

"Quite all right," replied Laming, a little petulantly.

The woman washed her hands of him on her flowered apron.

But then a police constable materialized.

"Had a little too much?"

Laming thought it best to nod.

"Work near here?"

Laming nodded again.

It was fortunate that all the partners had left together for luncheon before Laming was brought back to the office by an arm of the law.

The next day, Saturday, Laming's leg was suddenly much worse. Indeed, it hurt so much that he could hardly walk the short distance to the park, and the American Garden was, of course, on the far side. His mother looked extremely anxious as she stood on the porch, kissing him good-bye again and again. It was quite terribly hot.

Still, much was at stake, and Laming was determined to meet Ellen, even if he did himself a permanent injury. He would be most unlikely ever again to find anyone like Ellen in his entire life, so that, if he lost her, a permanent injury might hardly matter. Confused thinking, but, as with so much thinking of that kind, conclusive.

When he arrived, he found that the railwaymen were actually lying on their backs upon the grass. They were in their braces, with their eyes shut, their mouths sagging. It was like the end of a military engagement, the reckoning.

And, this time, there was no sign at all of Ellen, who had previously been there first. Laming looked in vain behind all the shrub arrangements and then lowered himself onto one of the seats which the railwaymen normally occupied. He extended his bad leg, then lifted it horizontally onto the seat.

A fireman in uniform sauntered past, looking for dropped

matches, for tiny plumes of smoke. There was a sound of children screeching at one another, but that was over the brow of the hill. Laming would have taken off his jacket if he had not been meeting a lady.

"Hullo, Laming."

It was Helen's voice. She had crept up behind his head in complete silence.

"Ellen asked me to say that she can't come today. She's so sorry. There's a difficulty in the shop. We're both a bit early, aren't we?"

Laming pushed and pulled his bad leg off the seat, and she sat beside him.

She was in the brick-wall dress with the mesh of white foliage: She looked cool and dry as ever. How could Laming be there early? He must have made too much allowance for infirmity.

"Say something!" said Helen.

What could anyone say? Laming felt as if he had suffered a blow on the very center of the brain from a lead ingot. His leg had begun to burn in a new way.

"I'm sorry if I frightened you," said Helen.

Laming managed to smile a little. He still knew that if he said anything at all, it would be something foolish, ludicrously inappropriate.

"Please take me to Kelly's flat." It seemed to be a matter of course.

"Kelly?" Even that had been copycatted without volition.

"Where you usually go. Come on, Laming. It'll be fun. We might have tea there."

"I can only walk slowly. Trouble again with my leg."

"Ellen says it's just around the corner. We can buy some cakes on the way."

They set forth, a painful journey, where Laming was concerned. They circumvented the inert railwaymen. In one or two cases, Helen stepped over them, but that was more than Laming cared to risk.

Helen spoke. "Won't you take my hand, as it's Saturday?"

"I'd like to, but I think I'd better concentrate."

"Take my arm, if you prefer."

Orsino, Endymion, Adonis: how differently one feels about these heroes when one re-encounters them amid such pain, such heat!

Nor did they buy any cakes; there was no shop, and Laming did not feel like going in search, even though he realized it might be wise to do so.

"I forgot," exclaimed Laming, as they turned the last and most crucial corner. "I haven't got any keys. I think we need two at least."

"Ellen lent me hers," said Helen. She had been carrying them, not in her handbag, but all the time in her hand. They were on a little ring, with a bauble added. Helen's gloves were white for the hot weather, in lacelike net.

Helen and Laming were inside the flatlet. Helen sat on the huge divan, not pulling down her dress, as she usually did. Laming sat on one of the little white chairs, at once bedroom chairs and informal dinner-table chairs.

"What do you and Ellen usually do first?" asked Helen. She spoke as if she had kindly volunteered to help with the accounts.

"We talk for a bit," said Laming, unconvincing though that was when everyone knew that Ellen seldom spoke at all.

"Well, let's do that," said Helen. "Surely it can do no harm if I take off my dress? I don't want to crumple it. You'd better take some things off too, in all this heat."

And, indeed, perspiration was streaming down Laming's face and body, like runnels trickling over a wasteland.

Helen had taken off her white shoes too.

"Do you like my petticoat?" she inquired casually. "It came from Peter Jones in Sloane Square. I don't think I've ever been in North London before."

"I like it very much," said Laming.

"It's serviceable, anyway. You could hardly tear it if you tried. Have you lived in North London all your life?"

"First in Hornsey Rise and then, after my father died, in Drayton Park."

"I adored my father, though he was very strict with me."

"So *your* father's dead too?"

"He allowed me no license at all. Will you be like that with your daughter, Laming, when the time comes?"

"I don't expect I'll ever have a daughter, Helen." Because of his leg, he would have liked a softer, lower chair and, for that matter, a more stoutly constructed one. But the springy, jumpy divan would not be the answer either, unless he were completely to recline on it, which would be injudicious.

"Do take something off, Laming. You look so terribly hot."

But he simply could not. Nor had he any knowledge of

how men normally behaved, were called upon to behave, in situations such as this. Ellen had made all easy, but the present circumstances were very different, and of course Ellen herself was one of the reasons why they were different.

"I *am* looking forward to *Careless Rapture*," said Helen. "I adore Dorothy Dickson's clothes."

Laming had never to his knowledge seen Dorothy Dickson. "She's very fair, isn't she?" he asked.

"She's like a pretty flower bending before the breeze," said Helen.

"Isn't she married to a man named Souchong?"

"Heisen," said Helen.

"I thought it was *some* kind of tea."

"After a week without leaving the department, it's so wonderful to talk freely and intimately."

There it was! A week without leaving the department, and he had supposed himself to have seen her yesterday, and twice the day before, and all over London!

As well as feeling hot and tortured, Laming suddenly felt sick with uncertainty; it was like the very last stage of *mal de mer*, and almost on an instant. Probably he had been feeling a little sick for some time.

"Laming!" said Helen, in her matter-of-fact way, "if I were to take off my petticoat, would you take off your coat and pullover?"

If he had spoken, he would have vomited, and perhaps at her, the flatlet being so minute.

"Laming! What's the matter?"

If he had made a dash for the bathroom, he would have been unable to stop her coming in after him, half-dressed, reasonable, with life weighed off—and more than ordinary people, it would seem, to judge by her excessively frequent appearances. So, instead, he made a dash for the staircase.

Holding in the sick, he flitted down the stairs. At least, he still had all the clothes in which he had entered.

"Laming! Darling! Sweetheart!"

She came out of the flatlet after him, and a terrible thing followed.

Helen, shoeless, caught her stockinged foot in the nailed-down landing runner and plunged the whole length of the flight, falling full upon her head on the hall floor, softened only by cracked, standard-colored linoleum. The peril of the fall had been greatly compounded by her agitation.

She lay there horribly tangled, horribly inert, perhaps with concussion, perhaps with a broken neck, though no blood was visible. Her petticoat was ripped, and badly, whatever the guarantee might have been.

Laming could well have been finally ill at that point, but the effect upon him was the opposite. He felt cold and awed, whatever the hall thermometer might show; and he forgot about feeling sick.

He stood trembling lest another tenant, lest the wife of a caretaker, intrude upon the scene of horror. There was a flatlet door at this ground-floor level, and a flight of stairs winding into the dark basement. But there was no further sound of any kind; in fact, a quite notable silence. It was, of course, a Saturday, the weekend.

Laming opened the front door of the house, as surreptitiously as one can do such a thing in bright sunlight.

There was no one to be seen in the street, and about eyes behind lace curtains there was nothing to be done before nightfall. Laming could scarcely wait until nightfall.

When outside the house, he shut the door quietly, resenting the click of the Yale-type fitment. He felt very exposed as he stood at the top of the four or five North London steps, like Sidney Carton on the scaffold, or some man less worthy.

He dropped down the steps and thereby hurt his leg even more. Nonetheless, he began to run, or perhaps rather to jogtrot. It was hot as Hell.

He cantered unevenly around the first corner.

And there stood Ellen; startled and stationary at his apparition. She was in a little blue holiday singlet, and darker blue shorts, plain and sweet. Apart from Ellen, that thoroughfare seemed empty too.

"Laming!"

She opened wide her arms, as one does with a child.

Matted and haggard, he stared at her. Then he determinedly stared away from her.

"I waited and waited. In the American Garden. Then I thought I'd better come on."

She was adorable in her playgirl rig, and so understanding, so truly loving.

But Laming was under bad influences. "Who's Kelly?" he asked.

"A friend," she replied. "But you haven't seen him."

He glared brazenly at the universe.

MARRIAGE

Then he pushed rudely past her, and all the way home his head sang a popular song to him, as heads do in times of trouble.

His mother spoke with urgency. "Oh, Laming. I'm so glad to see you back."

He stared at her like a murderer who had the police car in the next street.

"You look tired. Poor Laming! It's a girl isn't it?"

He could only gaze at the floor. His leg was about to fall right off. His brain had gone rotten, like an egg.

"There's always the one you take, and the one you might have taken."

He continued to stare at the eroded lentil-colored carpet.

"Lie down and rest. I'll come back for you soon."

Agonizingly he flopped onto the hard chesterfield, with its mustard-and-cress covering, much worn down in places.

In the end, she was with him again. She wore a short-sleeved nightdress in white lawn, plain and pure. Her hair had long been quite short. She looked like a bride.

"It's too hot for a dressing gown," she said, smiling. He smiled wanly back.

"Let me help you to take your things off," she said.

And when they were in bed, her bed, with the windows open and the drawn blinds carelessly flapping, she seemed younger than ever. He knew that she would never change, never disappoint. She did not even need to be thought about.

"Laming," she said. "You know who loves you best of all."

He sank into her being.

His leg could be forgotten. The heat could be forgotten. He had sailed into port. He had come home. He had lost and found himself.

DAW BOOKS

- [ ] **THE 1979 ANNUAL WORLD'S BEST SF.** The latest "World's Best" with David Lake, C. J. Cherryh, Ursula K. Le Guin, and more. (#UE1459—$2.25)

- [ ] **THE 1978 ANNUAL WORLD'S BEST SF.** Leading off with Varley, Haldeman, Bryant, Ellison, Bishop, etc. (#UJ1376—$1.95)

- [ ] **THE 1977 ANNUAL WORLD'S BEST SF.** Featuring Asimov, Tiptree, Aldiss, Coney, and a galaxy of great ones. An SFBC Selection. (#UE1297—$1.75)

- [ ] **THE 1976 ANNUAL WORLD'S BEST SF.** A winner with Fritz Leiber, Brunner, Cowper, Vinge, and more. An SFBC Selection. (#UW1232—$1.50)

- [ ] **THE 1975 ANNUAL WORLD'S BEST SF.** The authentic "World's Best" featuring Bester, Dickson, Martin, Asimov, etc. (#UW1170—$1.50)

- [ ] **THE DAW SCIENCE FICTION READER.** The unique anthology with a full novel by Andre Norton and tales by Akers, Dickson, Bradley, Stableford, and Tanith Lee. (#UW1242—$1.50)

- [ ] **THE BEST FROM THE REST OF THE WORLD.** Great stories by the master of sf writers of Western Europe. (#UE1343—$1.75)

- [ ] **THE YEAR'S BEST FANTASY STORIES: 3. Edited by Lin Carter,** the 1977 volume includes C. J. Cherryh, Karl Edward Wagner, G.R.R. Martin, etc. (#UW1338—$1.50)

If you wish to order these titles,

please see the coupon in

the back of this book.

DAW BOOKS

GREAT NOVELS OF HEROIC ADVENTURES ON EXOTIC WORLDS

- ☐ DINOSAUR BEACH by Keith Laumer. (#UW1332—$1.50)
- ☐ THE GODS OF XUMA by David L. Lake. (#UW1360—$1.50)
- ☐ THE BIG BLACK MARK by A. Bertram Chandler. (#UW1355—$1.50)
- ☐ THE WAY BACK by A. Bertram Chandler. (#UW1352—$1.50)
- ☐ THE GRAND WHEEL by Barrington J. Bayley. (#UW1318—$1.50)
- ☐ THE OVERLORDS OF WAR by Gerard Klein. (#UW1313—$1.50)
- ☐ BENEATH THE SHATTERED MOONS by Michael Bishop. (#UW1305—$1.50)
- ☐ EARTHCHILD by Doris Piserchia. (#UW1308—$1.50)
- ☐ ARMADA OF ANTARES by Alan Burt Akers. (#UY1227—$1.25)
- ☐ RENEGADE OF KREGEN by Alan Burt Akers. (#UY1271—$1.25)
- ☐ KROZAIR OF KREGEN by Alan Burt Akers. (#UW1288—$1.50)
- ☐ ALDAIR IN ALBION by Neal Barrett, Jr. (#UY1235—$1.25)
- ☐ ALDAIR, MASTER OF SHIPS by Neal Barrett, Jr. (#UW1326—$1.50)
- ☐ WARLORD OF GHANDOR by Del DowDell. (#UW1315—$1.50)
- ☐ THE RIGHT HAND OF DEXTRA by David J. Lake. (#UW1290—$1.50)
- ☐ THE WILDINGS OF WESTRON by David J. Lake. (#UW1306—$1.50)
- ☐ KIOGA OF THE WILDERNESS by William L. Chester. (#UW1253—$1.50)
- ☐ ONE AGAINST A WILDERNESS by William L. Chester. (#UW1280—$1.50)
- ☐ KIOGA OF THE UNKNOWN LAND by William L. Chester. (#UJ1378—$1.95)
- ☐ INTERSTELLAR EMPIRE by John Brunner. (#UE1362—$1.75)
- ☐ THE PRODUCTIONS OF TIME by John Brunner. (#UW1329—$1.50)

To order these titles,
see coupon on the
last page of this book.

DAW BOOKS sf

ANDRE NORTON
in DAW BOOKS editions

- ☐ **YURTH BURDEN.** Two human races vied for control of that world—until a terror from the past threatened both! A DAW Andre Norton original! (#UE1400—$1.75)

- ☐ **MERLIN'S MIRROR.** A new novel, written for DAW, of science-lore versus Arthurian legendry. (#UW1340—$1.50)

- ☐ **SPELL OF THE WITCH WORLD.** A DAW exclusive, continuing the famous Witch World stories, and not available elsewhere. (#UW1430—$1.50)

- ☐ **THE CRYSTAL GRYPHON.** The latest in the beloved Witch-World novels, it is an outstanding other-world adventure. (#UE1428—$1.75)

- ☐ **HERE ABIDE MONSTERS.** Trapped in a parallel world, just off Earth's own map and right out of legend. (#UW1333—$1.50)

- ☐ **THE BOOK OF ANDRE NORTON.** Novelettes, short stories, articles, and a bibliography make this a treat for Norton's millions of readers. (#UW1341—$1.50)

- ☐ **PERILOUS DREAMS.** Tamisen crosses four worlds in her Quest for reality ... A DAW exclusive. (#UE1405—$1.75)

DAW BOOKS are represented by the publishers of Signet and Mentor Books, THE NEW AMERICAN LIBRARY, INC.

THE NEW AMERICAN LIBRARY, INC.,
P.O. Box 999, Bergenfield, New Jersey 07621

Please send me the DAW BOOKS I have checked above. I am enclosing
$_____ (check or money order—no currency or C.O.D.'s).
Please include the list price plus 35¢ a copy to cover mailing costs.

Name _____

Address _____

City_____ State _____ Zip Code _____
Please allow at least 4 weeks for delivery

THE DIVERSITY OF HORROR

In his introduction to this, the seventh series of the only anthology in America regularly presenting the best of the year's tales of terror, Gerald Page writes:

"The hallmark of any form of imaginative writing is diversity. You never truly know where a good imaginative story will take you, whether it's science fiction, fantasy or horror. And that's true not only of the genre, but of the best writers. Diversity was the rule for Poe, H.G. Wells and John Collier, and it remains the rule for Fritz Leiber, Richard Matheson, Robert Aickman, Ramsey Campbell and the rest of today's best writers. Good horror fiction may be good fiction of any type, and no editor who wants the best he can get his hands on will reject a good story simply because it's horrifying."

Included among the gems in this book will be found stories from many sources, some well known, some very obscure. Regardless . . . they have in common the ability to terrify!

Anthologies from DAW

THE 1974 ANNUAL WORLD'S BEST SF
THE 1975 ANNUAL WORLD'S BEST SF
THE 1976 ANNUAL WORLD'S BEST SF
THE 1977 ANNUAL WORLD'S BEST SF
THE 1978 ANNUAL WORLD'S BEST SF
THE 1979 ANNUAL WORLD'S BEST SF

WOLLHEIM'S WORLD'S BEST SF: Vol. 1
WOLLHEIM'S WORLD'S BEST SF: Vol. 2

THE DAW SCIENCE FICTION READER

THE YEAR'S BEST HORROR STORIES: 1
THE YEAR'S BEST HORROR STORIES: II
THE YEAR'S BEST HORROR STORIES: III
THE YEAR'S BEST HORROR STORIES: IV
THE YEAR'S BEST HORROR STORIES: V
THE YEAR'S BEST HORROR STORIES: VI

THE YEAR'S BEST FANTASY STORIES: 1
THE YEAR'S BEST FANTASY STORIES: 2
THE YEAR'S BEST FANTASY STORIES: 3
THE YEAR'S BEST FANTASY STORIES: 4

THE BEST FROM THE REST OF THE WORLD

HEROIC FANTASY
ASIMOV PRESENTS THE GREAT SF STORIES: 1